GRACE SEES RED

Center Point
Large Print

Also by Julie Hyzy and available from
Center Point Large Print:

The Manor House Mysteries
   Grace Interrupted
   Grace Among Thieves
   Grace Takes Off
   Grace Against the Clock
   Grace Cries Uncle

**This Large Print Book carries the
Seal of Approval of N.A.V.H.**

GRACE SEES RED

JULIE HYZY

CENTER POINT LARGE PRINT
THORNDIKE, MAINE

This Center Point Large Print edition is published in the year 2016 by arrangement with The Berkley Publishing Group, an imprint of Penguin Publishing Group, a division of Penguin Random House Company LLC.

The text of this Large Print edition is unabridged. In other aspects, this book may vary from the original edition. Printed in the United States of America on permanent paper. Set in 16-point Times New Roman type.

ISBN: 978-1-68324-177-5

Library of Congress Cataloging-in-Publication Data

Names: Hyzy, Julie A.
Title: Grace sees red / Julie Hyzy.
Description: Center Point Large Print edition. | Thorndike, Maine : Center Point Large Print, 2016.
Identifiers: LCCN 2016034841 | ISBN 9781683241775
    hardcover : alk. paper)
Subjects: LCSH: Women detectives—Fiction. | Murder—Investigation—Fiction. | Large type books. | GSAFD: Mystery fiction.
Classification: LCC PS3608.Y98 G7285 2016 | DDC 813/.6—dc23
LC record available at https://lccn.loc.gov/2016034841

For Paul and Mitch with special thanks for all the Dymphna Dust. Love you guys!

Acknowledgments

For this book, Grace and I owe a debt of gratitude to both old friends and new. Sending giant "Room 32" hugs to one of my oldest and dearest friends, Maureen Komperda, for her guidance and advice on all things medical. Any errors, misstatements, or exaggerations are wholly mine. Love you, Corky! Thanks, too, to my good friend and go-to legal expert, David Eppenstein, who put me in touch with awesome North Carolina attorney Rick Schulz (via another North Carolina attorney, David Erdman) when I had questions about procedure in that state. Thanks for the assists, David and David. And special thanks, Rick, for your quick and enthusiastic support.

I'm extremely grateful to my luminous editor, Michelle Vega; her fabulous assistant, Bethany Blair; and the wonderful people at Berkley Prime Crime, including Robin Barletta, Stacy Edwards, and Erica Horisk, for bringing these books to life. All are awesome supporters of this series, some from the very beginning.

Heartfelt thanks, as always, to my fabulous family. Hugs and love to my ever-patient husband, Curt, and my strong, independent, and compassionate kids, Robyn, Sara, and Biz.

GRACE SEES RED

Chapter 1

A SMILE BROKE OVER BENNETT'S FACE AS he sipped coffee from his china cup. "Take a look," he said, gesturing over my shoulder.

Seated on the persimmon sofa in his study, I balanced my own cup and saucer as I twisted to see. "What?" I asked, noticing nothing out of place.

"Outside," he said.

Sunlight sliced across the oak floor, sending a warm glow up the nearby bookcase. I leaned sideways to get a better view of Marshfield's extensive grounds stretching out below. Landscapers dotted the yellow-gray vista, coaxing green out of hibernation with every optimistic sweep of their rakes.

"Spring is coming," Bennett said.

"It's about time." Turning back to face him, I took a sip from my cup, quite proud that I hadn't spilled a drop in the process.

Bennett breathed deeply, almost as though the windows were open and he was taking in the delicious fresh air. "I can't imagine a better time of year for our new beginning." Returning his cup to its matching saucer on the low table between us, he leaned forward and regarded me with his bright blue stare. "Everything that has come before this happened for a reason. I sincerely believe that."

I nodded acknowledgment of the sentiment though I didn't entirely agree. "We could have done without a couple of incidents." Using my cup to point, I said, "You getting shot, for instance."

He waved away my concern. "Patched up and good as new." My septuagenarian boss, Bennett Marshfield, a man I'd come to love as family even before recent DNA results had confirmed our uncle-niece relationship, had, indeed, recovered from the gunshot wound he'd sustained less than two months earlier. He patted his chest where the bullet had gone through. "It was a painful lesson but an important one: Savor each day. Tomorrow is not guaranteed. Take nothing for granted. Speaking of which, are you ready for your next lesson?"

"You know I am."

"Good. Let's get started. The house will be crawling with tourists before we know it."

Bennett's butler, Theo, bustled in to clear away our breakfast dishes as we got to our feet. "It's Sunday," he reminded us unnecessarily. "You have an extra hour before the mansion opens for the day."

"That we do," Bennett said. Turning to me, he

asked, "You're sure this early-morning excursion isn't interfering with your weekend plans?"

"Not at all." Although I generally opted to spend Sunday mornings lounging in my kitchen, trading newspaper sections with Bruce and Scott, my roommates had gone in early to their wine shop today. Two days ago, their shop's landlord had delivered some distressing news about the building's structural integrity. Today, Bruce, Scott, and their landlord were holding an emergency meeting at Amethyst Cellars before it opened for customers. I knew my friends were eager to find a workable solution to their problems before tourist season began.

Bennett and I set out from the study, walking side by side to his apartment's main entrance. His rooms took up most of this wing's fourth floor. Marshfield business offices took up all of the wing's third level and a portion of the second. The rest of the mansion served as a combination tourist attraction and museum. Thousands of visitors streamed through our front doors every day eager to stroll the home's opulence and marvel at Bennett's eclectic collection of antiques.

"There's no one special in your life right now?"

I nudged his arm. "You'd know if there were."

He winked at me. "Can't blame an old man for asking. Just envisioning the future. It's been a long time since this house had children running around in it. I should know. I was one of them."

13

"You are not old," I reminded him. "I'll thank you to stop saying that."

I had no idea where we were headed for today's lesson, but as Bennett held open a stairway door, he said, "I do feel younger these days. More vital than I have a right to, considering."

"I'm glad to hear it."

"You take your time, Gracie. Find the right fellow. And I'll wait patiently for youngsters to spoil."

"Marriage and kids are not even on my radar at this point," I said. "We have a lot more to worry about than my love life."

"We do. But you and I are up to the challenge. Don't you agree?"

"We are, but . . ." I let my thought trail off.

Years ago, convinced that he was the sole surviving member of the Marshfield family, Bennett had bequeathed that, upon his death, ownership of the estate would transfer to the village of Emberstowne. Once we discovered that Marshfield blood ran through my veins, however, he'd completely revised his will. The details were numerous, but it boiled down to this: Upon Bennett's death, I would become the sole owner of Marshfield Manor and would maintain control of the estate for my entire lifetime. If I had children, I could—but would not be required to—grant them control of the estate upon my death. No matter who sat at the family helm, whether now or a hundred years hence, if the Marshfield bloodline died out, the estate was to be turned over to the village and preserved as an historic site.

This change had resulted in a couple of immediate consequences: Not only had Bennett turned me into a very wealthy young woman, I'd become a mini-celebrity in our small town. I'd also drawn the ire of Emberstowne officials who watched as their expected windfall dissolved before their eyes. That they now needed to wait for *my* demise or, heaven help them, that of my descendants, was too much for some of the town elders to bear.

Emberstowne lawyers had argued against Bennett's decision, citing the city's expectation of inheritance, but the courts had swiftly dismissed such suits as without merit.

I'd balked at the change myself, but as I came to understand my uncle's motivations, I'd relented. Bennett wanted family to control his fortune until there was no family left. Being able to provide for me and my future children gave him enormous pleasure. I'd come to realize I couldn't deny him that.

Still, I had one major reservation and it involved my sister.

"What about Liza?" I finally said. "No matter how many assurances you offer, I'm terrified of the day she finds out."

Bennett and I had discussed the "Liza situation"—as we'd taken to calling it—at length. Even though his lawyers had taken every possible precaution when drafting the updated will—going so far as to bequeath her a small annual stipend—there was no telling what schemes she'd dream up to increase her share once she discovered the truth.

Bennett led me out of the stairway at the second floor. Again, he held the door open. "Our attorneys and advisers will help us break the news to her when the time comes. Have you heard from your sister lately?"

"Not since the sentencing."

Liza's role in a major antiquity theft should have landed her in prison for more than ten years, but because she'd cooperated with authorities and had no prior convictions, she'd been given a mere two-year sentence with the potential for early release if she behaved herself.

I shrugged as though I'd gotten past my sister's betrayals. "She blames me, of course."

"We know better."

This time of the morning the glorious mansion was quiet and still, as though the grand dame was breathlessly awaiting her first guests of the day. Barring the handful of security guards completing preopening inspections, Bennett and I were alone.

I inhaled deeply—history and wood polish. No matter how meticulously our staffers cleaned, they couldn't clear hundred-year-old dust from every crevice. Nor would I want them to.

Never in my life could I have anticipated the future that now stretched before me. Except for my wariness with regard to Liza, I was as content as I could ever hope to be. I loved wandering this house. Assuming Bennett stayed healthy and strong, we could conceivably enjoy decades running the estate together.

Lamps on the public floors wouldn't be switched on for another hour but there was enough ambient light streaming in from the tall windows to allow us to safely navigate the second-level living room's furniture. I brushed my fingers along the back of a golden wing chair, following Bennett as he traversed the room's forty-foot length.

"What is today's lesson?" I asked when he took a sharp right into a hall that formerly housed Marshfield guests. From the moment he'd returned home from the hospital after being shot, Bennett had undertaken the job of educating me in all things Marshfield. Over the past weeks he and I had pored over photo albums and scrapbooks and together we'd investigated areas of the house that had been closed off for years.

There was a playful glint in his eye as he pointed farther down the long corridor. "You tell me. What's at the end of his hallway?"

"An open stairway. Your grandfather originally

designed it to allow guests and family easy access to all floors without having to traipse all the way back to the center of the house." I paraphrased information provided via headsets on visitors' self-guided tours.

"And beyond that?"

"There's an odd-shaped area around the stairs. A dead end."

"Sure about that, are you?"

Bennett's teasing tone stopped me in my tracks. The reason this corridor dead-ended was because the library below was two stories tall. Once one reached the stairway, there was nowhere to go but up or down.

I felt myself smile. Although I was familiar with Marshfield's floor plans, past experience taught me that there were secret passages and hidden rooms whose details had been omitted when original documents were filed with city authorities.

"Is there a way to get into the library from this level?" I asked.

"What I'm about to show you is much more than that." He started moving again. I followed.

The far end of the hallway I'd described was cordoned off by velvet ropes to keep guests safely on the tour. Bennett tilted one of the brass uprights to the side and gestured me through. Three steps later, we stood at the foot of a gorgeous oak stairway that stretched upward to my right. Behind it, an identical structure led down to the first floor.

"I know how much you enjoy exploring Marshfield's secret rooms," he said.

"And there's one here?"

"Think a little bigger, Gracie."

I studied the fawn-colored walls around me. There was a skinny window in a narrow alcove to my left and a wide window far behind the stairway to my right. The eastern wall ahead of me curved dramatically, following the lines of the library below. I skimmed my hand along its length, walking slowly, scrutinizing the long blank expanse and eager to find a clue.

Coming up empty, I took a step back and perched my hands on my hips.

"Giving up so soon?" Bennett asked.

I was about to answer when my cell phone rang. "Who could be calling me on a Sunday morning?" I asked rhetorically as I pulled it from my pocket. A second later, I had my answer. "It's Frances."

"Frances?" Bennett frowned. "On a weekend?" As I tapped the screen to connect with my assistant, I heard him mutter, "Something must be wrong."

I pulled the device to my ear. "Frances?"

"Who else would be calling from this number?" she asked. Before I could respond, she followed up with "What are you doing right now?"

My assistant's acerbic attitude clearly remained intact. "I'm surprised to hear from you today," I said. "What's up? Are you all right?"

"What are you doing right now?" she asked again. "Are you busy? If you're busy, don't worry about it."

"No, I'm not busy," I said with an apologetic look to Bennett. Still frowning, he waved away my concern.

Frances started to speak but stopped herself.

"Are you sure you're okay?" I asked.

"Give me a minute, would you?"

I pulled my lips in to stop myself from asking more. On a good day, Frances could be ornery. Today, she was off the charts.

"Take your time," I said.

"What's wrong?" Bennett mouthed.

I shrugged and shook my head. He stepped closer and leaned in to hear.

"Okay, here it is." Frances huffed, but spoke haltingly. "I need a favor. Can you do me a favor?"

I had no idea what this favor entailed, but I knew my assistant wouldn't be asking for help if it wasn't serious. "Anything, Frances. What do you need?"

Though I couldn't see her, I could sense her relief. "I need you to come out here. I'm in Rosette."

"Sure." I was confused but willing to roll with it. "Where's that?"

"It's a small town. I'm not surprised you haven't heard of it. I'll give you the address. You have a pen and paper?"

"No, but I'll record it in my phone," I said. "Let me put you on speaker."

Her heavy breathing was hard to miss in the few seconds it took me to pull up my mapping app. "Go ahead," I said. "I'm ready."

She provided an address and spelled the street name as I typed in the information and the app determined my route. "How soon can you be here?" she asked.

"My GPS estimates about an hour," I said. "I'm leaving Marshfield now."

"What are you doing there?" she asked. "I thought you were at home."

"Bennett and I are walking through the—"

"He's with you?" Her pitch rose to panic level. "And you have me on speakerphone? Is the Mister hearing all this?"

Bennett stepped closer to the phone. "Are you all right, Frances? What happened? Were you in an accident?"

She made a sound I couldn't decipher but which clearly wasn't an expression of joy. After a few more puffs of angry breathing, she said, "Should have known better than to ask for help."

Bennett and I stepped past the velvet ropes to head back the way we'd come. There would be no

21

exploring of secret rooms today. "We're on our way, Frances," I said.

"Both of you?" she asked.

Bennett nodded. "Both of us."

"Swell," she said, and hung up.

Chapter 2

I PULLED OUT OF THE LOT AT MARSHFIELD with Bennett in the passenger seat, surprised to see storm clouds forming in the otherwise bright sky. "She was awfully cryptic on the phone," I said as we set off. "I wonder what's up."

"Apparently we're about to find out where Frances goes on weekends," he said. "Although it's evident she would have preferred to keep the information from me."

"I always thought you knew but that you didn't think it was your place to share her secrets."

As we sped along the local access road that led to the interstate, Bennett shook his head. "A suspicion or two. Nothing more."

Sunday-morning traffic was light, making for an easy merge onto the expressway. "What kind of suspicions?"

Bennett smirked. "The romantic kind, of course. What better options are there? I've always believed that Frances spent her weekends with a gentleman friend."

Keeping my eyes on the road, I nodded. "That's my best guess, too. But why the cloak-and-dagger approach?" A second later, a thought hit me. "You don't think it's because he's married, do you?"

"No." Bennett bunched his lips. "At least I hope not."

Heavy raindrops splashed my windshield, smacking out a slow, rhythmless beat. I flicked on my lights and wipers.

"There goes our sunshine," Bennett said.

The rain velocity continued to increase. I adjusted the wipers' tempo to keep up. "Has Frances ever been married?" I asked. "She's so stingy with personal information that I've been afraid to ask."

"Testing my memory, are you?" He frowned at the silvery, gleaming road ahead. "You need to understand that Frances came to work for us when I was in my thirties. She's younger than I am by quite a few years, and she wasn't always the powerhouse she is now."

"I find that hard to believe."

Bennett snorted. "What I mean to say is that she was originally brought on as an assistant clerk or bookkeeper, I believe. Because I was busy growing the business and she was busy with her life, she remained under my radar for a good many years."

He shrugged. "That said, I know she has a sister in Emberstowne. They lost their parents about fifteen years ago, one right after the other. No idea if there are any other siblings." He made a thoughtful noise, then spoke slowly. "I do seem to recall learning that Frances had been married briefly and suffered through a particularly acrimonious divorce."

"I'm sorry to hear that. I take it she never had children?"

"No." He sighed deeply. "I wonder if having children might have softened her outlook at all. Frances is possibly the most cynical human being I've ever come across."

"Every experience and person we encounter in life helps shape us. Kids included."

"Frances may have been an exemplary parent. Or she may have been the worst," he said. "But we'll never know, will we?"

I exited to my right to merge onto another expressway. "No, we won't."

"By the way." Bennett raised his voice to be heard above the downpour. "How is the situation with Bruce and Scott? Have they heard any more from their landlord?"

I grimaced. "Yes, unfortunately. They're meeting today about it. The structural issues are worse than the landlord first led them to believe. Instead of dealing with core problems over the years, apparently he's done only the bare minimum to get by, patching things and making superficial repairs."

"You'd never know it. Their wine shop is impeccably maintained."

"That's because they've taken on the

responsibility for keeping the customer areas pristine. It's costing them far more than it should and the landlord isn't offering them any rebate on the rent."

"That's wrong," Bennett said. "Can't village inspectors force the landlord to make repairs?"

Road signs above let me know that we were less than five miles from our exit. "That's exactly what's happened. Inspectors are threatening to shutter the entire building until repairs are complete. The landlord has thirty days to comply or the shop will be closed down."

"Thirty days? Is that long enough?"

"Hardly." I glanced over to Bennett. "That's barely enough time to put the contract out for bids. Tourist season starts in a couple of months and it's almost a certainty that Bruce and Scott will lose business this year."

"That's a shame."

We were silent as I exited the expressway and drove for several miles. I made a soft right onto a two-lane road.

"There's an idea I've been meaning to broach with you," I said.

"Go ahead."

We were within ten minutes of our destination. Not nearly enough time for the discussion I had planned. "It'll keep until the ride back," I said.

"Fair enough."

At the next intersection, I slowed the car to a full stop.

"I'm supposed to take a right here," I said. "But this looks like private property."

Two concave stone signs flanked the wide driveway on our right. Bennett read the engraved words aloud. "Indwell Estates."

We both leaned forward to peer around the massive entranceway, but there was nothing much to see. Trees bursting with pale green buds lined a long, paved road that curved out of sight behind a forest of evergreens.

"Is this someone's home?" Bennett asked.

"I have no idea." I shrugged and turned the wheel. "I guess we're about to find out."

The gentle ride leading us deeper into Indwell property reminded me of Marshfield's welcoming roadways. Verdant, smooth, and winding, they looked as though they could have been transplanted here, down to the small blue signs alerting us to the 15-miles-per-hour speed limit. As we progressed, however, all resemblance faded away. The number of signs and their size increased exponentially. Some offered instructions for visitors, others for doctors. Another directed ambulances to silence sirens and alarms before proceeding farther.

Two cars, both with elderly drivers at the wheel, and both traveling well under the speed limit, passed us going the opposite direction. When we approached a hilltop clearing with no one behind us, I slowed to a crawl, coming to a full stop at a vista that provided an overview of the property.

"If this is a hospital, it's certainly a swanky one," I said.

Six M-shaped buildings lay in the gray lowland before us, forming an enormous circle around a small, restless lake. Separated by wide stretches of rain-slicked lawns, the sprawling brick-and-stone structures reminded me of Italian piazzas, or perhaps outbuildings at an upscale resort. With their narrow, curved back sides facing the lake and wide entrances facing outward, the buildings appeared to have been designed to resemble rays of the sun.

Bennett seemed stymied as well. "It's enormous."

"The GPS tells us we have another two miles," I said. "I assume our destination is that very last building. The one with its back to us."

"This is all very odd."

I agreed, and accelerated onto a path that ran counterclockwise around the grounds. "What in the world is Frances doing here?"

Just past the turnoff for the second-to-the-last building on our left, we encountered an orange-and-white construction sawhorse blocking the street. A rain-battered cardboard sign with a hastily drawn arrow had been duct-taped to the horse, directing us to TEMPORARY VISITOR PARKING.

We pulled into a small, packed lot tucked into a low nook next to our destination. This sign read EMPLOYEE PARKING ONLY. Shrugging, I angled into one of the few open spots. "It seems we don't have much choice."

Soggy, warm air rolled in when we opened our doors. The rain had stopped and the sun had returned to reclaim the sky. Temperatures had definitely climbed since we'd left Marshfield.

This building was two stories, constructed on a slope. We'd parked along the lowest level, between the southern edge of the building and its nearest neighbor. The main entrance sat up one level and faced east, or possibly northeast. I couldn't tell for certain.

I pointed. A nearby stone stairway led up the grassy incline. "You up for walking?" I asked.

"Of course." Bennett took a long look around, a puzzled expression on his face. "Are we sure this is the address Frances provided?"

I rechecked my phone and the GPS instructions. "This is it."

"Then she must be here." Bennett started for the stairs.

New mulch, wet dirt, and warm greenery combined to give the damp air an earthy freshness. I breathed deeply as I hurried along the building's side. "Whatever this place is, it's beautiful."

With wings emanating from a circular hub at its

center point, the brick structure featured gorgeous stone accents and clean lines. The grounds immediately surrounding the simple design included the lake behind us and a wide walking path with gardens that featured both marble statues and old-fashioned oil lamps. I wondered if the architect hadn't been able to decide between Renaissance Florence and eighteenth-century London. It didn't matter, however. All this, set against a distant blue-purple mountain backdrop made Indwell Estates a postcard photographer's dream.

Even the steps we climbed were lovely, with ornate curlicue handrails. As we crested the top of the incline, I grabbed Bennett's arm. "Uh-oh."

He'd seen it, too. Two squad cars sat along the front sidewalk, one of them blocking an accessible entrance ramp. A coroner's van idled behind them. Two more dark sedans—with oversized spotlights mounted next to their side-view mirrors—were parked along the far walkway.

A young, uniformed police officer leaned against the coroner's van. The moment he spotted us, he jogged over.

"Can I see some ID?"

"What's going on?" Bennett asked as he drew out his wallet.

"Hang on." After a squinting study of Bennett's information, the cop ran his index finger down a list of names in his notebook, apparently looking for a match. Finding none, he repeated the process with me. "You here to visit a patient?" he asked.

My first instinct was to explain Frances's phone call, but at the last second thought better of it. "Yes, a visit," I said. "What happened?"

He offered a perfunctory smile. "Steer clear of the ruckus inside and you'll be fine."

"Ruckus?" I asked. "Is there some emergency?"

"All clear now." The cop waved us on.

As soon as we were out of earshot, Bennett made a low noise deep in his throat. "Let's find Frances."

Chapter 3

ANOTHER OFFICER, THIS ONE HEAVYSET and older, held up a hand as we entered the facility's honey-hued reception area. He pointed to our left. "All visitors that way," he said, indicating a long hallway across the circular lobby. "No exceptions." About thirty feet to our right, yet another cop stood with his arms folded, blocking anyone from entering the east wing.

I tried to get a better look. "What's going on?" I asked.

The cop wore an implacable expression and an air of impatience. Pointing again, he said, "That way." He took a menacing step forward. "Either follow orders or leave. Your choice."

I had no doubt that Frances's phone call had something to do with the police presence here and that the answers we sought were down that blocked-off wing. Tempting though it was, I decided not to try an end run around the sentry.

"Understood," I said, tugging Bennett's sleeve. "We're going."

At the mouth of the far hallway, two women wearing bright-colored medical scrubs called to us, waving. "Over here."

We skirted an abandoned welcome desk and crossed the chilly, spacious circle in about fifteen strides. There was no longer any doubt in my mind as to what sort of facility this was. Although traditional-style furniture clustered around the lobby fireplace and silk flower arrangements sat at the center of every end table, there were two wheelchairs and an unused IV pole outside the far elevator bank, looking as though they were waiting for a lift. This was an assisted-living facility—though an upscale one, to be sure.

"What's going on?" I asked when we reached the two women.

The one nearest me held a clipboard close to her ample chest. Fifty-ish with angled platinum hair that came to little points at either side of her chin, she wore an unabashedly eager look as she repeatedly clicked her ballpoint pen. "Sorry for the disturbance," she said. "We've had an incident."

"We noticed," I said. "What happened?"

"We're not sure. Not exactly," she said. "I mean, it might be an incident." She stressed the word *incident* with a lowered voice and wide eyes. "Or it might be nothing. It's probably nothing."

"Cathy," the other woman warned. "Let's not overreact."

"What kind of incident?" I asked.

"Nothing. Nothing." The second woman waved the air, as though to erase what Cathy had said.

33

"At least I hope it's nothing." Though this woman's pale, lank hair was pulled back in a low ponytail, she repeatedly tucked stray strands behind her right ear. The badge hanging from her lanyard indicated her name was Debbie and that she was a nurse. "We're not supposed to talk about it."

Cathy waggled her head. "Give me a break." When she turned a shoulder to her colleague I got a glimpse of her badge: aide. She whispered conspiratorially, "People die in this place all the time. But calling in the homicide cops? Yeah. That doesn't happen every day."

At the word *homicide* my stomach dropped. Bennett wrapped his fingers around my forearm. didn't know whether he did it to steady himself or me. "Who's dead?" I asked.

The nurse ignored me. "Cathy, stop." Her voice was a warning. "They told us—"

"Oh come on, Debbie," she said in that bored, singsong cadence popular with middle-schoolers. "It's not like I'm sharing privileged information." She wiggled her fingers to indicate the far side of the facility. "There are half a dozen investigators here. Maybe more. Anybody can see this isn't business as usual."

Debbie forced a tight smile. "I'm sorry," she said, addressing me and Bennett. "We haven't had a lot of visitors since they evacuated the East Wing." She rapped a knuckle against the back of

Cathy's clipboard, causing the other woman to jump. "Quit gossiping and record their names."

"Oh, yeah," Cathy said, and clicked her pen a few more times.

"Until they allow us back to the desk, you'll have to sign in here," Debbie went on. "I know, I know," she continued, despite the fact that we hadn't said a word, "visitors usually come and go here without all this hoopla. But until further notice, we have to take down your information before we can allow you into any residents' rooms. But first: Who are you here to visit?"

Bennett and I exchanged a puzzled glance, which clearly had a bewildering effect on the women. "We're not here to see a patient," I began. "At least, I *assume* she isn't one."

Bennett chimed in. "One of our employees asked us to meet her here. Her name is Frances Sliwa."

Debbie gave a little yelp and Cathy's eyes nearly pulsed out of her face. She clicked her pen ferociously. "What do we do?" she asked Debbie. "Who do we call?"

My stomach jolted. "What happened?" The coffee I'd enjoyed earlier began re-percolating in my gut. "You obviously know who Frances is. Is she all right?"

Even though Debbie appeared as rattled as Cathy was, she raised a hand. "I don't believe there's anything to worry about. Really."

Somehow her assurance didn't do it for me.

"Take us to her." Bennett said.

Cathy squeaked. "We can't."

"She's tied up at the moment," Debbie said.

Reminding me of a spy from some melo-dramatic 1940s-era film, Cathy ducked her head a bit and looked both ways. She pointed surreptitiously toward the East Wing. "She's down there. With the police."

From behind me: "Is there a problem here?"

All four of us jumped. I turned. The cop from the front door was making his way over. With his chin held high, he walked with his arms curled about four inches out from his sides, like he was forming flesh parentheses around his uniformed girth.

"What's the problem?" he asked again.

"These folks came to see one of the people from the East Wing," Debbie said.

Cathy had been following the exchange with her giant eyes. "One of the witnesses," she added helpfully.

Witnesses? I sucked in a breath and took a step closer to Bennett. "What is going on?" I asked quietly.

Cathy shoved the clipboard into Debbie's hands. "I can escort them over there, if you want," she said.

"Hang on. What are your names and who are you here to see?" The cop wrote our information down, then held up a finger as he spoke into his radio, conveying a terse summary of the situation to the person on the other end.

The voice crackled back that Ms. Sliwa was currently providing a statement, and further instructed the cop to have us wait in the holding room.

He signed off. "You heard the boss. Your friend is busy for now. These ladies will show you to the holding area."

"The Sun Gallery," Cathy said.

The cop looked at her. "What?"

"That's where we put the people you send over here. It's called the Sun Gallery."

"Yeah, okay." To us: "They'll show you where to wait."

"What is going on here?" Bennett asked. "I demand answers."

Except for blinking slowly a couple of times, the cop didn't react. "Nothing I can tell you, sir. Now, if you'll follow these women, they'll get you settled until your friend is free."

Bennett was unused to such flat-out refusal. While he wasn't the sort of person to exercise his considerable influence unnecessarily, he was accustomed to people bending over backward for him. I knew that as much as he relished his position of power in town, he was always happy to step back whenever he sensed that one of his requests pushed too hard. But this wasn't some ordinary entreaty. Whatever was happening here involved one of our own.

I was close enough to him to feel him quiver with frustration, but the patrol officer was simply doing his job. More important, it was clear that this officer did not possess the authority to disobey orders.

"We'll take your suggestion and wait in the holding area," I said to him. "But could you please let Frances know we're here?" When he nodded and ambled back to the front doors, I turned to Cathy. "Which way is the Sun Gallery?"

"I'll take you." She started off at a brisk pace, talking over her shoulder. "We're using it to house patients the police kicked out when they evacuated the East Wing." She wrinkled her nose and shook her head somberly. "They don't seem to be worried about the people on this end of the building, though. I guess because most of the residents here are too out of it to even know something's going on."

Sharp tangs of disinfectant rolled over us in waves as we strode past doors dotting both sides of the wide corridor.

"Sundays tend to be quiet," she said. "A lot of families come by to take their loved ones out for the day. That's why it's so empty this morning. After all the excitement though, visitors are allowed only in this wing. After we record their names for the police, of course."

She stopped long enough to clap a pink hand next to her mouth and stage-whisper, "This end of the building is for the really sick residents. Some of them got moved to this side *from* the East Wing." She waggled her brows at us as though that was supposed to mean something.

"Everyone who lives here is wealthy, I take it?" I asked.

She smirked. "You have to be to afford this place."

Bennett and I exchanged yet another glance. None of this made sense.

Cathy resumed walking and chatting. "At least the Sun Gallery is a nice place to wait. Even the East Wing residents come down here when it's nice out. The view over the lake is really pretty." As we took a hard right turn, she extended an arm, pointing farther down the hall. "Percy's already there. They finished with him about ten minutes ago."

"Percy?" I asked. "Who's that?"

She stopped to face us, wrinkling her nose again. "How can you know Frances but not know Percy?"

Bennett appeared as puzzled as I was. Offering an exaggerated shrug, I said, "Frances doesn't talk about her personal life."

For the first time since we'd met, Cathy regarded us with suspicion. Folding her arms, she asked, "Then why are you here?"

39

"Because she asked us to come," I said. "She gave us this address but didn't say a word about what was going on."

Cathy gave a careless little head bobble. "That's weird, but people are weird." She started down the hallway again. "Percy's her husband."

"Husband?" Bennett and I repeated in unison.

With a fresh swagger in her step, Cathy grinned over her shoulder. "Come on. I'll introduce you."

Chapter 4

"HERE WE ARE," CATHY SAID AS WE stepped through a double-door entryway.

The Sun Gallery turned out to be a basketball court–sized room with a long wall of screened sliding glass doors, offering a wide view over the lake below.

A dozen people were scattered about the spacious area, most in small groups of two or three. Two elderly residents, heads down, sat knee-to-knee in a far corner, passing playing cards back and forth. Almost everyone glanced up at our arrival, faces suffused with curiosity. A couple of awkward seconds later, all of them returned to whatever they were doing. One hunched-over man with a blanket on his lap lifted his hand in a hesitant hello. I waved back. He squinted at us, dropped his hand, and turned away.

I could imagine how on a summer day, with its windowed doors thrown open and a warm breeze drifting in through its many screens, this room could serve as a cheery porch-like vista to enjoy the sun. But today, with inky storm clouds rolling in over the lake, the darkening room gave off an electric buzz.

Cathy wound her way toward the windowed wall through a sea of wide-set pedestal tables, all of them featuring inlaid checkerboards. "This serves as our game room, too."

"Very nice," I said, because she seemed to expect it.

"Isn't it? Our guests are so fortunate to have such a lovely place to call home. Indwell is state-of-the-art." She stopped long enough to whisper again. "Poor things. But when people can no longer take care of themselves, this is an ideal alternative." She delivered this line with a beaming glance at Bennett. A second later, she called, "Percy," to the man with his back to us, sitting farthest from the door.

He didn't respond.

As we made our way over, we passed a young man in a highly mechanized wheelchair. He rolled his head against the back of the chair's extended neck brace to face us. With curly black hair and a chin lined with facial scruff, he looked to be about twenty-five years old.

"Hey," he called to us in a slurred but friendly manner. His eyes were a deep-set warm brown, and wide with interest. "You here to see Percy?"

Cathy dismissed him with a wave. "I'll be with you in a minute, Kyle."

Kyle nudged a curled hand against the chair's controls, spinning to face us. "You have to be Frances's friends, right?" he asked.

Bennett and I stopped. In my peripheral vision, I noticed Percy perk up.

"We are," Bennett said. "Do you know what's going on? Can you tell us?"

Kyle blinked and shot us a full-wattage grin. "Sure, I can."

"Hold up there, kid." Percy rotated his own motorized chair and whirred across the room to join us, parking himself between me and Bennett. "These folks are here to see me."

Actually, we're here for Frances.

With his heavily freckled bald crown and smirking, what's-it-to-you expression, Percy was a doppelgänger for the actor Gene Hackman. He had a similar nose and lots of laugh-line wrinkles, but didn't seem particularly jolly right now.

"Hello," I said, "I'm Grace Wheaton."

He raised an elbow the way most people might shoo a fly. "I know who you both are. Nice to finally put faces to names." He turned to Bennett, squinting up at him. "So you're Marshfield. I thought you'd be taller."

Cathy giggled. "Isn't this funny? You know them but they don't know you. Why on earth did Frances keep you such a secret, Percy?"

"I'll tell you why." Percy's deep, gravelly voice would be ideal for narrating luxury car commercials. "Because of this." He winged both arms this time, twisting to face me. "She's embarrassed."

I didn't know what to say, though clearly he expected some response. "I'm sure that's not—"

"You can't be sure. You don't know." Though he cut me off, he didn't do so unkindly. Nodding toward the front of the building, he said, "Until five minutes ago you didn't even know I existed." He turned to face Bennett. "Did you?"

Kyle inched his chair closer. "Frances talked about you two all the time. You think maybe when the police release her, we can discuss me coming out to visit Marshfield Manor? I'd really like to see it for myself one of these days."

I tried to ignore my churning gut. "Why are the police talking with Frances?" I asked. The coroner out front, the mention of homicide detectives, Cathy referring to Frances as a "witness"—this was not good.

"Now, now, let's not get ahead of ourselves." Cathy leaned in closer. She slid a glance toward the hallway. "We're not supposed to talk about any of this." Her body language screamed that she was ready to spill.

A crack of lightning zinged across the gloomy sky. Before I could expel a breath, thunder rattled the windows.

"Young woman," Bennett said. "I ask you to take pity on an old man's nerves and please tell us what's going on here and how Frances is involved."

"Well," she said, drawing out the word, "this morning—"

"Cathy, what's taking you so long?" I glanced up to see Debbie calling from the Sun Gallery entryway. "I need help up front."

"Oops. Gotta run." Cathy's grin never dimmed. "I'll catch up with you later."

When she was gone, Percy gestured with his eyes. "Have a seat, both of you," he said. "I'd offer to pull out a chair for you, Grace, but"—he winged his elbows again—"gallantry doesn't come easy for me these days."

Although he delivered the words with self-deprecating humor, there was distinct sadness in his eyes.

Using the thumb and index finger of his right hand, Percy manipulated his wheelchair's joystick, deftly maneuvering the conveyance to a nearby table with his back to the windows. While Bennett and I dragged wooden chairs from the room's perimeter to join him, Kyle zoomed over to settle across the checkerboard from Percy. Parked sideways, Kyle beamed like a kid who'd just graduated to the adults' table and couldn't wait to make a mess.

Thunder continued to crash outside as we settled ourselves. Flashing twigs of light skittered across the murky sky.

Nearly out of patience, Bennett leaned forward, keeping his voice low, his attention lasered on

45

Percy. "Right now I don't require an explanation as to who you are or why Frances comes to visit you here. All I care to know is where she is and what's going on."

"It's going to be fine. I'm sure it is," Percy said. "That is, if she can keep her wisecracking to a minimum."

"I don't want empty assurances. I want facts."

"I can tell you," Kyle said.

"One step at a time, kid." Percy gave a very Gene Hackman–like wink. To Bennett, he said, "It would help if you didn't interrupt."

Bennett's eyes blazed, but he sat back and drew in a deep breath. "Very well." He splayed his hands atop the checkerboard tabletop. "You have the floor."

I guessed Percy to be about ten years younger than my uncle, but whatever health issues he faced aged him. I found him attractive in an older-man sort of way—but then again, I'd always harbored a secret crush on Gene Hackman.

"First of all, although I am able to use my hands and fingers, doing so requires considerable effort. I tend to use my elbows to gesture when I talk."

Bennett said nothing but his expression spoke volumes.

"I tell you this so you don't get worried that I'm having a seizure or something." He shot me a crooked grin. "People do."

It took all my restraint to calmly urge, "Go on."

Percy pointed with his chin. "Kyle over there and I live in the East Wing. As does—well, er, did—a guy named Gustave Westburg. We call him Gus. He was old, crabby, and a real pain to have around, wasn't he, Kyle?"

"I liked him." The younger man cackled. "Never had a nice thing to say about anybody else, though."

"He didn't belong here," Percy said.

"Who didn't belong here?" I asked. "Gus?"

"Right. He shouldn't have been allowed to live with us. He had serious health issues."

"He probably shouldn't have been allowed in our wing at all," Kyle added.

Perhaps reading the confusion on my face, Percy explained, "This isn't a nursing home. Not in the typical sense." He rolled his gaze up and around the room. "Each building tends to specialize in some affliction. Except ours. We're the mishmash, aren't we, Kyle?"

He grinned. "A real melting pot."

"Indwell maintains state-of-the-art facilities for all its patients," Percy said. "One of the buildings you passed on the way is a mental health facility. Another one is for little kids, and another is a rehab center for amputees. People go in and out of that place all the time. No long-term patients there. Not like here."

"Mishmash," Kyle repeated. "This wing is for non-ambulatory patients, but our wing is for people like us who can do most things themselves and who don't need round-the-clock medical attention. I guess it kind of averages out that way."

"Our wing is designed for people like me and Kyle here," Percy said. "Our rooms are different from the ones at this end. More like small apartments. Our mobility issues are severe enough that we can't live on our own but we're both basically healthy. Gus wasn't. He shouldn't have been with us, but when money talks, people listen. It's different in the East Wing."

"More space, more autonomy," Kyle said.

"More expensive, too. Our rooms are specially outfitted." Percy flailed again as he talked. "I'm telling you, Gus didn't belong there. He was already going downhill by the time he moved in."

"But money talks?" I prompted. Bennett caught my eye and nodded approvingly. I knew he'd picked up on that comment, too. "What did you mean by that? I get the impression everyone who comes to live here is wealthy."

"Not everyone. Not me, for sure. As with anything, there are degrees," Percy said with a sly grin. "Gus and a buddy made a fortune investing in business together. He's not a gazillionaire like you"—this directed to Bennett—"but he was rich. And then, as the story goes, he got sick. Like me and Kyle, he couldn't live on his own. But, unlike us, he has kids."

"He didn't want to live with one of them?"

"They didn't like him very much." Percy barked a laugh. "Nobody did. So the kids decided to bring him here. Thing is, once Gus toured the place and saw how much better the apartments were than the regular rooms, he refused to live anywhere else."

"If the apartments are as nice as you describe, I'm surprised more people don't make that choice."

"They can't." Kyle shook his head like a toddler refusing to eat green beans. "Percy and I don't require constant medical care. Gus did. People that sick can't live in the apartments because it's too hard on the nursing staff."

"But again, unlike us, Gus was ambulatory," Percy said, pulling the conversation back to his side of the table. "He didn't need a wheelchair. Not even a cane. He moved slowly and he usually carted an oxygen tank behind him, but he could get around on his own. He should have been assigned to *this* end of the building but after Gus pressured them, the administration agreed to make an exception and allow him on our side. For a reasonable fee, of course." Percy dug his elbows into his seat back to readjust himself. "When Frances and I left Indwell this morning, Gus was alive. When we got back, he was dead."

"Where did you go?" I asked.

"Church. There's a chapel in one of the other

buildings, but we don't go there. Frances takes me to a parish about ten minutes away and then out to breakfast."

"*Hmph,*" Bennett said. "That explains a lot."

"It does?" I asked.

"You know how Frances is," he said. "She doesn't have a lot of friends at Marshfield. Years back, when she first started leaving for the weekend, everyone was atwitter that she wasn't attending church in Emberstowne anymore. Many unkind remarks were whispered behind her back. I did my best to put a stop to it, but there was only so much I could do."

"That's terrible," I said. "Frances's choice to worship, or not, is no one's business but her own."

"True," Bennett agreed, "but because Frances pokes her nose into everyone else's affairs, I think they felt turnabout was fair play."

"She wasn't always like that." Percy frowned. "As far as the church stuff goes, I think it's a colossal waste of time, but it's important to her that I atone for all my sins. Of which there are many, as I'm sure you'll soon learn. But once that woman sets her mind to something, she won't be convinced otherwise. Every week she packs me up and off we go. I don't have it in me to walk away." Using his chin to gesture toward his lifeless legs, he smirked. "Literally."

"If you and Frances were gone when Gustave

died," Bennett asked, "why is she considered a witness? What could she possibly have seen?"

An uneasy glance passed between Percy and Kyle. "It isn't what she saw," Percy said. "It's what the cops think she *did*."

Bennett stiffened.

"What are you saying?" I asked.

"I'm not sure, but . . ." Percy flexed his jaw.

Kyle interrupted. "Frances may have killed Gus."

Chapter 5

"WHOA, WHOA, WHOA," I SAID WITHOUT even attempting to keep my voice down. "No way. No. Way." Though Frances had never been a suspect in any of the murders around Marshfield Manor, she was abrasive enough that Detectives Rodriguez and Flynn—Flynn, in particular— would have leapt at the chance to lock my assistant up. Who knew how she was handling herself with these Rosette cops? This was not good. At all. "How long has she been in with them?"

"Fifteen, twenty minutes?" Kyle said. "Not long."

In the world of interrogations, twenty minutes was an eternity.

Bennett got to his feet. "This is preposterous. Let me talk to the officer in charge. They've made a grave mistake."

"We know," Percy said. When Bennett paid him no heed, Percy raised his voice. "Please, sit. It's going to be fine. They're questioning everyone who was around this morning. They questioned me and Kyle, too. I'm sure this is all routine and she'll join us here soon."

"But you said she's been in there for twenty minutes," I reminded him.

"Yeah," he agreed. "They have a little more to cover with Frances."

"I don't like this," I said. "Should we call a lawyer?"

Bennett had already pulled out his cell phone. "I'll get one down here immediately. Gracie, go talk with the officer at the door. Tell him that Frances refuses to answer any more questions until her attorney is present."

I got up, even though I knew the mission would be a futile endeavor. Neither Bennett nor I could prevent the police from questioning Frances. If she wanted counsel present, Frances would have to demand that herself.

"Wait a moment," Bennett said. "There's no signal here. I'll go out front to make the call myself and discuss this matter with the officer in charge. You stay with these two gentlemen and find out all you can about what happened here today."

Kyle rotated his chair to observe Bennett's progress out of the Sun Gallery. "You guys don't mess around, do you?"

I didn't bother answering. "You said they have more to cover with Frances. That she might be a suspect. What do you mean?"

Percy hunched a shoulder. "I'm telling you she's going to be released any second now."

His confidence was beginning to gnaw on my nerves. "And I'm telling you that it isn't always that simple. What more can you tell me? How did Gustave die?"

"They won't give us specifics," Percy said. "When Frances and I got back to the apartment, police were swarming the East Wing and wouldn't let us back into our room. That's the first we heard about Gus being dead. When they shuttled us over here, Cathy told us she heard them use the word *murder*. But you've met Cathy. She exaggerates."

I turned to Kyle. "Where were you?"

"Physical therapy. I left about the same time Percy and Frances took off for church. So I heard the fight."

"Fight?" I asked.

"Frances and Gus got into it, big-time," Kyle said. "Their worst one ever."

I dropped my head into my hands. "Oh no."

"It's not like that," Percy said. "Everyone knew that Frances and Gus didn't like each other very much, but today's argument was normal. Nothing special."

I lifted my head. "Except this time one of the combatants is dead."

"That's beside the point." Percy worked his lips. "You gotta understand, the guy was sick. I mean, seriously ill. Congestive heart failure, emphysema, and who knows what else. The fact that he croaked this morning shouldn't have triggered anything more than a call to the funeral home for a pickup."

"Yeah," Kyle said. "People die here every day. Like, literally."

"No, *you* don't understand," I said. "If foul play is suspected, and Frances is involved, this is serious. I need answers."

Percy stared out over the top of Kyle's head. "And here they come. See, what did I tell you?"

Bennett accompanied Frances as the two made their way toward us. Her gaze was fixed on our table, but one look at her fisted hands, pursed lips, and storming gait, and I knew she wasn't actually seeing any of us.

I got to my feet. "What's going on, Frances?"

"How dare they?" she asked rhetorically. "I didn't kill that old bag of bones. How do they know he didn't do it himself? I'll bet that miserable, selfish, ignorant lump finally decided he'd had enough and figured he could blame it on me."

Bennett pulled up another chair. "Have a seat, Frances."

Outside, the thunder and lightning had finally let up, but in here, Frances's stormy fury was about to be unleashed. "You think I can sit after what I've been through?"

Perspiration speckled the chest of her violet blouse. Her steel-gray hair poufed out at both temples as though she'd recently been yanking it out.

"Talk to me, Frances."

Normally, Frances eschewed all physical contact. When I touched her arm, I expected her to draw back. She surprised me by taking a sharp breath. She worked her jaw as though to collect herself. After a swift glance around the Sun Gallery, she faced me. "This is ridiculous."

"I know it is. And we're here to help. But we need to know what's going on."

She cocked an eyebrow at me, then turned to Bennett. "Sorry for snapping. I'm a little stressed right now."

Bennett waved off the apology. "Perfectly understandable." He nudged the chair a little closer to her. "But now that you've been released, things are looking up. Let's all take a deep breath and sort this out, shall we?"

Frances nodded. She tucked the hem of her blouse into her slacks' elastic waistband and took a seat in the proffered chair. "Stupid cops."

When we were all settled, with Frances between me and Kyle, Bennett gave me a nod. I decided to tread gently. "Percy and Kyle said that their roommate is dead and the police suspect murder. Is that right?"

Frances leaned forward, smashing a fingertip against one of the black checkerboard squares as though testing its rigidity. "As far as offing that old curmudgeon, the nurses probably have a sign-up sheet at the front desk for people eager to do the deed," she said. "Don't know why they spent so much time talking to me." She shot me a sideways glance. "I didn't do it."

"We know you didn't." Keeping calm took every bit of resolve I could manage. Questions scrambled my thoughts and a thousand prickles of worry tap-danced along my spine. I wanted answers so badly I was tempted to shake everyone around me until the right words fell out. But Frances was as worked up as I'd ever seen her. Next to me, under the table, her knee bounced. And though she poked at the same square over and over, exerting so much pressure that her fingernail reddened, she couldn't keep her hand from shaking.

She looked up, thrusting her chin toward Percy. "So you're probably wondering why I never told you about him."

"Right now, all we care about is that you're free to go," Bennett said. "Are you?"

Frances snorted. "Who knows? They may need to 'follow up' with me." She gave a haughty little head-waggle. "These guys are barking up the wrong tree, thinking I had something to do with any of this." Curling up one side of her mouth, Frances added, "These cops are even bigger idiots than Flynn and Rodriguez back home."

"I'm relieved that you're out of interrogation,"

Bennett said. "As an added precaution, I've contacted one of my attorneys. She'll meet us here shortly."

"I don't need an attorney. Then for sure they'll think I'm guilty."

"It doesn't hurt to cover our bases, Frances," I said. "And it makes Bennett feel good to be able to help."

She settled both chubby arms on the table. "I suppose."

With a nod, Bennett encouraged me to go on.

"I have a couple of questions," I said.

Frances squinted at the tabletop. "Go ahead."

"First of all, your husband says—"

Frances jerked like a folded marionette suddenly brought to life. "Hold up right there, missy." Flipping her fingers to point gunlike at Percy, she said, "That lowlife across the table is not my husband."

"Oh, come on, Frances," Percy said in a gently teasing tone. "If you're not my one and only, then why do we have the same last name?"

"Did he *tell you* we were married?" she asked.

"Actually . . ." I was about to explain that Cathy had identified him, when Frances interrupted.

"Let me clarify. It's true that Mr. Tall Tales over there *was* my husband, but that was a couple of lifetimes ago. Lucky for me, I wised up and divorced him. Probably back when you were still in diapers."

"Got it." I wondered why, if she despised the man so much, she continued to visit him every weekend. "Can we get back to why the police believe Gus was murdered?"

"Fine." Frances huffed out a breath and glared at Percy. "I'll wait 'til later to set the story straight."

"I can't believe you think I'd lie to your friends," he said, feigning hurt.

She snarled at him. "Wouldn't be the first time."

Percy didn't seem the least bit perturbed. "All I told them was that Gus was alive when we left the apartment this morning and dead by the time we got back. You take it from there, sweetie."

"Hold your tongue." If Frances could have shot poison darts straight from her eyes to his heart, she wouldn't have given it a second thought. "What's wrong with you?"

"That's my little pistol." Percy turned to Bennett. "I knew she was in there somewhere. Come on now, out with the rest of the story. What did the police ask you?"

Whether it had been a result of Percy's teasing or the fact that she was finally able to catch her breath after being questioned by the police, Frances's mood had done a complete turnaround. Instead of leaning heavily on the table, she sat back, arms folded across her chest, regarding us all with mild annoyance. This was the Frances I knew.

"They thought they were being so clever," she said. "But Grace and I know how cops operate. They thought they could trap me into admitting something I didn't do." She gave a quick, humorless laugh. "They don't know who they're up against."

Relieved to finally be on track, I asked, "What do you know about how Gus died?"

She made eye contact with Percy and Kyle. "You know that tube thing Gus had attached to him all the time?" She pointed to the back of her left hand. "Right here?"

"The heparin lock?" Kyle asked.

"Yeah, that's it." She turned to me. "It's for shooting medicine into him without always having to stick him with a needle every single time."

Percy gestured with his elbow. "There's nothing dangerous about those."

"I didn't say there was." More poison darts.

"What about it?" I asked.

Frances resumed the story. "One of the nurses came in to flush it—they have to do that every couple of days so it doesn't get infected—and that's when they found Gus dead."

"Which nurse?" Kyle asked.

"That skinny male nurse. The tall one with the bad complexion," Frances said. "His name is Santiago something-or-other."

"So how do they know Gus was murdered?" I asked. "I can't imagine a gunshot would go unnoticed around here. Was he stabbed? Smothered?"

"They didn't give me specifics. All I know is that they found something in Gus's room that shouldn't have been there."

"What did they find?" Bennett asked.

"They wouldn't tell me."

"That's not very helpful," I said.

"You think?" Frances grimaced. "They were waiting for me to say something that would prove I was there, so that they could claim I had insider knowledge. But I can't give them information I don't possess." She tightened her arms across her chest and twisted around to face the rest of the room. Raising her voice, she said, "You all heard that loud and clear, right? I didn't do it."

A few of the room's inhabitants shot furtive glances to one another and pretended not to be paying us any attention. A couple of people shifted in their seats.

Cathy came hurrying over, slightly out of breath as though she'd run the entire way down the hall. "Just so you know," she said when she got to our table, "the police said they don't know how soon they plan to allow you back in your rooms. So if you need something, you'll have to ask one of us to get it for you."

"Kyle and I aren't sleeping in here tonight," Percy said. "Not a chance."

"Of course not." Cathy giggled, which seemed an odd reaction, given the events of the day. "We're looking into options in case the police stay here really late."

"There aren't any open apartments in our wing," Percy said. "They better not stick us together in one of those dorm rooms where we have to share a TV and a bathroom. I don't want to listen to the kid snore all night."

"I don't snore," Kyle said. "I breathe heavily."

"It's not for sure. And it would only be temporary," Cathy said. "We'll have to make do until we get the all clear from the police."

Percy shook his head. "No way. Frances pays an arm and a leg for me to stay in the apartment." He flailed his elbows. "And it took two arms and two legs—mine—to get me in here in the first place."

Cathy was the only one who laughed at Percy's attempt at humor. "Oh, you," she said with a flirtatious giggle. To Frances: "He's so funny."

"Funny doesn't begin to describe him," Frances said.

"Anyway, I came to give you both that update. If anything else comes up, I'll be sure to let you know."

A moment later, she was gone.

"She certainly is chipper," I said.

"Cathy's all right," Kyle said. "I'll take her over Santiago any day."

"You mean the nurse who found Gus," I said. "What's wrong with him?"

"He's nosy." Frances leaned forward again. "Always butting into everybody else's business. I'd like to open his closet and see how many skeletons tumble out."

I resisted the urge to make eye contact with Bennett. I knew at that moment we were both thinking about pots and black kettles. "Did he have a grudge against Gus?" I asked.

Frances snorted. "Everyone had a grudge against Gus."

"Uh-oh," Percy said.

I turned to follow his gaze. The nurse we'd spoken with earlier, Debbie, led an elderly gentleman into the room. She rested one hand on his shoulder and patted his arm with the other. The man was tall but stooped. Wearing a heavy rain jacket and carrying a small, weighty bag, he used his free hand to shield his eyes. Although he didn't appear to need the support Debbie offered, his body language suggested that he appreciated her presence.

"Who is that?" I asked.

Kyle had turned his chair enough to see where we were looking. "Anton," he said in a hushed tone.

"Gus's best friend," Percy said.

"Best friend?" Kyle asked. "Don't you mean contraband smuggler?"

"More like a little of both." Percy waved an elbow dismissively. "Either way, it looks like he just heard the news."

Chapter 6

DEBBIE SHOT US A SILENT PLEA FOR HELP. Percy nodded and the nurse brought Anton to our table. Reading the situation, Bennett got up to bring over yet another chair. He positioned it to his right, next to Percy. Our group had swelled to six around a table designed for two.

"Why don't you sit with Kyle and Percy for a while, Anton?" Debbie said as she helped him into the seat and patted his shoulder. "The police will probably want to speak with you. I'll let them know you're here."

Eyes red, he looked up to thank her before turning his attention to the rest of us. Though my presence and Bennett's seemed to confuse him, he mumbled a greeting. When he placed his bag in front of him, it hit the table with a heavy *thunk*.

"We're all very sorry," Percy said. "This must be a terrible shock."

Anton blinked glassy eyes. "What happened?" When he spoke, his voice cracked. The man was about Bennett's age and just as tall. Where Bennett was athletic to the point of slim, however, Anton was bulky. He had a ruddy complexion, a wide, flat forehead, and a full head of gray hair. "Why are all the police here?"

I held my breath, but before Percy or Kyle had a chance to answer, Frances said, "They believe Gus was murdered, and they think I did it."

Anton's grief-stricken expression shifted from bewilderment to surprise before settling on outrage. "They are mistaken," he said. There was a trace of Eastern Europe in his manner of speaking. "This is not possible."

"Frances and Gus had another blow-up this morning," Kyle said. "That makes her Suspect Number One."

Anton reached a furry hand across the checkerboard to rest it atop Frances's. "But of course you didn't hurt Gus," he said. "Why would anyone? He had no enemies."

Frances looked ready to argue the point, but my swift kick under the table warned her off.

Anton evidently hadn't expected an answer. He sat back again and turned to the group. "Why do the police suspect murder? What don't I know?"

Under the table, Frances returned my kick before getting to her feet. "I need to visit the ladies' room." She turned to me. "You probably ought to come along so you know where it is. We may be here a while."

Nothing like a subtle hint. "Sure," I said. "Good idea."

Frances took off out of the room at a speedy pace. I caught up with her in the hallway. She didn't break stride even when I fell into step next to her. Her hands were fisted, her brow tight. "Not a word. Not yet."

Three-quarters of the way down the long corridor, she made a sharp left and pushed her way into a door marked WOMEN.

Three cream-colored stalls lined the right side of the utilitarian room. Frances placed her hands on her knees and half-bent, half-crouched to check under each of the closed doors.

I pushed at all three doors, one at a time, satisfied when each of them swung wide open before banging shut once again. "No one here."

"You do it your way, and I'll do it mine." Frances's face was red when she righted herself. "Can't be too careful."

"What's going on, Frances?" I asked.

She scanned the tops of the walls as though looking for security cameras.

"We're in a washroom," I reminded her. "Nobody's going to spy on us in here."

"You're so naïve." Satisfied with her scrutiny, she folded her thick arms across her chest and positioned herself in the middle of the room. "First things first: Out with it. What did Percy tell you about me?"

"Nothing at all. It's all been about Gustave," I said. "Talk to me, Frances. Bennett and I are completely in the dark here. What couldn't you tell me at the table?"

She chewed on her lower lip for a moment before answering. "They're being careful not to tell me much, but you and I know how these things work." She dug one hand out from its perch inside her elbow to wag a finger between us. "We've been through this before. Police making foolish mistakes. Bad information. *Pheh.* That busybody nurse is the one I'm mad at. When he found Gus dead, he should have called the morgue attendants, not the police."

"You don't believe Gus was murdered?"

"It doesn't matter what I think. But now, because that nosy Santiago found a cap in Gus's room, everybody's all hysterical, thinking that I dosed Gus with Percy's medication."

"Wait. What are you talking about? You said that the police didn't tell you anything."

Frances's brows jumped so far up her face I thought they might spring off the top of her head. "You think I'm going to spill everything I know the first time somebody asks?" She harrumphed. "Give me a little more credit than that. I lied when we were at the table."

I brought my hands to my head. "Frances, we aren't playing a game here. If the police suspect you, we have to take this seriously."

"It's pretty clear to me that I'm taking this far more seriously than you are." She lifted her chin.

68

"Why do you think I pulled you in here? Why do you think I'm telling you about the insulin syringe cap? It's purple, by the way." She raised her hands in the air. "It's purple. Of course it is."

"What in the world are you talking about?"

Frances's voice had begun to rise as she spoke and she gave a self-conscious glance around the room before continuing in a quieter tone. "On top of all his other health issues, Percy's a diabetic. We keep insulin in his room for when he needs it."

"Wait," I said. "Stop right there. Why is Percy allowed to keep medication in the apartment? He clearly can't self-administer."

"Don't let him fool you; he's fully capable," Frances said. "He can't manipulate his hands as well as you and I do, but he's not as weak as he tries to pretend." She muttered something about Percy's predilection for enlisting help from attractive young women before adding, "You probably didn't notice that he keeps an injector in the chair next to his leg. We tuck one in there for emergencies. The rest are in his room."

"That doesn't explain why the facility allows patients to keep their own medication. Isn't it their job to deliver dosages?"

"Just because he's disabled doesn't mean he's helpless." Frances ran her fingers up both sides of her head, clearly losing patience. "Percy's here for assisted living, not critical care. There's a difference. He needs help getting in and out of bed sometimes and he can't prepare his own food, but mostly he manages on his own. Indwell provides him a measure of autonomy, but help is here if he needs it. That's the whole point: to allow residents to live as normal a life as possible. That's why it costs so much to get into this place. And don't even get me started on the monthly fees."

"Got it. I'm sorry. Go on."

Jamming a finger into her chest, she said, "I didn't kill the old geezer, but if somebody did, it looks like they used Percy's insulin."

"That's ridiculous. There's no way to know that before lab results come in. They haven't even taken the body away yet."

"The police are *speculating*," she said with an emphatic lilt to the word. "Nosy boy Santiago found a bright purple cap rolling around under Gus's bed when he went in there to do the heparin lock flush. He picked the cap up, recognized it, and planned to ask us about it later. But when he saw Gus was dead, he freaked out and called the police instead."

"That's hardly proof."

"Yes, but he was quick to alert the authorities about the individual who'd argued with Gus this morning—a person who conveniently has access to Percy's medicine. Guess who he was talking about?" She hit herself in the chest again, this time with both hands. "Me. That's who."

"What did you argue about?"

"Does it matter?" A moment later, she added, "Like usual, he started complaining about the 'mess' I made. All I did was leave my purse and coat on the sofa. It's where I always leave them. But I guess he wanted to sit there right at that very moment. I told him if he didn't shut up, I'd give him a whole lot more to complain about."

I winced. "Couldn't the cap they found have been accidentally dropped by another nurse visiting Gus's room? I'm sure they deal with insulin every day for plenty of patients."

"Percy's the only diabetic in that section, apparently." Frances shook her head. "But, more than that, Gus was a whack job about cleanliness. Nothing ever out of place. And he was completely ambulatory. Believe me, if he'd seen that cap on the floor, he would have pitched a fit you'd have heard back in Emberstowne."

"Still, that's circumstantial."

She started to pace the tile floor. "Yeah, until you get to the part where you find out that one of Percy's insulin syringes is missing."

"Are you sure?"

She stopped pacing to glare at me. "Yes, I'm sure."

There had to be another answer. "Could Gus have taken the insulin himself?"

"You mean could he have committed suicide?" She shrugged. "Anything's possible, but I doubt it. The guy may have been a lousy lunkhead, but he firmly believed in his right to be here."

"So how did the cap get there?"

"That's the million-dollar-bail question," she said. "And when they find the syringe, guess whose fingerprints will be all over it?"

My heart sank. "Yours."

She pursed her lips. "Yesterday, I realized I hadn't checked the expiration on Percy's meds for quite some time, so I pulled everything out. None of it was out-of-date, so I put everything back."

"Who knew you did that?" I asked.

"I know where you're going," she said, waving the air between us. "Nobody's trying to frame me."

"How can you be sure?"

"Nobody knew I handled the insulin. Not yesterday specifically, at least. Everyone here knows that I take care of Percy's share of the apartment and make certain his room is clean and his supplies are in place. I've done that since he moved in. Yesterday's inventory was nothing special. Nothing missing."

"How long has Percy been a resident?"

She pulled her mouth to one side. "A little short of ten years. He was one of the first residents when Indwell opened."

"What happened to him?" I asked. "I mean, what brought him here in the first place?"

"I brought him here," she said with a fiery spark in her eyes. "After he lost control of his motorcycle and slammed his spine into a cement barrier."

"Oh, I'm sorry. That had to be devastating."

"I don't know what hurts him worse: not being able to move his legs or the fact that there was no one willing to help him. No one but me, that is."

"He's lucky to have you."

"Too bad he didn't realize that when we were still married." Her eyes still blazing, she added, "Where were all those swooning women when he needed them? Not one of them stuck around when his life fell apart. Took a life-threatening accident to wake him up."

"I'm sorry, Frances," I said.

She glared again. "Don't you dare pity me. I made my bed, I'm lying in it. Nobody's business but my own, you understand?"

"Yes. Got it."

"If it weren't for that stupid nurse sounding the alarm, I'd have been able to keep you and the Mister out of all this. Now everyone in Emberstowne will know that I'm stuck taking care of the jerk who broke my heart all those years ago."

"No one has to know," I said. "Bennett and I won't tell a soul."

Her mouth turned down sharply. "This news will get out. Mark my words."

Chapter 7

WHEN FRANCES AND I RETURNED TO THE Sun Gallery, only Percy and Kyle remained at the table.

"Where's Bennett?" I asked as Frances and I reclaimed our seats.

"The lawyer showed up; they're talking." Kyle twisted to look around the room. "Don't know where they went."

"What about Anton?"

"Police are questioning him," Percy said.

I pointed to the bag Anton had *thunked* onto the table when he'd arrived. "Looks like he forgot something."

"Yeah, right." Kyle laughed. "I'm sure that was no oversight." He grinned across the table until he caught Percy's eye. "What do you think the police would make of his contraband?"

Percy wore a thoughtful look. "Maybe we should tell them about Anton's regular deliveries."

"No, I was just kidding," Kyle said. "There's no way Anton killed Gus."

"Doesn't matter." Percy sent an exaggerated loving gaze to Frances. "All I care about is getting the focus off my sweetie."

She rolled her eyes but her cheeks warmed.

Not understanding the conversation, I decided to find out exactly what contraband they were talking about. I picked up the heavy brown bag and wrapped my fingers around the neck of the bottle inside. "You're kidding me," I said when I pulled out a factory-sealed fifth of scotch. "Anton brought this for Gus?"

Percy and Kyle were unfazed.

"He brings in a bottle at least twice a week," Kyle said. "They share whatever it is. But they're not very picky, are they, Percy?" Without giving his roommate a chance to answer, he continued. "Scotch, gin, bourbon, you name it, Anton brought it in. Sometimes—if Gus was in a good mood—they'd even share."

"With you," Percy said. "Gus didn't like me."

Appalled, I turned on Frances. "We should tell the police."

She waved the air. "Anton wouldn't kill Gus."

"Neither would you, but that isn't stopping them from suspecting you." I hefted the bottle. "What if he died from something he drank?"

Percy fidgeted in his chair. "Gus kept the liquor in a cabinet so that the nurses wouldn't see it and dump it out." He blinked a couple of times, as though a thought had suddenly occurred to him. "But that doesn't mean Anton couldn't have added something to one of the open bottles when Gus wasn't looking." He locked eyes with Kyle.

"You know how Gus liked to start every morning with a healthy swig."

"Healthy?" I asked. "Hardly."

"I don't know," Kyle said, twisting his mouth. "Anton's a heck of a good guy. I can't see him doing anything to hurt Gus. Besides, that bottle hasn't even been opened."

"Doesn't matter. The cops need to know about his habits." Percy curled his fingers around the wheelchair's joystick. "Put the bottle on my lap," he said to Frances. "I'll take it with me."

Just then, Bennett returned. A short, heavyset woman wearing a plum skirt suit accompanied him. Though Bennett took his customary long-legged strides to cross the room, the diminutive woman managed to keep pace.

She sharply scrutinized our little group, her deep-set eyes missing nothing. Agewise I assumed she fell between Frances and me, but whether she'd hit forty or fifty at her last milestone birthday was impossible to tell. Her bob-length hair was a rich auburn, her skin smooth.

"This is Lillandra Holland," Bennett said without preamble when they reached us. He then introduced me, Percy, and Kyle. "Frances," he said, "Ms. Holland will be representing you in this matter."

The lawyer held up two pillowy palms. "Call me Lily, please," she said. "Makes life much easier for everyone." Turning to Frances, she extended a hand. "Pleased to make your acquaintance, Ms. Sliwa."

The quick seconds it took for the two women to shake provided Frances ample opportunity to invite the lawyer to call her by her first name. She didn't.

Unruffled, Lily continued. "I've spoken with the detectives in charge and convinced them to allow you to return to Emberstowne. You may have to make yourself available for further questioning at some point, but we'll worry about that when it happens."

Frances gave a satisfied nod. "It's about time they realized they were wasting their efforts."

Lily waved a chubby finger. "So that there are no misunderstandings, let me assure you that while you're free to go now—and I do mean that we ought to leave *right now*—the police have not completely eliminated you as a suspect. You're not in the clear. Not yet."

Frances looked away. "Stupid cops."

Lily shot Bennett a glance. I had no doubt he'd forewarned the attorney about Frances's prickly nature.

"I'd like you out of here before they change their minds." Lily gestured Frances to follow. "We can talk on the way back to Emberstowne."

"What about my car?" Frances asked. "I'm not leaving it here."

"Gracie or I can drive your vehicle back,"

Bennett said. "We'll drop it off in front of your house."

Grudgingly, Frances reached into her cavernous vinyl purse and dug out keys. "You can keep this set until I come in tomorrow. I have spares at home."

She then shot a look to Percy, who still waited with the bottle on his lap. He lifted his chin. "Go," he said. "We'll talk later."

I WOULD HAVE PREFERRED TO DRIVE back to Marshfield with Bennett so that we could compare notes along the way, but he took off in Frances's Buick, while the two women left in Lily's Lexus, and I drove home alone.

Surprised to find both my roommates' cars in our driveway, I parked behind Scott's and let myself in through the back door.

"What are you guys doing home so early?" I asked.

They both looked up at me. I took in the papers strewn across our kitchen table, the open laptop, and their wan, distraught faces and got the impression that my arrival had jolted them both out of a dream. From the looks of it, a nightmare.

"What happened?" I asked.

Bootsie curled around the doorway, saw it was me, and hurried back out of the room. Neither Bruce nor Scott noticed her.

"We're done." Scott's voice was lifeless, flat.

I pulled out a chair and sat across from them, not even bothering to peel off my jacket. "What happened to the thirty days?"

"Thirty days turned into zero days," Bruce said, making a circle with his fingers, "today, when the village inspector shut us down."

"But . . . it's Sunday," I said, as though that solved anything. "Village inspectors don't work on weekends."

"They do when a building collapses," Scott said. He pantomimed the sky falling. "You know our second floor? Where we kept office supplies and stuff?"

"Yes."

He smashed his hands together. "All part of the first floor now." Anticipating my next question, he hurried to add, "No one was hurt, thank goodness. Most of the damage is at the rear of the building. But we lost a lot of our inventory underneath it."

"A lot," Bruce said. "There's wine everywhere."

"Everywhere," Scott echoed. "There's a river of wine winding across the floor. Like that scene from *A Tale of Two Cities*, but without all the people lapping it up off the ground." He turned to Bruce: "It's a good thing we never utilized that second floor fully, the way we talked about. Can you imagine how much worse it would have been with extra weight up there?"

Eyes glazed, Bruce stared at the laptop's

screen. "Probably would have happened sooner, is all," he said without looking up. "We knew the building was a ticking time bomb. We just didn't realize how short of a fuse we were dealing with."

"We got lucky," Scott said. "This could have been much worse."

"I know you're right." Bruce blinked himself back into the conversation and offered a weak smile. "But at the moment, I'm not feeling very lucky at all."

Scott laid a hand atop Bruce's and squeezed. "No one on our staff was injured, we hadn't opened for business for the day yet so there weren't any customers in the place, and you and I are still here to clean up the mess. I think we need to count our blessings."

Bruce nodded, but I could tell he was unconvinced.

Scott was usually the naysayer of the two, Bruce more of a Pollyanna. It was unsettling to see them reverse roles.

"I'm so sorry," I said. "What can I do to help?"

"There's nothing anyone can do. Not now." Bruce went back to studying his laptop. "Our landlord should have taken care of these repairs years ago."

"At a minimum, he ought to be fined," I said.

Scott nodded. "Believe me, he will be."

"Not going to do us any good, though," Bruce said. "We're moving into tourist season with no shop and no prospects. I'm looking at our cash reserves, and I don't think we'll be able to make it through the summer with no income." Again he tried to smile. "By the way, how did your meeting with Bennett go?"

I remembered my promise to Frances to keep her situation on the down-low. "We had a nice chat."

Bruce glanced at the clock. "Long chat." He nodded absentmindedly. "That's good."

Scott had gone back to tapping on a calculator and scribbling notes on the papers before him. "We have enough to pay our living expenses," he began. "But that's about it."

"I can help with that," I said. "You know that I don't need rent from you two anymore."

Scott shook his head. "Didn't you insist on continuing to work for Bennett even after you found out you were related? You could have easily stepped away and lived a luxurious life without having to work for your income," he said. "You told him you didn't want a handout. Neither do we."

"Then call it a loan, if you like," I said. "But from now until Amethyst Cellars is back up and running, I refuse to accept a penny from either of you."

When they started to protest again, I said. "Please, let me do this much. It means a lot to me."

They exchanged a glance. Scott gave a quick nod, Bruce a small smile.

"Thanks, Grace," Bruce said. "But we owe you."

Chapter 8

AT MARSHFIELD EARLY THE NEXT morning, I crossed through Frances's office into mine, dropping off my purse and hanging up my soon-to-be-unnecessary trench coat. Yesterday's storms had passed and I took a moment to gaze out my giant mullioned window, hoping that the day's cheery forecast bode well for both sunny skies and good news for Frances.

Frances usually started coffee for us when she got in but I decided to take over that responsibility today. After the weekend she'd had, I wanted to do whatever I could to make life a little easier for her. I hurried back through her office and out into the corridor. Our entire floor remained deliciously deserted at this early hour. I enjoyed the morning quiet and guessed that I had at least another twenty minutes before other staffers began showing up.

At one time, before I was born, this section of the house had been designated for overnight guests. Now as I walked along the quiet hallway, passing rooms that had been converted into staff offices, I tried to imagine what this wing had been like back during its glory days. When

Bennett's father—my grandfather—had entertained here.

This home was Bennett's. And now—as he'd repeatedly made clear—it was mine, too.

Though much of the hallway's carved oak embellishment—from the crown molding to the wainscot—remained intact, the guest rooms had been transformed over the years from opulent to utilitarian. This area was no longer a place where wealthy industrialists and their families cavorted; this was where work got done.

It would be nice to see these rooms returned to their former splendor. To rip out the harsh lighting and replace fluorescent fixtures with vintage accessories or, at a minimum, high-quality reproductions. I ran my fingertips along the top of a metal filing cabinet that had been relegated to the hallway because we'd run out of office space. Squat, gray, and ugly, the cabinet was nonetheless sturdy and did its job well. Whoever had outfitted the work areas, sometime in the middle of the last century, had done so with an eye to durability but with little regard for aesthetics.

The high-ceilinged employee lunchroom had, at one time, served as a guest parlor. Now the space featured a linoleum floor, 1960s-era kitchen cabinetry, bronze appliances, and a mosaic tile backsplash in three shades of ochre. Over the sink, two unadorned windows faced north, and I stared out over the front of the estate—a very different view from that in my office—while I turned on the faucet to fill the coffeepot's reservoir.

As the water splashed in, an idea began to formulate. What if we relocated our personnel outside the mansion and kept only necessary staff on the premises? Assuming a suitable office location could be found nearby, the move itself could be accomplished with relative ease. We could even build new, if need be. We had acres of open space.

Except for a few key players, our office workers were never required to put in an appearance in the public part of the mansion. The docent staff, of course, was always present, but there was no need for accounting, marketing, or outside sales staffers to be on-site every day.

The world had changed a great deal since these rooms had been repurposed into offices. With the advent of e-mail and the ability of personnel to work remotely, we could probably bring this area back—restore it to its former brilliance. I'd have to remember to mention the idea to Bennett one of these days. But not until after we got Frances through this current crisis.

"What in the world are you doing?"

I spun to find my assistant glaring at me from the doorway. Hand on her hips, she wore an expression of surprised disbelief.

I shut off the faucet. "You still have your coat on."

She still had her purse, too, and it swung from the crook of her arm as she marched across the small room. "You didn't run the water ahead of time, did you?"

"What do you mean?" I asked, hefting the reservoir, which was now pretty weighty. "How could I have filled this *without* running the water?"

She shook her head as though annoyed, snatched the reservoir from me, and upended it, sending its contents glugging down the drain. "This is an old building. A very old building," she said as she placed the empty container to the side and turned the faucet back on, full force. "There's most likely lead in the pipes. I let the water run for a full minute each morning before I start the coffee." She yanked up one sleeve of her coat, frowned at her watch, and said, "Lead accumulates in a body, you know. I read that on the Internet. Can't be too careful."

My first thought was to argue that the small amount of lead that we might be ingesting—and there was no proof for certain that we were—probably wasn't enough to cause harm. But the truth was I knew nothing of toxic lead levels. And I didn't want to start out the day bickering.

"Good plan." I leaned a hip against the speckled Formica countertop and asked, "How did your talk with Lily go?"

She continued to study her watch. "Stupid."

"You don't like her? Or you don't believe she's an effective lawyer?"

"She's competent enough, I'm sure," Frances said without looking up. "But I don't understand why she needs to ask me so many personal questions. It's like a body can't have any privacy anymore. Some of the things she wanted to know . . ." Frances shook her head.

"What did she say about your situation?" I asked. "How soon will you be in the clear?"

"Time's up," Frances said, raising her eyes from her watch and turning back to the sink.

While she refilled the reservoir, I pulled out a coffee filter and began spooning in grounds. "There's nothing special I need to know at this step, is there?"

She glanced over. "Three rounded scoops, and a half-scoop more."

When we finished setting up, I gestured toward our offices. "Let's talk while we wait for it to brew."

She made the typical Frances face of disapproval. "I don't plan to tell you any more than you need to know," she said.

"I wouldn't dream of prying."

I led the way and as she fell into step behind,

I heard her mutter, "Not that you don't already know it all now, anyway."

Back in our offices, she waved me away. "Go ahead, get started on whatever you need to do. Once I get myself settled, I'll come in and tell you everything Lily and I talked about. Will that satisfy you?"

"Completely," I said.

"And I suppose you expect me to bring in the coffee when it's ready."

"I'll be happy to get it."

She glowered. "Why? Am I suddenly incapable of doing my job?"

I opened my mouth to argue that getting coffee for me was not actually part of her job description, but then thought better of it. "Of course not."

"Pheh." She hung up her coat, sat at her desk, placed her purse in a drawer, and began studying papers on her desk. "I'm not accused of anything yet, you know. I'm not an official suspect. Just a person of interest."

None of this had anything to do with getting coffee. "I know that."

"Don't start treating me differently."

"Not a chance, Frances."

"You'd better not," she said gruffly. Then she met my eyes. Though her brows were as carefully penciled in as ever, they were lifeless and flat, no longer bouncy tadpoles. Her eyes held none of their usual sassy sparkle. My heart lurched. Frances was far more frightened than she was letting on.

"Bring me up to speed whenever you're ready, then," I said with all the breezy calm I could muster. I knew instinctively that the less pressure I put on her, the easier it would be for her to open up. "You know where I'll be."

Chapter 9

SEATED AT MY DESK WITH MY FINGERS clasped atop my head, I swiveled to stare out the window at the sunny landscape. More than anything, I wanted this cloud of suspicion to go away. And I wanted it gone now. The best way I could think to accomplish that was to track down as much information about the situation as I could, using every means available.

My first instinct had been to alert our favorite private investigator, Ronny Tooney. Catching myself, I silently mouthed, "Bronson." It was taking me a long time to get used to using his real first name. The man had provided invaluable assistance to us over the years. Even if nothing could be done to dissuade the police from investigating Frances, Tooney—I was sure—would be able to come up with some interesting way to help prove her innocence.

Even though I knew he could be trusted to keep our confidence, Frances's admonishment to keep the story to myself prevented me from alerting the resourceful detective. But I had to do something. Deep in thought, I bit my lower lip. We couldn't let Frances twist in the wind until the police cleared her. I knew from experience how long that could take. Though perennially cranky, and quick to criticize others, Frances was not nearly as indestructible as she pretended to be.

"I know you're a lady of leisure these days, but do you think you could pretend to be working instead of daydreaming?"

I sat up, dropping my hands to my lap. "Where's the fun in that?"

Frances crossed my office carrying a tray. On it were two steaming mugs of coffee, a pitcher of cream, and two plated croissants as well as necessary silverware and linens.

She placed the tray on my desk, took one of the mugs, one of the croissant plates, and sat down across from me. "Help yourself. I'm not going to spoon-feed you."

"Thanks, Frances." Gentle heat radiated off the golden-brown pastry and I got a warm whiff of yeasty deliciousness as I brought the croissant to my side of the desk. I added cream to my mug then took a sip of the brew. "Excellent coffee."

"Three-and-a-half scoops of grounds. After you let the water run for a full minute." She held her cup so close to her face that I could only see her eyes over the top of its rim. "Remember that in case I get hauled off to prison and you're stuck making it yourself."

"That's not going to happen," I said. "You do know that, don't you?"

"I know that the two geniuses who run Emberstowne's homicide department are always ready to jump at the obvious answer. If it weren't for you and me, there's no telling how many innocent people they'd have locked up and how many murderers would still be running free."

"Rodriguez and Flynn aren't that bad."

"They're not that good, either."

"Regardless," I said, "we aren't dealing with them this time. I'm sure that the officers in charge of the investigation at Indwell will either determine that Gus died of natural causes, or that—if someone did kill him—it wasn't you."

She gave an indignant snort. "I almost wish it *had* happened in Emberstowne. At least we can handle those two goofballs. We have history with them."

"I was thinking," I began gently, "of bringing Tooney in on this."

"No."

"You know he wouldn't breathe a word."

"No."

"Why not?"

She placed her mug on my desk with a *thud*. "It's bad enough you and the Mister are involved. When I said that I don't want anyone else in town to know, I meant *nobody* else. You know as well as I do that the minute even one other person gets wind of what went down at Indwell yesterday, my reputation is shot."

"Not at all, Frances." Though tempted to break into my croissant and enjoy its flaky goodness, I pushed the plate aside. "There's not a soul here at Marshfield and there's not anyone in town who'd believe you capable of murder."

She waved the air. "Well, of course they know I didn't murder anyone. That's not what I'm talking about."

I sat back. "It's that important to you to keep your relationship with Percy a secret?"

"Nobody can know about him."

"Why not?"

"Get your mind out of the gutter. It's not like he's got another wife in town or anything like that." She chewed the inside of her cheek. "I just don't want people around here to find out that I spend so much time taking care of him."

I waited.

She picked her mug back up and took a long sip before answering. "You always ask how I know things before I'm supposed to know them. You always give me grief about my grapevine."

"I find it uncanny how much you come up with, and how fast."

"What you don't know is that those grapevine people will gleefully turn on one another in an instant if the scoop is juicy enough." She took another sip of coffee. "Sometimes, even if it's dull as nuts. Trust me, I've known these people for decades. Loyalty goes out the window when there's a good story to tell."

"Decades?" I picked up on the word. "If you've been friends with these folks that long, they must know you were once married to Percy."

"Who said they were friends?" Frances snorted. "Just because I've known a few of them most of my life doesn't mean I trust them. Let me tell you—they're masters at making you believe they're sincerely interested in your life and happiness. But that's only to butter you up and get you to talk. And while you're spilling your soul, they're soaking up details to share later."

"Details they share with you."

Frances acknowledged that without comment. "Information is like currency. It's power. They hold it, they wield it. They almost ruined you, you know."

"What?" Even though I knew shouldn't, I asked, "When?"

"When Abe was murdered, right after you first started working here, a couple of them tried to get people to believe that you were responsible. They started spreading rumors about how you staged the whole ruckus in the Birdcage Room just to give yourself an alibi."

"That's ludicrous." Despite the fact that the case had been solved a few years ago—with my assistance, no less—I felt a rush of anger. "How could anyone suggest such a thing?"

"Don't worry; I shut that one down." A ghost of a smile crossed Frances's lips—the first hint of reduced tension I'd seen from her since her coffee-making lesson this morning.

"You stood up for me?"

"Don't get all sappy." She rolled her eyes. Another good sign. "I may not have liked you very much back then, but anybody with a brain could see that you didn't kill Abe."

"Why do you bother with these folks if they're so bad?"

Frances shrugged. "Hard to resist good gossip."

"I don't believe you."

She shrugged again. "What can I say? I'd rather be an ally than a target."

Frances must have sensed the pity I was feeling for her because she shot me a warning look. "Enough about all that. You and I need to talk about how soon this lawyer woman, Lily, can clear my good name."

"What did she tell you on the ride back?"

"Mostly she explained procedures and told me what to expect." Frances barked another laugh. "Like I haven't seen a homicide investigation in action before. She says she'll call me today after she's had a chance to consult with the detectives. She wants to feel them out to see what we're up against. I told her we shouldn't be up against anything because I didn't do it."

"It's a ridiculous situation, we all know that.

But I'm glad Bennett called her in. It's good that you have an advocate."

I stopped when I heard Frances's office door open. She frowned.

I asked, "Are we expecting anyone?"

"Not that I know of."

As Frances got to her feet, our unexpected guests appeared in the doorway.

Rodriguez and Flynn strode in, Rodriguez breaking into a wide smile the moment he spotted Frances. "There you are," he said, pointing triumphantly. The middle-aged homicide detective—once obese—had worked hard to trim himself down to pleasantly chubby after a near-fatal heart attack the previous year. His weight had dropped off as his zest for living skyrocketed. Turning to address his partner, he added, "Told you we'd find her here, safe and sound." To us, he said, "Morning, ladies. Mind if we come in? We'd like to hear about all your excitement yesterday."

Frances's cheeks were bright red, her expression fierce. Rather than speak, she sputtered, "What are you talking about?"

Flynn scowled. "You're a wanted woman. Don't tell me this comes as a surprise."

She spun on me. "Did you—?"

I held up both hands. "Not a word, Frances. I swear."

"There you go again," Flynn said, "jumping

to conclusions. Grace has nothing to do with us being here this morning. Your little skirmish in Rosette, however, does." Thinner and far more fidgety than the older detective, Flynn crossed his arms and tried to stare us down. If we hadn't known him as well as we did from so many prior entanglements, the two of us may have been intimidated by the tall, angry detective with the shiny shaved head. As it was, Frances looked ready to deck him.

Rodriguez laid a hand on his partner's shoulder. "The department in Rosette notified us. Professional courtesy, you understand. We decided to stop by to see how you were doing."

"Yeah, that's it. We're here to make sure you're okay." Flynn didn't even attempt to mask his sarcasm. He spied the mugs of coffee and croissants and asked, "Mind if we have a little chat?"

Chapter 10

I IGNORED FRANCES'S GLARE OF DIS-approval. "Have a seat, gentlemen," I said. "Would you like coffee?"

Rodriguez broke into a wide smile. "If it wouldn't be too much trouble."

With a huff, Frances started for the door.

"Where are you going?" I asked.

She flung her hand out. "Coffee doesn't magically appear by itself, you know."

"Please," I said, "have a seat. I'll get something sent up from the Birdcage Room kitchen. I think we can find someone willing to bring us a carafe and a couple of pastries."

She pursed her lips but didn't argue.

I picked up the phone. Remembering that the staff in the Birdcage Room probably wasn't at full force for the day yet, I made a quick last-minute decision and opted to call Theo, Bennett's butler, instead. We spoke for less than a minute and he promised he'd be down with my request shortly.

In that brief space of time, we settled ourselves in our usual positions: me behind the desk, Rodriguez across to my left, Flynn across to my right, and Frances to my far right, perched on the small sofa against the north wall. She sat with her ample arms folded across her chest, looking ready to head-butt the first person who spoke.

"What do you know?" I asked the detectives. "What did the other police department tell you?"

Flynn jerked his thumb toward Frances. "They wanted to know if we were acquainted with Suzy Sunshine over there."

"Let me handle this, amigo." Rodriguez repositioned his chair to be able to address both me and Frances at the same time. He wiggled his hand, silently directing Flynn to scoot back out of his sight line. Once that was complete, Rodriguez laced his fingers across his midsection. Although he no longer possessed a triple-extra-large body, he still shifted slowly, as though he hadn't yet become accustomed to his trimmer frame.

"That's better," he said.

"What *I'd* like to know is what they told you about the actual crime," I said. "And how soon they think Frances can be cleared."

"Doesn't work that way." Rodriguez shook his head. "They were looking for information from us. We didn't get much from them. Other than learning that our friend here is a person of interest in their homicide investigation, that is."

"She didn't do it, you know."

"Knowing something and proving it are two different animals."

"Whatever happened to innocent until proven guilty?"

"Don't get all worked up yet, Miz Wheaton," Rodriguez said. "We told Rosette's officers that we knew Miz Sliwa very well and that she'd even assisted us in several of our investigations."

"Assisted." Frances snorted. "Did your jobs for you, you should have said."

Flynn about flew off his seat. "We vouched for your character, lady. We can take it back. How do we really know you didn't have anything to do with this homicide? Maybe you saw your chance and took it. Maybe you thought that because you've been up close and personal with so many of *our* investigations that you could outsmart their police department and get off scot-free. Is that it?"

Frances had a wide, wobbly neck. I'd never seen veins stand out in it before now.

"Cut it out, Flynn. That's no way to talk to one of our friends," Rodriguez said. Addressing Frances, he added, "We know you're innocent, but we're officers of the law and our job is to follow where the evidence takes us. We plan to ask you a few questions, check out a few leads, and then report our findings to the guys in Rosette."

"Guys?" Frances asked. "For your information, the homicide detectives there are female."

Rodriguez drew in a sharp breath. "Yes, we've spoken with one of them. I assure you, I meant no disrespect. We often use 'guys' without specifying gender. But thank you for the clarification." Continuing smoothly, he went on, "We would appreciate your full cooperation, Miz Sliwa."

She squared her shoulders. "If they told you what happened yesterday, then you already know everything."

"Yeah, right." Flynn edged forward in his seat. "We didn't even know you were married. Thanks a lot for that. Made us look like idiots."

Cutting Frances off before she could make a snarky comment, I jumped in. "Enough. We're not getting anything accomplished here."

At that moment the outer office door opened.

"That must be the coffee," Frances said, getting to her feet.

"Sit down, Frances," I said. "I'll take care of it."

From the low voices filtering in, I could tell that two people had arrived. "In here," I called.

Theo carried a silver tray laden with a selection of breakfast pastries; a large carafe; and assorted cups, plates, and silverware.

Bennett came in behind him. "I hope I'm not intruding," he said. "Detective Rodriguez, you're looking well. Detective Flynn, good to see you again. I trust you're both here to help us prove Frances's innocence in the difficult matter we encountered this weekend."

Both Rodriguez and Flynn got to their feet to shake hands with the mansion's owner. "We'll do our best," Rodriguez said.

Flynn tilted his head to indicate Frances. "Assuming she cooperates."

Bennett fixed his gaze on Frances. "We will all cooperate," he said as he shifted his focus to Flynn. "Frances's well-being is paramount here, and we trust that you will do your utmost to help uncover the truth in this situation. If you find that you cannot perform your duties—for whatever reason—let me know now. I would be happy to engage professionals to pick up your slack."

The tip of Flynn's nose went pink. He worked his jaw. "No need for that."

"Good to hear," Bennett said as he pulled a chair over from across the office.

Tension in the room lessened as Theo cleared away the mugs Frances had brought for us and began setting new cups and saucers on the empty edges of my desk. Silently, we all waited for him to complete the task.

"Speaking of other professionals," I said the moment Theo left us, "I suggested bringing Ronny Tooney in at first. But Frances said she'd rather not."

Flynn gave a mirthless laugh. "That guy."

Bennett had positioned his chair between Flynn and Frances. Facing Flynn again, he asked,

"What did we just say about cooperation? Mr. Tooney has proved to be an invaluable asset to Marshfield Manor." Bennett softened his words with a fleeting smile. "As have you, Detective Flynn. Right now one of our trusted employees— a friend—is in trouble. I repeat, if you find that this particular situation is too difficult to manage, please tell us now."

Chastised a second time, Flynn flushed again. "I say things to let off steam sometimes." He shrugged. "I don't really mean anything by it."

Bennett turned to Frances. "I believe it would be a good idea to bring Mr. Tooney in on this matter. He is very discreet."

Frances grumbled. "So much for keeping this quiet," she said. "Fine. Call him. If these two already know what went on at Indwell, probably everybody in Emberstowne does, too."

Rodriguez helped himself to coffee then settled back in his chair. "Neither Flynn nor I have any reason to discuss the matter with anyone outside our department," he said. "And even though we don't have jurisdiction in Rosette, we may be able to offer suggestions to help you navigate this situation. At least until you're cleared of suspicion." He regarded Frances with warm compassion.

She squirmed.

The detective kept his gaze trained on her. "Why don't you tell us what happened? Everything you know, starting from the moment you arrived at Indwell Estates yesterday."

"I got there Saturday, not yesterday. I always get there Saturday and leave Sunday," she said.

"All right, good. You arrived at Indwell on Saturday. Take us through it."

She did.

As she recounted her experiences, Flynn—making short work of three pastries between sips of coffee—interrupted twice to ask questions. Rodriguez remained silent, taking notes. When Frances got to the part where Bennett and I entered the scene, she invited us to chime in. All in all, there was very little she divulged that I didn't already know.

To her credit, Frances had delivered facts objectively, and—with few exceptions—had refrained from shading her narration with color commentary.

I hadn't known she had it in her.

Almost as though she'd heard me voice the sentiment, she added, "That lawyer Lily Holland warned me that I need to keep emotion out of this." She shot me a silent query that asked "How did I do?"

I nodded approval.

Rodriguez shut his notebook and got to his feet "We'll stay in touch with Rosette's department and keep you all apprised as much as possible." As the rest of us rose, some silent signal passed between the two detectives. "Flynn," he said, "why don't you get Miz Sliwa's home contact information, in case we need to reach her during off-hours?"

Flynn nodded and started for the door, fully expecting my assistant to follow.

"Where are you going?" she asked. "I know my own phone number. You can write it down here."

Flynn scratched the back of his bald head. "I keep my contacts in an old-fashioned Rolodex," he said, then pointed toward her office. "I'd prefer a business card. Do you have any?"

"Of course I do."

"Let me have one of those, then. I'll jot your home info on the back."

My assistant huffed, but trundled toward the door with Flynn in tow.

As soon as they were gone, Rodriguez stepped up to my desk and invited Bennett to come closer. "Listen, I've been a cop most of my adult life. I know how we operate." Speaking quietly, but faster than I'd ever heard him before, he flicked a glance between us and continued. "Our girl here is in trouble. Rosette's department has their sights set on her and even though the evidence is circumstantial right now—the argument she had with the victim, her husband's missing medication, and finding the cap in the victim's room—if toxicology comes back positive for insulin, she's going down for this."

"Her lawyer—" I began.

"Can only do so much," Rodriguez finished. "She can't stop them from arresting her, and she can't convince the cops they have the wrong person if there's no one else with means, motive, and opportunity."

"This is ridiculous," Bennett said, raising his voice. "What can we do?"

"Keep her calm." Rodriguez held an index finger to his lips. "She's on her best behavior but we can all see the strain taking its toll. There's no point getting her riled up. Let's just hope the autopsy results confirm a natural death."

"I wish this had all happened here," I said. "I trust you and Flynn. I trust our people. I don't know those detectives in Rosette."

Pain crossed Rodriguez's face. "One more thing," he said. "Flynn and I are sworn to uphold the law. Even though we don't have jurisdiction, we can't ignore evidence if it's presented to us and we can't share information with you and Frances if it compromises Rosette's investigation."

I drew in a sharp breath. Bennett frowned.

Rodriguez's words came out very quickly. "We know Frances well enough to believe she's innocent. But none of us really know for certain that she didn't kill the victim."

I opened my mouth to protest, but Rodriguez held up a placating hand.

"Flynn and I truly believe she's being unjustly accused, but I need you both to know that while he and I can advise you about rights, and suggest courses of action, we cannot do anything to jeopardize the process."

Flynn poked his head in, locked eyes with Rodriguez, and asked, "Are you done socializing? We've got work to do."

"Coming, amigo," Rodriguez said with a wink. "Just enjoying a little more of this delicious coffee before we leave."

His hands on the doorjamb, Flynn nodded. "Anything else we need from Ms. Sliwa while we're here?"

Rodriguez ran a hand along his chin. "Have her jot down the names of everyone she encountered at Indwell on Saturday and Sunday. Just in case we happen to talk to a few of them."

Flynn gave him an "Are you kidding me?" look. Rodriguez shrugged.

When Flynn disappeared again, Rodriguez turned to me. "You have a talent for getting into the middle of these things, Miz Wheaton. I have an idea of how to put that to use." He shot a quick glance toward the open doorway between the offices. "You've met the new coroner, haven't you?"

"Just once. When you and Flynn were investigating the victim in our backyard over the winter, he let me sit in his van and keep warm." Even though that single interaction had been brief, I clearly remembered two things: the new coroner had required the assistance of a cane to walk, and he possessed a dry sense of humor.

"Dr. Bradley," Rodriguez said. "Joe. Give him a call."

"What can he do? He doesn't consult in Rosette, does he?"

"Not that I'm aware of, but—"

Bennett finished the thought. "He could be another ally."

Rodriguez nodded. "Tell him what's going on; he'll have a unique take on all this. And if it turns out that the victim did die from insulin poisoning, Frances's lawyer will try to argue it was a suicide. You're going to want someone to tell you what to look for in an autopsy to prove or disprove that theory."

"What if someone else killed Gus and is trying to frame Frances?" I asked.

Rodriguez rubbed his forehead. "Let's hope it was a suicide. But either way, Joe could be a big help."

Though unconvinced, I said, "Okay, I'll call him."

Flynn's voice drifted in. "Get me out of here."

"I gotta run before I have to arrest my partner for homicide." Rodriguez squeezed my shoulder. "We'll be in touch. Hang in there."

Chapter 11

LATER, WHEN FRANCES LEFT THE OFFICE to take a washroom break, I put in a quick call to Bronson Tooney. Even though she'd given approval to bring the private investigator into the fold, I knew that overhearing me talking to him would cause her aggravation. Contacting him was better shared after the fact.

"How are you?" I asked when he answered.

"Always better when I'm talking with you, Grace." I could hear the smile in his voice. "But I'm pretty sure you're not calling just to chit-chat. This is about Frances's situation, isn't it?"

"How did you know?"

"Word gets around."

That was fast. "She stepped out for just a couple of minutes, so I don't have long to talk."

"She doesn't want you to bring me in on this, does she?"

"At first she didn't. But we can use the help. She really wants to keep this on the down-low."

He made what sounded like a growl.

"Is there a problem?" I asked. "Don't you want to help Frances?"

"It's not that," he said quickly. "It's about keeping this quiet. I think it's too late."

"Oh no. Any idea where the leak started?" I asked.

"Where do they ever start?" he asked. "But that's not as important as helping Frances. I already started looking into Percy's background."

"You knew Frances was married?"

"Yeah."

"And that she visited Percy at Indwell every weekend?"

"I only found out about that a few years ago."

"A few years ago?" I repeated. "And you never told me?"

He gave a soft laugh. "You know I'd do anything for you, Grace, but this was Frances's secret and I saw no reason to share it with anyone."

"You're a good man, Bronson."

He cleared his throat, and I could imagine his soft face glowing pink the way it always did when someone paid him a compliment. "It might be a good idea for Frances to come up with a list of people she knows," he said. "She's been visiting there for what, about ten years? I'm sure she's amassed a collection of friends as well as foes. That will give me a place to start. You never know what might turn up."

"That's a great idea," I said. "I'll suggest it to her."

"Listen," he said, "I know you said she'll be back any second, so how about I stop by your house tonight to go over the details?"

I thought about it. "You've heard about what's going on at Amethyst Cellars, haven't you?"

He said he had.

"That means Scott and Bruce will probably be home. And even though word of Frances's trouble is spreading around town, I don't want anyone hearing it from me. Would you mind if I swung by your house after work instead for a few minutes?"

The question seemed to take him by surprise. "Sure," he said. "No problem. Sounds like a great idea. I'd like that."

"Good, I'll see you then."

When Frances returned, I got up and headed into her office, taking a seat across from her. "When do you meet with Lily Holland again?" I asked.

"She's supposed to call me today."

"She seems very capable."

The phone rang. Frances leaned close to peer at the caller ID. Her brows shot up. "Speak of the devil." Frowning, she picked up the receiver. "Hello?"

I boosted myself, intending to give her privacy but she waved me back into my seat with an impatient glare.

"Yes," she said into the phone. "I do. Yes, I am. Yes, they have."

Frances was clearly on her best polite behavior.

After a couple of seconds, she said, "Would you mind if I put you on speaker? Grace Wheaton is here in the office with me and I'd like her to hear what you have to say."

Frances pressed the button to engage the speakerphone. As soon as I heard background noise, I said, "Good afternoon, Lily. Thanks for keeping in touch."

"I have only a few minutes right now," she said quickly. "I plan to chat with a colleague in Rosette later today. She's very familiar with their judges and courts. It's always good to have as much insider information as possible."

Barely pausing to take a breath, she went on, "What I was telling Ms. Sliwa is that Gustave Westburg's autopsy took place this morning, but results from toxicology may not be in for a little while longer."

"So there's still doubt that he died of natural causes?" I asked.

"Until evidence proves otherwise, the police are investigating this as a possible homicide."

"How many homicides a year does Rosette usually experience?" I asked.

Lily gave a quick laugh. "You and I are on the same page, Ms. Wheaton. Zero murders. Squeaky clean for as far back as records go. Believe me, Rosette is pinning its hopes on this being a false alarm. Even one homicide in Rosette spoils its pristine record."

From her end of the line, I heard a door open in the background.

"Hang on," Lily said, and we could tell by the sound that she'd covered the mouthpiece. Seconds later, she came back. "I've been called into a meeting, but I wanted to stress a few things before you and I talk again. Are you still there, Ms. Sliwa?"

Frances made a face at the phone. "Oh, for crying out loud, go ahead and call me by my first name."

"Good. That's a start, at least." Was that impatience in Lily's tone? "I told you yesterday that I don't want you discussing this matter with anyone beyond Ms. Wheaton and Mr. Bennett."

"Call me Grace," I said. "But our local homicide team already knows. They paid us a visit this morning."

"I'd be surprised if they didn't know. That's fine."

I had to chime in again. "And the private investigator Marshfield keeps on retainer."

Frances shot me an inquisitive look. I mouthed, "I called him."

Lily drew in a deep breath and asked, "Anyone else?"

"No," we said together.

I leaned over to scribble a quick note to my assistant. "Give Tooney names." I double-underlined: "From Indwell. Everybody involved."

Frances rolled her eyes and frowned.

"Good. I have no doubt the story will leak," Lily said. "That's inevitable. But Frances, under no circumstances should you speak with the media. No newspaper interviews, no phone calls. Is that clear?"

"Yes," she said. "Perfectly."

"And under no circumstances are you to speak to the police without me. You understand?"

Frances's patience was wearing thin. "Of course," she said with a labored sigh. A split-second later she blinked, then stared at me, as though a thought had just occurred to her.

"All right then," Lily said. "I'll be in touch as soon as—"

"Hang on a minute," Frances said, sitting up straighter. "I know you don't want me stirring up trouble at Indwell but there aren't any restrictions on Grace, are there? She's free to go out there and talk with people, isn't she?"

"Legally, there are no restrictions on either of you, but I believe it's in your best interests to—"

"All I'm asking is if Grace can go out there and look into this for me."

"I cannot condone interfering with a police investigation."

Frances swatted the air. "I'm not talking about

meddling. I just think it wouldn't hurt for her to ask a few questions. Get to know the people involved."

"Again, Frances, I cannot condone—"

"Yeah, yeah, yeah," Frances said. "We got it."

I couldn't see Lily's face, but I could tell from the tiny sounds coming from her end of the line that she was more than a little annoyed. "There are safeguards in place to protect the innocent," she began. "There is no need for individuals to involve themselves in the justice system."

"Loud and clear," Frances said. "Anything else before we hang up?"

"As always, if you have any questions, or need me, please feel free to call."

"Great. Thanks. Go ahead to your meeting." Frances grinned at me. "Bye," she said. And hung up.

I stared at her. "She's your lawyer. You don't want to make her your enemy."

Frances looked happier than I'd seen her all day. *"Pheh,"* she said. "It's her job to represent me whether she likes me or not."

"That's no excuse for rudeness."

"I wasn't rude," Frances said, looking genuinely taken aback. "I'm efficient. And I think Lily will come to appreciate that. But that doesn't matter right now. Did you hear what she said?"

"I heard everything she said."

Frances shot me a scathing look. "I mean about

you being free to go investigate. I won't be there to help you, of course, but if you bring back your findings, we can discuss it all here. Before you know it, you and I will have this case solved."

Chapter 12

TOONEY'S HOUSE SAT NEXT DOOR TO mine. Bennett had purchased the home for our loyal investigator about a year earlier, almost immediately as soon as its prior owner, Todd Pedota, had put it up for sale. The discovery of an underground tunnel that linked our two homes probably had something to do with my former neighbor's quick departure. That, and the fact that a killer had used the passageway to frame Todd for murder. The moment charges were dropped, he left town. And the moment he was gone, Bennett snapped the place up.

It was no secret that, after all the frightening situations we'd faced the past few years, Bennett's primary goal was to keep me safe. Having Tooney right next door—willing and able to be at my side in the few minutes it took to traverse the tunnel—gave Bennett extraordinary peace of mind. And, after having seen the hovel Tooney had lived in, it did my heart good to see my friend enjoying more comfortable accommodations.

I parked in my own driveway, noting that—again—both Scott's and Bruce's cars were there.

Until Amethyst Cellars reopened, the boys would probably be home every night.

Crossing the yards, I made my way over to Tooney's and hurried up the steps to his front door. Though the days were getting longer and the sun was finally beginning to show signs of wanting to stay, the late-afternoon breeze made me wish I'd thrown on my trench coat instead of leaving it in the car.

Tooney answered the door before I had a chance to ring the bell. "Right on time," he said. The big man's expression didn't often shift, but whenever he smiled I was startled by how completely his features transformed from homely and plain to genuinely handsome.

"Thanks for letting me stop by." I didn't bother to ask how Tooney knew what time I usually arrived home after work; the man made it his business to know everything going on in Emberstowne. In fact, I believed that his knowledge of the town's goings-on rivaled Frances's. Not that I'd ever suggest such a travesty to my assistant.

"Anytime, Grace. Anytime at all." He ushered me through the small front foyer and led me deeper into the house. Even though I'd been here a handful of times during its renovation, the floor plan, flip-flopped from mine, always took a little getting used to. My parlor was to the right, Tooney's to the left. I followed him in.

My first thought was to wonder if anyone, including Tooney, had ever stepped foot in the parlor since the new furnishings had arrived. This elegant room, with its raspberry walls, overstuffed upholstery, and decorating magazines fanned carefully on each end table "just so," had originally been staged for a portfolio photo shoot months ago. From the looks of it, nothing had changed since then. The place even still smelled new.

Although these living conditions represented a huge improvement for Tooney, I wondered if the middle-aged bachelor ever truly felt comfortable in his new digs.

"Have a seat," he said, extending a rough hand toward the wing chair nearest the fireplace, "Or would you be more comfortable in the living room?" He took two steps sideways and switched directions with his hand.

Before I could answer, he asked, "Would you like something to drink? I have fresh coffee made. And I still have those two bottles of wine that Hillary gave me as a housewarming gift. They're from Amethyst Cellars, so I know you'll like them."

Despite myself, I grinned. I was here to discuss Frances's plight, but Tooney's attempts to play host touched my heart. "I'd be too afraid I might spill," I said with a laugh. Having perused the parlor, I turned around and peered into a navy blue–themed living room. "Look at this place. It's

as gorgeous and clean as the day you moved in."
I crossed the living room to run my hands over the
cream-colored sofa's seat cushions. "Has anyone
ever sat here?"

Tooney's cheeks colored. "I don't get a lot of
company."

I spun, surveying the rest of the space. "Where
do you watch television?"

He gestured upward with his eyes. "My room.
It's comfortable up there."

"I'm sure it is, but it doesn't look like you enjoy
the rest of your house."

"Eh . . ." He gave a one-shouldered shrug. "No
sense in messing up all the new things. I'd rather
keep everything clean so that if Mr. Marshfield
ever wants to sell the place, he won't have to
redecorate again."

"Tooney." I crossed to him and laid both hands
on one of his forearms. He tensed. "Bennett has
no intention of selling. He bought this for *you*.
This is your home for as long as you care to live
here. Don't try to keep it nice for someone else.
Live in it. Enjoy it."

His cheeks burned brighter than ever. "I am."
He shifted his weight. "In my own way."

Acting on impulse, I said. "How about we talk
in the kitchen? Would you mind?"

I got a quick impression of panic on his part.
As though he hadn't ever considered the heart
of the home to be a suitable location for guests.

Before he could refuse, I trotted past him through the dining room, marveling again at how peculiar it felt to be walking through a house that was identical to mine, yet not.

"Grace, just a second—"

When I stepped into the kitchen, I smiled. "Now this is more like it."

"I'm sorry about the mess," Tooney said, coming around from behind me. He rushed ahead of me to pick up the shirts and jackets he'd draped over the backs of a few chairs. "I wasn't expecting you to come in here."

"This isn't so bad," I said. It really wasn't. Other than the clothing—which he snatched up, zip-zip-zip—the only additional "mess" to speak of included a newspaper spread across the tabletop, two empty beer bottles next to it, and a small pile of dishes soaking in the sink.

Tooney scooted past me to open the basement door. He threw the bunched-up garments down the stairs and turned to face me again, chagrined. "I try to keep things clean around here but some-times—"

"Bronson," I said, remembering to use his real name. "This is great. I feel much more at home in here."

"You do?" he asked.

I laughed as I dropped my purse on one chair, pulled out another, and sat down. "You should see our house sometimes. Bruce and Scott stay on top of things way better than I do, but there are days when it's simply too much for all of us. Messes build fast, don't they?"

Looking a bit more relaxed now, he started to lower himself into the chair across from mine. "Hang on," he said, stopping himself. "Did you want coffee? Or I'd be happy to open up that wine I mentioned. I don't know when I'll ever have a chance to serve it otherwise."

"I'm fine," I said. "Honest."

He looked so profoundly disappointed that I stopped him before he sat down. "On second thought," I said, "after the past couple of days, a glass of wine would be perfect. But only if you'll join me."

His soft features creased into a wide smile. "Great," he said. "I'll be back in a second."

He disappeared into his dining room, returning moments later carrying a bottle and two stemmed glasses. He placed the glasses on the tabletop and squinted at the wine's label. "This one's a tempranillo," he said. "Is that okay? Or would you prefer the merlot?"

"Tempranillo is one of my favorites."

He opened and poured the wine with a deftness that surprised me. I'd often wondered about Tooney's past. Had he ever been married? Had a serious sweetheart? The one or two times I'd tried to tease information out of him, he'd clammed up and become noticeably uncomfortable.

When he sat across from me, I lifted my glass to tap his. "To helping Frances," I said.

"Yes, and . . ."

"And what?" I prompted when he let the thought trail off.

He hesitated. "And to finding out what really happened to the victim."

I got the impression he'd intended to say something else but I went along with it. We tapped glasses again. "That would be ideal, but the sooner we get Frances extricated from this mess, the better. That's my number-one goal."

Tooney and I spent the next half hour discussing what we knew thus far, what we needed to find out, and the best methods for following up. "It will be tough for you," I said. "There's no way the police in Rosette will bring you in on this—they'll know that you're biased. And I don't know how much Indwell will cooperate, either."

"I intend to keep a low profile," he said. "With any luck, no one will even know I'm around."

"Before I forget." I reached into my purse. "Here are those names you asked Frances to come up with."

"Thanks," he said as he read over the list. "I'll get started right away. Anyone in particular she wants me to focus on?"

I shook my head. "The sons, Harland and Dan, probably stand to inherit. So that makes them suspects in my eyes. But both, apparently, have solid alibis."

"I'll shadow them. See what kind of people they are. See if anything pops."

"Whatever you can dig up will be greatly appreciated."

When I mentioned Frances's fears about her grapevine finding out, he flinched.

"I don't blame her," he said. "That group of busybodies is not nice."

"Who are they?" I asked.

He shared a few names, none of which I'd ever heard before.

"I've lived here long enough to know most of the movers and shakers in town. How can I have not met any of these people?"

"Can't say. But they know you."

I frowned. "So I've gathered."

The moment I drained my last sip of wine, Tooney reached for the bottle to pour more.

I laughed, placing my hand over the top of my glass. "What are you trying to do, Tooney? Get me tipsy?"

He froze, mid-movement, alarm in his eyes. "No, of course not. I would never do that to you." He sat down, cheeks red again. "I'm sorry. We were having such a nice time, I just thought you might like to keep talking a little bit." With a shrug, he added, "Plus, I won't drink any more of this by myself. I wouldn't want it to go to waste."

"You're right. We *are* having a nice time." I removed my hand. "A half glass, then. Good thing I'm not driving."

He poured carefully, giving me a fraction of the amount I'd had before, then topped off his own. "This is really excellent wine," he said. "Bruce and Scott have a good thing going with Amethyst Cellars. I hope they're able to keep the place alive, even with these new obstacles."

"Me, too," I said, sipping slowly. "They work so hard."

Tooney nodded.

Finished with business now, we were simply two friends enjoying a quiet moment together after a long day. Tooney swirled the ruby liquid in his glass before taking a sniff and sipping. When he caught me watching, he grinned good-naturedly.

"You're a wine drinker?" I asked.

"I am."

I flicked a glance toward the two beer bottles by the sink. "Then why did you say that you probably wouldn't have opened the tempranillo on your own?"

He gave a very Tooney-like shrug. "Wine tastes better when it's shared."

I smiled. "I like that. Fair enough."

"Today's a treat for me," he said. "This is special."

"How so?" I asked.

"You and me," he said, "we're always running around or busy or catching up in the middle of some crazy business. There's been a lot going on here in Emberstowne and at Marshfield these past few years. You and me," he said again, this time lifting his glass to gesture, "we don't take time to sit and talk, you know, just for the heck of it."

"You're right," I said. "We haven't made time to hang out together."

"I'm not looking to be your BFF, or whatever the word is these days." He gave a sad smile. "But I'm enjoying this small chance to talk without Rodriguez and Flynn beating down the door."

I laughed out loud at that. My friend Bronson Tooney, the slightly pudgy, middle-aged private investigator who'd been there for me every time I'd needed him was telling me that he needed me to be there for him once in a while as well. I could do that.

I leaned across the table and patted his hand. "You're a treasure, Bronson," I said. "We're lucky to have you in our lives."

"I'm the lucky one," he said. "If it hadn't been for you believing in me, I'd still be trying—and failing—to get my private-eye business off the ground. You changed a lot of lives when you came to Marshfield. Mine included."

It wasn't the wine—it was more the warm camaraderie—that spurred me to draw him out.

"It wasn't that long ago that you finally told me

that your first name wasn't Ronny," I said. "What else don't I know?"

He shrugged again, this time looking confused. "Nothing that would make any difference."

"No, no," I said. "That's not good enough." I drained my glass again, stood, and poured us both a full measure, which garnered me a look of surprise from Tooney. "Come on, tell me about you. Where did you grow up? What are some of the big moments in your life?"

"I grew up here, in town. No big moments to speak of."

I favored him with a withering glare. "Work with me," I said. "You know so much about me, but I know little about you."

"Not much to tell."

I glared again. "Tooney."

I couldn't tell if he was enjoying the attention or if my prying made him uncomfortable.

Leaning forward, I decided to push—just a little bit. "Take me back," I said. "Senior year of high school. Start there. Tell me all about it."

To my surprise, he did.

Chapter 13

I LEFT TOONEY'S HOUSE LATER THAN I'D planned, but when I did I was filled with a feeling of immense satisfaction. Although Tooney hadn't gotten past college in his recitation of the story of his life, I did feel as though I knew the man a little bit better. Who would have imagined that he'd played the lead in a school musical or that he'd double majored in Spanish and German, hoping his language skills would eventually earn him a spot in the Secret Service?

He'd ended his story there, not because he had no more to tell, but because the wine had run dry. Smiling, he protested that he'd bored me enough for one night.

"Promise we'll do this again soon," I said when I left.

"Anytime, Grace."

"YOU'RE HOME," BRUCE AND SCOTT chorused when I stepped through the back door.

I sniffed the air's savory warmth. "Sorry I'm late."

"That's okay. So is dinner." Scott grinned.

"*Celebratory* dinner," Bruce said.

Scott nodded. "Right. We have lots of updates to share."

I hung up my purse. "It smells heavenly in here."

"Beef stroganoff," Bruce said. "Your mom's recipe."

One of my favorites. "Then we *are* celebrating," I said as Bootsie wandered into the kitchen to rub against my legs. I picked her up. "What's the good news?"

Had it only been yesterday that I'd found them at the kitchen table poring over distressing financial statements? Tonight my roommates were busy preparing dinner. And smiling. A lot.

Sporting one of his favorite aprons—the one that looked like a Scottish kilt—Bruce waved his spatula in the air and adopted a singsong tone. "We may have an opportunity to move to a new building."

"Not new-new," Scott said from across the room. "It's pretty old, in fact. But new for us. Why don't you open a bottle of wine while I finish setting the table? Pick whatever suits your mood, Grace. We'll tell you all about it."

Because I'd already enjoyed two full glasses of wine over at Tooney's house, I almost protested that I couldn't handle any more. But the looks on their faces and their contagious good cheer convinced me to hold my tongue.

I released Bootsie to the floor in the dining

room as I scrutinized the contents of our wine rack. "Excellent," I whispered to myself when I spotted what I was looking for. "Tempranillo sound good to you both?" I asked.

"Perfect," Scott called. "Bruce says dinner's almost ready. Your timing is incredible."

"I would have been home a lot sooner," I said as I uncorked the bottle and pulled out three glasses, "but I stopped next door to talk to Tooney for a bit. I had to bring him up to date on a few Marshfield matters."

Bruce turned to face me. "This wouldn't have anything to do with Frances, would it?"

I stopped mid pour. "What do you know about that?"

"Everyone's talking about it," Scott said. "We've heard at least three different versions about an incident yesterday involving Frances, a long-lost lover, and a murder victim. We assume the lover and the murder victim are one and the same."

"They're not." I blew out a long breath. "Poor Frances."

"Why didn't you tell us?" Bruce asked.

"She asked me not to. She was hoping to keep all this safe from the grapevine's clutches."

"We wouldn't have told anyone, Grace. You know that."

"I do," I said. "But I gave my word."

"Got it." Bruce nodded. " 'Nuff said."

I resumed my wine-pouring duties. "Seeing as how Frances's secret is out, I'll give you the real story. But not until you two tell me all your news."

Over dinner, Bruce and Scott did exactly that. "The bank foreclosed on a piece of property years ago that's remained vacant all this time. You know that building about three blocks up the street from our current location?"

I tried to picture the area. "The old glass factory?"

"That's the one," they said in unison.

"You plan to buy it?" I asked.

"No way we could afford that mortgage." Bruce shook his head. "But we're in negotiations to rent it out. We got a look inside today and the space has so much potential."

"Brick walls, exposed beams, concrete floors," Scott chimed in. "A perfect backdrop for our new site."

"This sounds wonderful," I said sincerely. "But the first floor alone has to be five times the size of your current location. Would you be able to make such a big space work?"

"I'm glad you asked," Bruce said. "We hope to section off a portion and rent only as much as we need. That'll give us room to expand as our business grows."

Scott's eyes glinted. "We could possibly, even, someday, consider opening a restaurant. There's huge opportunity here."

"And the best part is that we can probably afford it," Bruce said. "We went over the numbers today. Based on average per-square-foot leasing prices, with what we're saving in rent from our current location, we can easily pay for the amount of space we need at the old glass factory."

"That's the best news I've heard all day," I said.

Over dinner they told me about how they expected the bank to work with them. Among other things, I learned that the former factory had an actual name: the Granite Building.

"Christened in honor of our state rock?" I asked.

Bruce shrugged. "Doubtful. I think our state rock and state precious stone and such were decided in the nineteen seventies. The building is at least twenty years older than that."

"Do you have to worry about preservation?" I asked.

"We got lucky there," Bruce said. "Although the building's old, it's not historically significant. We can do as we please. And if all goes smoothly, we'll be able to sign an agreement within a week."

"But we're not taking anything for granite." Scott giggled around a cheekful of stroganoff. "See what I did there?"

I laughed.

"But . . ." Bruce said warily, "we're thinking of bringing Hillary in for the renovations. Would you be okay with that?"

"Hillary?" I asked, startled by the mention of Bennett's stepdaughter's name. But a second later, I got it. "Sure, if that's who you really want. She's certainly qualified in home restoration." I held up my hands as though to encompass our entire house. "And she was surprisingly easy to work with. But industrial design is very different."

"We know," Scott said. "And when we expand, we'll bring in architects who specialize in restaurant design for the layout and setup. But for the moment, with only interior design and furnishings to worry about, we think Hillary is a good choice."

"Who knows?" Bruce chimed in. "Maybe she'll turn us down because this project is too far out of her wheelhouse. But we didn't want to even approach her until we talked with you about it."

"I would never stand in your way," I said.

"You've barely touched your wine," Bruce said. "Something wrong?"

I laughed. "Hardly. It's just that Tooney brought out a bottle while I was there and if I over-imbibe I won't sleep well tonight. This glass"—I held mine up again—"represents my limit for the evening."

The two of them stared at me as I put the glass down and picked up my fork.

"What's wrong?" I asked.

"Who else was there with you?" Scott asked.

"No one. It was just the two of us. Talking about Frances." I shrugged.

With the looks I was getting from them I thought better of mentioning my attempt to draw out Tooney's personal stories.

"It was just the two of you. Discussing business." Bruce's brows tightened. "And he opened a bottle of wine?"

"Guys." I leaned back. "He got it as a gift from Hillary—the same wine we're drinking tonight, in fact—and said he'd probably never open it on his own. My being there gave him an opportunity and he took it."

In tandem, the two gestured helplessly. "Grace," Bruce began slowly, "the man is in love with you."

"No, no." I put my fork down. "No. He's fond of me. I know that. Everyone knows that. And I'm fond of him, too. We're friends. That's all it is."

They both frowned. "Spending time with him, over wine?" Scott shook his head. "You're encouraging him."

"He doesn't think of me that way." I rubbed my forehead. "I certainly don't think of him like that. And even if I did, he's at least twenty years older than I am."

"You've never heard of a May-December romance?" Bruce asked.

I stared at the ceiling. If the boys were right, my pestering Tooney for personal anecdotes would have definitely sent our private investigator down a path I hadn't intended. "I can't deny that Tooney and I have a special bond, but there's no way he thinks of me romantically." I shook my head, knowing in my heart that I was speaking the truth. "I'm sure he loves me exactly the way I love him. But he's not in love with me. Nope."

"I hope you're right," Scott said. "We'd hate to see him get hurt."

"I am right. And I wouldn't hurt him for all the world."

My roommates exchanged an uneasy glance.

I was about to protest further when the house phone rang. Bruce was closest to the handset, so he got up and read the caller ID. "Why would anyone from the county be calling us this late in the day?" he asked rhetorically with a glance at the kitchen clock. "Aren't all their offices closed by now?"

"Maybe it's about the Granite Building," Scott said. "The bank said they planned to expedite the process."

Bruce answered the phone and after a quick exchange, held the handset out to me. "It's the coroner. He wants to talk to you."

The wonderful stroganoff I'd eaten moments earlier began roiling around my stomach, sloshing through a giant puddle of wine.

I accepted the phone and cleared my throat. "This is Grace."

135

"I hope I'm not interrupting dinner."

Of all the things a coroner might begin with, that wasn't exactly what I would have expected. "No, not at all," I lied, with a "What the heck is this all about?" shrug to my roommates. "What can I do for you?"

"I don't know if you remember," he said, "but you and I met a few months ago. In your backyard, or at least close enough."

"Of course," I said as the shock of having him call wore off and a rush of recollection brought me fully into the conversation. "Dr. Bradley."

"Call me Joe," he said. "My patients prefer to use my title, but I like keeping things less formal between colleagues."

In spite of myself, I snickered.

"Did I say something funny?" he asked.

Bruce and Scott watched me with wide-eyed puzzlement.

"I'm sorry. No, not funny at all," I said, mortified. "It's just—your patients. They can't actually call you *anything,* can they?"

He had a big, booming laugh, one that made me feel far less self-conscious about my unintentional giggle moments earlier. "Not those patients," he said. "I'm talking about the living, breathing ones who walk into my office of their own volition. Or those who are carried in, kicking and screaming. Toddlers are notoriously reluctant to come visit me."

"I don't understand," I said.

"My coroner duties require only a few hours each week, and not every day. Sometimes I work in the morning, sometimes in the evening, like tonight. In real life I'm a family physician. I belong to a group of four doctors in town."

"I didn't know."

"There's no reason you should." He chuckled. "But introducing myself isn't my motive for calling today. Detective Rodriguez thought I could be of some help to you. He gave me your number. From the stories he and Detective Flynn tell, you've developed quite a reputation for crime solving. And I understand this latest incident hits rather close to home."

"Of course." Belatedly I remembered Rodriguez's suggestion to contact him. "That's so nice of you to call."

I pointed to the handset and mouthed, "It's about Frances." Bruce and Scott visibly relaxed. Thank goodness my roommates had already gotten the lowdown, otherwise I'd have had a hard time explaining why our county coroner had called to chat.

"What can I do for you?" Joe asked.

"At this point, I don't know," I said. Bruce and Scott shooed me out of the room, pantomiming so I'd know that they would clean up the kitchen. I wandered into our parlor and plopped into my favorite wing chair. "As I'm sure Detective

Rodriguez told you, the autopsy was supposed to take place today. The victim—who probably died of natural causes—will be tested to determine if there's any insulin present in his body. The man wasn't a diabetic, and if they determine he was overdosed, things won't look good for Frances."

"Frances is your assistant, isn't she? The older woman from Marshfield who helped you solve all the recent murders out there?"

"She'd probably prefer it if you gave the two of us equal credit, but yes, that's her. She's not guilty. We all know that."

He made an indecipherable noise, and I could tell that he was taking notes. "Do you know what else, aside from the insulin, that they intend to test for?" he asked. "I mean, beyond what's standard."

"I have no idea. I don't even know what is standard. No one's talking to me. Not yet, at least."

I intended to correct that soon.

"But you plan to correct that soon, I'll bet," he said.

I half laughed. "You read my mind."

"I'd appreciate it if you'd keep me updated," he said. "Do you have a pen?"

I hurried back into the kitchen, where I grabbed one, along with a pad of paper. "I do now."

He had me write down three phone numbers. "The first one is my cell. I shut it off while I'm with patients, but I check messages and texts

138

regularly. The second is my extension here at the morgue, and I always do my best to pick up. Those patients don't complain about interruptions. The last one is my main office. If you ever need to reach me immediately, or there's an emergency, call that number. Either my receptionist or my answering service will know how to get in touch."

"I don't anticipate any emergencies," I said.

"Neither do I, but it pays to plan ahead."

"I appreciate it," I said. "Here's my cell."

"Got it," he said as he wrote it down. "As I'm sure Detective Rodriguez told you, I'm here to help."

Chapter 14

"IT'S ABOUT TIME YOU GOT HERE," Frances said when I walked into her office the next morning. She stood in front of her desk, arms folded, one sensibly shod foot tapping impatience.

"About time?" I asked. I was early. And she was still wearing her coat. "What's going on?"

"Lily said they need me back in Rosette for another statement. She's meeting me at their police department. I figured you'd want to come along."

"Of course I would, but I have three meetings scheduled for today." One of them was with Bennett's financial planner, a notoriously picky man who'd confirmed our appointment no fewer than three times last week. "Give me a few minutes to reschedule—"

"Already done," she said. "I forwarded all the changes to you via e-mail and updated your calendar. And I told the Mister that we'd be out for the morning. Maybe longer. He said he'd stay back to meet with his adviser, but that we should keep him informed." She nodded as though that settled everything. "You ready?"

Did I have any choice? "Let's go."

"Good. You can drive."

Frances kept quiet until we'd exited Marshfield's front gate. As I took a right onto the main road, she twisted in her seat to stare behind us.

"Forget something?" I asked.

Righting herself, she shook her head. "I don't usually come through the front gate in the morning. I use the employee entrance."

"So do I. But this way's faster to the expressway."

"I forget how pretty the entrance is."

Startled by such an uncharacteristic observation, I took my eyes off the road long enough to make sure it was Frances, and not an impostor, sitting in my passenger seat.

"Our new landscape architect has really upped her game," I said. "I can't wait to see her plans come into full bloom this season. We'll have to come out this way more often when the weather starts warming up."

Frances gave an impatient sniff. "Maybe *you'll* come out this way to enjoy the pretty flowers. I'll probably be locked up in some windowless jail cell with a roommate who never bathes."

"We won't let that happen."

"How many times have Rodriguez and Flynn arrested the wrong person?"

I didn't want to answer that.

"Exactly," she said as though reading my mind.

"And they're decent human beings, the two of them." Leaning slightly toward me, she lowered her voice. "Don't ever tell them I said such a thing. Especially Flynn."

"Your secret's safe with me." As we followed the road that would take us to Rosette, I scrunched my nose. I knew this next part would be tough. "Speaking of secrets," I said, "it seems that your story has gotten out. Bruce and Scott came home knowing most of it, even though I never said a word."

Frances flinched, but only slightly. "Guess I'm not surprised."

"I'm sorry, Frances."

She slid me one of her trademark glares, but whatever message she'd intended to convey fell flat.

We traveled quietly for a while. Unlike Sunday's trek to Indwell, today's weather was mild and sunny, with the promise of a warm-up.

"Everything will work out," I said. "It may take a while, but I have faith in the system."

"I'm not worried."

I didn't believe her for a second. "Good."

"Knowing these quick-to-judge detectives believe I could have done it—that's what's got me steamed. They look at me like I'm their number-one target."

If Frances were anyone else, I may have reached over to pat her arm. But I kept both hands on the steering wheel and said, "Then we need to give them other options to consider."

She gave a brisk nod. "That's where you come in."

I knew she expected me to solve the mystery of Gus's death by lunchtime, but like Dorothy and Kansas, we weren't in Marshfield anymore. We wouldn't even be in Emberstowne. Although we had a network of professionals to call on for elp, they had no power, no jurisdiction. Frances and I were on our own.

"You know I'll do whatever I can, but my influence in Rosette will be limited. And I highly doubt that the police at the station will allow me to question them while you're being inter-viewed."

"The cops in Rosette don't know who they're bargaining with." Adjusting herself to face me, she said, "I've been giving this some thought. Instead of coming with me to the station—I can always tell you later about what happened there—why don't you drop me off and head back over to Indwell and see what you can dig up?"

"Happy to do that." I'd been considering a similar idea myself. "Mind you, I don't know how much they'll let me wander around, especially if I start asking questions about Gus."

"Tell them you're visiting Percy. He took a shine to you—he always likes to chat up the pretty ones—and he'll introduce you around. As long as you're there as his guest, they can't throw you out." She twisted her mouth to one side. "Unless you get belligerent." With a pointed glare, she added, "Don't get belligerent."

"I'll do my best." Taking a hand off the wheel long enough to point at her, I said, "And when you're in there with the detectives, I suggest you heed that advice as well."

Scooching to face forward again, she frowned out the windshield. "No need to get sassy."

"We still have a bit of a ride ahead of us," I said. "Tell me about the people I'll meet there. I want to know who's who."

She provided a wealth of information about the good folks at Indwell and by the time we exited the expressway, I had no doubt I'd be able to recognize each and every one of them on sight.

"Go." After alighting from the car, Frances leaned back inside the open passenger window and made shooing motions with her hands. "Go already. You're wasting time."

"Do you see Lily's car anywhere?" I shut off the engine and got out to look around. "I don't want to leave you here until I know she's arrived."

"I'll be fine," Frances said over the top of the car. "You think I can't handle these dim-witted detectives on my own?"

Not with an attitude like that, you can't.

"I'll feel better if we wait until Lily gets here."

Frances shielded her eyes against the sun as she surveyed the sea of dark Ford sedans. Nothing here remotely resembled the high-powered attorney's ride.

"Let's go in together," I said. "I'll wait with you until she shows up. Then I'll take off."

"Don't baby me. I'm twice your age. I know how to handle myself."

"You're not twice my age and this is hardly babying you." Despite my best efforts, my voice rose. "Think about it: I didn't abandon my sister until I knew she had proper representation for her trial. And you know how fond I am of her."

Frances grudgingly acknowledged my point.

I didn't know if the reason she so fervently wanted me gone was because of her eagerness for me to get started on my end of the investigation, or because she was frightened about her interview and didn't want me to see.

"There she is." Frances pointed a stubby finger at a shiny Lexus pulling into the small lot. With a glance at her watch, she added, "Right on time."

After parking in the farthest open spot, Lily Holland sprang from the driver's seat, retrieved a maroon briefcase from the back, and waved to us as she made her brisk way over. Her shiny auburn bob bounced in the sunshine. We exchanged quick greetings.

"I want to go over a few guidelines with you before we go in," Lily said to Frances. "Our goal is to answer all their questions accurately but to get you out of there as quickly as possible and without any discussion of arrest."

Frances folded her arms. "If someone did kill Gus, these idiots are wasting valuable time questioning me."

Lily nodded. "That's exactly the sort of sentiment I'd prefer you didn't voice once we're inside."

Before she could say another word, Frances flicked her fingers in my direction. "Go on, now. My lawyer's here. I'm safe."

I wished I could believe that. Although I knew Lily would do everything she could to expedite things, I worried that my assistant's sharp tongue might make the task more difficult.

"Call me when you want me to come by and pick you up," I said.

"Don't worry about coming all the way back out here. I'll be happy to drop Frances off when we're finished," Lily said.

When Frances told her that I wouldn't be coming all the way back from Emberstowne, that I planned to visit Percy at Indwell, Lily's eyes narrowed. "You're visiting Frances's ex-husband?"

"That's right," I said.

"A man you met for the first time on Sunday?"

Frances jumped in before I could respond. "Grace plans to have a look around and talk to a few people. No harm in that."

Lily shot me a piercing glare. "Do not insert

yourself into the police investigation. Do not make my job harder than it is."

"I won't," I said as I got back into my car.

Frances came around to my open window. "Don't listen to her," she whispered. "Sniff around. Dig deep. Find out as much as you can."

Chapter 15

DRIVING TO INDWELL ESTATES, I SLOWED once again at the vantage point overlooking the property. The facility's gardens were even more breathtaking than they'd appeared during Sunday's storms. Lush green lawns and sparkling fountains gave the impression of a paradise tucked away, hidden where no one—except wealthy patients, perhaps—might find it. People roamed the grounds this morning, mostly in small groups. Elderly folks, accompanied by aides or family members, either strolled or were pushed in wheelchairs, enjoying the morning's gentle sunshine.

I found a spot nearer the front door than last time and made my way in.

The busy lobby took me by surprise. In stark contrast to Sunday's quiet desolation, there were people present today. Lots of them—laughing, conversing, and sipping drinks from paper cups. A few residents sat by the fireplace, others clustered near the windows. Life had gone back to normal around here. And normal, apparently, included a lively lobby atmosphere; cool, mentholated air; and soft conversations.

Cathy, the ever-so-helpful chatty aide, sat alone at the front desk working at a computer. According to Frances, Cathy had once been a full-time registered nurse at a big university hospital. Widowed young, she subsequently married a man who owned a slew of convenience stores. They settled in Rosette, where she took her current, less stressful job as an aide. The couple had no kids, but Cathy doted on her three dachshunds.

As though feeling the weight of my scrutiny, Cathy glanced up and said, "Good morning." Her expression was guileless, bland. Not even a flicker of recognition.

There was a sign-in sheet on the desk in front of me and a basket of *Visitor* tags to its right. I leaned down, intending to print my name in the proper column of the sheet when Cathy, sensing my hesitation, asked, "First time visiting?"

"I was here Sunday," I said. "During all the commotion?"

She nodded, still oblivious.

"You and Debbie, the nurse, helped us. We were here with Frances Sliwa?"

Like curtains rising from a stage, bewilderment lifted from her eyes. "Oh," she said, drawing the exclamation out. "Yes. I remember. That was really something, wasn't it? Did the police arrest Frances yet? I heard they were going to, maybe even today."

Her careless inquiry made my stomach pinch.

"No," I said. "I'm sure they won't. They only want to talk with her. She's clearly an important witness, but there's no way she would have harmed Gus."

"Mm-mm," she said with a lilt that suggested she doubted me. "So then why are you here?"

"I'm visiting Percy. Her ex-husband."

"Really? I thought you didn't even know about him before Sunday."

With a high-wattage smile, I said, "I make friends easily."

She took a moment to connect the dots. "Wait a second. I'll bet because Frances can't be here, she wants you to deliver a message. Am I close?"

I forced a smile. "Something like that. She wants to know that he's all right. After all that excitement, she's nervous about him."

"Tell me about it. Everybody here has been on edge."

Sensing her warming up, I decided to push my luck a little. "I can imagine," I said. "That nurse, the one who started all this craziness, what was his name again?" I knew it, of course, but simple inquiries were often effective segues.

"Santiago," she said quietly, leaning across the desk to be heard. "And let me tell you, he's in love with all the attention. He keeps telling everyone how observant he was to have noticed the cap on the floor."

So the cap on the floor was now common knowledge. "I probably wouldn't have."

She grinned. "Me neither. But then again, with patients as nasty as Gus, I try to spend as little time in the room with them as possible."

"I wouldn't blame you. I never met Gus, but it sounds like he was a real curmudgeon."

Cathy held a hand next to her mouth and stage-whispered, "So is Santiago. Except he's about forty years younger."

"Good to know," I said. "He's not working today, is he? I'd rather avoid him if I can."

Or, seek him out. But no need to share that with Cathy right now.

"Not sure," she said, wrinkling her nose. "He usually works mornings, but I haven't seen him yet. Don't worry. If he's here, he'll find you."

"Why?"

"Fresh blood," she said with a grin. "Another person to tell the 'I was the person who discovered a murder' story to."

"We don't know for sure that Gus was murdered," I reminded her. "I'm betting they determine that he died of natural causes."

Cathy shrugged as though it made no difference at all. As though it didn't matter that someone's—Frances's—good name and freedom hung in the balance. Cheerfully, she said, "Don't let Santiago hear you say that. He prefers playing the hero."

After a little bit more small talk, I finished signing in, wished Cathy a good day, and headed into the East Wing, the area that had been off-limits when Bennett and I had arrived Sunday. Cathy assured me that the police had gotten all they needed from the crime scene (*alleged* crime scene, I silently corrected) and that Percy and Kyle had been allowed to return to their apartment.

"It's the last one at the end of the hall before you make a left," she said, pointing. "Straight on at the corner. You can't miss it. If Percy's not there, try the Sun Gallery. He loves playing cards and is always looking for someone to join him."

Percy played cards? Interesting. Frances had mentioned that even though he had severe physical limitations and his hands didn't always cooperate, he was still able to manage a self-injection when necessary. Apparently he managed other tasks as well.

"Thanks, Cathy."

"Let me know if you hear any news," she said as I walked away.

I smiled over my shoulder and waved. *Not a chance.*

As I pushed open the doors to the East Wing, I was struck by how very un-nursing-home-like it was. When Bennett and I had been shuttled to the Sun Gallery on Sunday, we'd traversed a wide, rather utilitarian hallway. It had been attractive enough—even homey—for an assisted-living facility. But nothing special.

This section, on the other hand, made me believe I'd stepped into a luxury hotel. From the high-quality paintings that hung along both long walls, to the cream-colored wainscoting, to the mini-chandeliers suspended from the coffered ceiling, to the gentle notes of classical music that accompanied me as I made my way down a golden hardwood corridor, the allure of this space took me by surprise.

Six-panel cherrywood doors ran along both sides of this hallway spaced about fifty feet apart. Closed, each sported a decorative brass knocker and had a cheery welcome mat placed on the floor out front. From the looks of the decorative wreaths, floor plants, and crafty personalization at each one, I got the impression that residents in this wing were allowed to enhance their abodes however they pleased.

I slowed my pace to peruse the names of the occupants. Three apartments belonged to married couples; the fourth displayed two female names.

Straight ahead, I spotted a fifth resident door exactly where Cathy had said it would be—at the far end of the hall where the corridor made a sharp turn to the left. That had to be Percy's place. I hadn't seen Gus's name on any doors thus far, and—come to think of it—hadn't seen Kyle's, either. Maybe their rooms were located farther down the hall to the left. I'd have to find out.

I reached to knock at Percy's door, then pulled my hand back in surprise. Percy's, Gus's, and Kyle's names were all listed there. The three men lived together?

"May I help you?"

I turned.

A workstation sat about fifty feet down the long hall to my left, staffed by two women and a man. One of the women, the younger of the two, beckoned me over.

As I made my way toward them, I replayed Frances's descriptions in my head. The thirty-something young man had a slim build, fresh acne lacing the hollows of both cheeks, and hipster chin stubble. He leaned against a tall cabinet. I had no doubt this was Santiago. Frances hadn't been able to provide much detail on the guy's personal life, but she'd eagerly shared her opinion, telling me that he was arrogant, snippy, and insincere. Worse, he had connections; his mother was on Indwell's board of trustees.

However unpleasant his personality, I was glad to see him. He was first on my conversations-to-have list today.

The twenty-something woman—the one who'd beckoned me over—had a dark complexion and the kind of skin that could sell beauty creams by the truckload. This must be Tara. I reminded myself: newly engaged to be married. Always professional. Always upbeat.

The final member of the trio—Debbie, the nurse we'd met Sunday—squinted at a computer monitor as she tapped at the keyboard. According to Frances, Debbie was divorced with no kids. She split her time between working at Indwell and taking care of an aged mother. Frances had told me that, like Tara, Debbie was always helpful, but more "down-to-earth." She apparently was one of the few staff members Gus had actually liked.

Cathy hadn't remembered me; maybe Debbie wouldn't, either.

"Hello," I said as I approached the trio. "I'm here to visit Percy Sliwa."

At the sound of my voice, Debbie looked up, taking an extra second to adjust her focus from the screen to me. "Oh, hi," she said. "Nice to see you again." She glanced over at the young man briefly and frowned.

"How are you?" I asked. "How did things go after we left?"

She stood up to come out from behind the desk. "Let me walk you over to Percy's room."

The black woman with the gorgeous skin looked confused by Debbie's offer. "It's right there." As she pointed, I caught a glimpse of her name tag. Yep. Tara. "It's not like she's going to get lost."

"But Grace and I have so much to talk about," Debbie said with a laugh.

Although it was nice that she'd remembered my name, it felt odd to have her scoop a hand through my elbow as though we were old friends. She tugged me away from the desk.

Debbie's demeanor practically screamed her intention to get me away from the young man. And he struck me as a person who didn't miss a beat.

He boosted himself from the cabinet. "Hello, there." His keen, dark gaze assessed me even as his thin lips stretched to reveal wide, yellow teeth. It looked as though the effort to be pleasant caused him pain. "You're here to see Percy?"

"I am."

"Interesting." The young man's eyes narrowed. "I've never seen you here before."

Debbie tugged my arm.

"What a coincidence," I said. "I've never seen you, either."

"Are you the woman Percy and Kyle were telling me about?"

I held up both hands, effectively dislodging Debbie's grip. "There's really no way for me to know, is there?"

When his eyebrows jumped, I got the impression he was amused. "True enough." He shot me another insincere smile. "Let me put it a different way. Are you the woman who works with Percy's wife at Marshfield Manor?"

I could feel Debbie's dismay as I abandoned the path to Percy's room and veered back to the desk. "First of all, Frances is Percy's *ex*-wife," I said with cutesy cheer, "but yes, I work with her at Marshfield. I'm Grace Wheaton." I extended my hand.

He shook it. "Santiago Perez."

"Nice to meet you, Santiago," I said, thinking: *Knew it!*

Debbie tapped my arm. I ignored her.

Santiago worked his big teeth over his bottom lip as he regarded me. "So how about Frances killing Gus?" he asked. "You know she would've gotten away with it if I hadn't been so observant."

I feigned ignorance. "That was you?"

"Yeah, and I have to tell you, I'm not the least bit surprised. From the day Gus moved in, Frances had it in for him." He bounced glances between Debbie and Tara. "Am I right?"

"I'm sorry to hear that you jumped to such a ridiculous conclusion," I said. "Frances may grouse like it's an Olympic sport, but she'd never hurt anyone." I maintained a tight smile. "Never."

"I've been in this unit for seven years. That's longer than anybody else at this desk," he said with another nod to the two women. "I've seen a

157

lot. More than you can imagine. And I can tell you, unequivocally, that Frances wanted Gus out of that apartment, even if it meant she had to kill him to do it."

"Santiago," Tara said, keeping her voice very low, "didn't the police tell you not to talk about this?"

He folded his arms across his chest. "I don't hear you complaining whenever I share my updates."

"Updates?" I asked. "There's more?"

"Lots more."

How could eyes that dead have such expressive brows?

"The police have been back to talk with me three times already," he said.

And? I wanted to ask. But this guy enjoyed the banter. Enjoyed playing too much. I suddenly felt empathy for Bootsie when I teased her with her feather stick.

I shook my head. "I heard about that injector cap you found on the floor." With a dismissive chuckle, I said, "I'll bet there are dozens—if not hundreds—of identical pieces of plastic in this building right now. The fact that one got kicked into Gus's room shouldn't surprise anyone."

"And it doesn't." The scary smile grew. "But all the missing insulin sure did."

I held up an index finger. "Only *one* injector is

missing. And that's assuming someone didn't miscount or misplace it."

"You haven't heard, then," he said with far too much glee for my taste. "That's what everyone thought at first. But when they took a closer look, they found out that at least *four* dosages are missing."

"I thought they said—"

"That only one was missing? Yeah," he said. "As for the other three?" He waited a long beat. "The injectors were right where they should be in Percy's room, but guess what? All three of them were empty."

I felt my jaw drop. "That can't be." Frances had told me that she'd done a quick inventory the day before. If the vials had been empty, surely she would have noticed.

Santiago added a smug nod to his repertoire of repugnant gestures. "You know what that means, don't you? This was no accident. Frances not only administered the fatal dose, she took precautions to cover her tracks. Premeditated murder." He held up both hands, mimicking helplessness. "Sorry."

"Three insulin vials were empty?"

"Yep," he said.

"That's despicable," I said. "What if Percy needed an injection? Or two? Whoever stole the medicine put his life in danger."

Santiago waved the air. "I'm sure Frances had a backup plan. She dotes on that man. And I'm sure she intended to replace what she used as quickly as she could."

"Frances didn't do this." My voice sounded as strained as I felt. "And I'm sure we'll find a reasonable explanation for the missing insulin." I worked hard to tamp down my frustration. "Plus, we don't even know for sure that Gus died from an insulin overdose. He could just as easily have died from natural causes."

"Yeah," Santiago said, stringing the word out. "And Tara here is going to be my boss someday." He missed Tara's annoyed reaction when he rolled his eyes.

"You never know," I said. "Hard work and perseverance are far better indicators of success than wild speculation and time-wasting."

He didn't like that one bit. "Like I said, I've seen a lot in my years here, but I never expected to get involved in a murder investigation. I'm not making anything up. I simply reported to the proper authorities."

His cell phone rang, interrupting his lecturing me further. Pulling the device from his pocket, he glanced at the display. "Got to take this one. Excuse me."

When he turned his back and started away with the phone jammed against one ear and a finger plugging the other, Debbie tapped my arm again. "I was trying to spare you. I knew that once he got started, he'd say something stupid."

Tara spun in her chair. "Don't mind him. He's convinced he's some sort of amateur detective." She tossed a frown over her shoulder and didn't bother to lower her voice. "And let's see who reports to who come next promotion." She fixed me with a direct gaze. "He's delusional, that one."

"Tara's not kidding," Debbie said. "Santiago loves being the center of attention."

"Is it true?" I asked. "About all the missing insulin, I mean?"

Debbie shrugged.

Tara said, "We only know what Santiago tells us."

"But I agree with you," Debbie said. "Gus died of natural causes. It's ludicrous to think otherwise."

Tara nodded. "Debbie thinks that Gus had a heart attack or a stroke."

"He was a prime candidate for either," Debbie said.

"When will full autopsy results be back?" I asked.

Tara shook her head. "We don't deal with autopsies too often around here. I'd be guessing."

"They should have a preliminary report soon," Debbie said. "But testing for certain drugs usually takes longer."

"And they'll be able to determine if Gus died from an insulin overdose?"

"Insulin is exceptionally hard to detect in an autopsy." Debbie said. "I'm sure there's nothing to find." She slid a glance back toward the desk. "I'll be happy to see Mr. Super Sleuth over there get his comeuppance."

Chapter 16

AS DEBBIE AND I MADE OUR WAY TO Percy's door, I asked, "Who else has access to patients' rooms and medications?"

"That's complicated. In this wing—where patients live as autonomously as they can—most handle their own meds. Staff members have access to everyone's apartment, of course, but there are strict rules about when and how often we can enter a resident's room."

That wasn't much help. "When you say that staff members have access," I asked, "does that apply to everyone? I understand medical personnel visits, but what about aides, volunteers, and the cleaning crew?"

"Part of the appeal of living here is that all residents' needs are provided for," she said, "so yes—even our cleaning people have access to rooms. But it's more considerate to knock first than to let oneself in unannounced. That's why patients use that." She pointed to the automatic door opener, a metal plate set about waist height in the wall next to us. "And we use this." She lifted the brass knocker affixed just above the three residents' names and let it drop. "But every employee—no matter their position—must submit to a background check before starting work here."

From inside, Percy shouted that he was coming.

"Even though we screen people," she continued, "we still advise residents to keep valuables locked up. Indwell is proud of the fact that none of our residents has ever had anything of value stolen. Items do go missing from time to time," she said with a wry smile, "but they're usually recovered quickly. Glasses are the biggest culprit. TV remotes and cell phones, too; those sorts of things. That's to be expected, especially with some patients suffering from memory loss."

I listened politely to her gentle boasting about Indwell's pristine reputation, but was more captivated by an earlier comment. "Let's go back to who has access to these rooms," I said. "You're telling me that if they find insulin in Gus's system, there are plenty of people who could have killed him. Frances isn't the only option."

"Don't let the wild claims get to you." Debbie crinkled up her nose. "They won't find insulin in Gus's system. The man just . . . died. As you might imagine, that happens pretty often around here. It bugs me that Santiago got everybody stirred up over nothing. This is a lot of ridiculous nonsense. My patients are very upset."

"But what about the missing medication?" I asked.

"I'm sure there's a perfectly reasonable explanation," she said. "Either that, or Santiago made that part up."

With a hiss, Percy's door opened, swinging smoothly outward. I stepped back to allow it to complete its full arc.

"Good morning." Percy grinned up at us from his wheelchair. "Come on in."

Another question occurred to me and I pointed to the door. "Can these be locked?"

"No." Debbie shook her head. "If there's ever an emergency, we need unrestricted access to the rooms."

"And I keep telling them that the doors shouldn't swing outward like that," Percy said with a glint of humor. "They tell me I should be grateful they don't swing inward. But they do swing inward if I'm on your side. Who designed this place, anyway? What were they thinking? Don't I keep saying that, Debbie?"

She smiled. "He never misses an opportunity to remind us that Indwell would be much more accessible for its wheelchair-bound residents if the doors opened sideways." She pantomimed the motion.

"Like on *Star Trek*," Percy said. "With a *whoosh*. The architects who designed this place could have used help from *Starfleet*'s engineers."

"And with that, I'll leave you two alone," Debbie said. "Let me know if you need anything."

"Come on in," Percy said. He used two fingers and an elbow to gesture me to follow him. As he rolled deeper into the apartment, I tried not to let my amazement show. A large, central space clearly served as a shared living area for the three men. Two closed doors to my right and one to my left probably led to their individual bedrooms.

"This looks more like a ritzy man-cave than a room in an assisted-living facility," I said in awe. "I've never seen anything like it."

Bright, neon beer signs—one in the shape of Texas—stretched across the wide charcoal wall to my left. Directly below the signs sat a red leather sofa that looked as though it had been ripped straight off the set of *Mad Men*. A giant flat-screen TV took up most of the wall opposite.

"Glad you approve," he said with a smirk. "We pay a hefty premium to live here. It better be nice. Come on in. I had a feeling you'd show up one of these days. How's my girl doing?"

It took me a half second to realize he meant Frances. "She was called down to the police station today."

He winced. "She's a trooper, that one. I worry more for the cops than I do for her." He snickered, but I didn't believe him for a second. Using his chin to indicate the sofa, he said, "Have a seat."

My skirt made squeaky sounds as I settled myself and placed my jacket and purse on the cushion next to me. I revised my original assessment. Not leather. Tight vinyl. Attractive, yes. Comfortable, no. "This place is . . ."

"Not bad for a prison cell?"

In spite of myself, I laughed. "I'd hardly call this a prison," I said, giving the apartment another quick perusal.

"Might as well be iron bars and bolts on the doors. I can't leave."

"Of course you can."

"Really?" The word came out sharply, but his expression flashed with melancholy, rather than anger. "Where would I go?"

I didn't have an answer for that.

"I have everything I need here. And, sure, the place is attractive enough. But make no mistake—I'm an inmate. In a prison of my own making."

Again, I didn't know what to say. "Given the circumstances, this is a beautiful place to live."

"I won't argue with you," he said. "I got lucky getting Kyle as a roommate. Before he came to Indwell, I had one of those smaller spots. You probably passed them on your way in."

"I didn't get to see inside any of them."

"They aren't bad, really. Compact and service-able." He lifted both hands, ever so slightly. "But no comparison to this place. Kyle's family is well-off. Really well-off. And because they feel guilty about leaving him here, they spare no expense. He and I hit it off, and he asked if I'd like to room with him. I'm no dummy. I jumped at the chance."

"How did Gus get in on the arrangement?"

"He's even more well-off than Kyle's family," Percy said. "This apartment has three bedrooms, three baths. I occupy the room on that side." He gestured with his head toward the lone door. "Gus and Kyle are opposite."

"How did you manage to snag the side by yourself? Kyle didn't call dibs on it?"

"My room's the smallest of the three. Kyle's and Gus's are a lot bigger."

"You said Kyle's family feels guilty and spares no expense." Judging from my surroundings, Percy wasn't kidding. "So why not keep him home? Wouldn't a full-time caregiver be a better option?"

"Kyle wanted out of the house just like any other kid his age would. His physical capabilities may be limited, but that doesn't keep him from wanting to be independent. He insisted on living on his own, but his parents are overprotective and didn't want him to leave. They settled on a compromise. This is it. Those of us in this wing are allowed visitors all day, all night. And Kyle makes good use of that privilege, trust me."

I wanted to get back to talking about Gus, but his offhand remark piqued my interest. "I had to sign in, up front," I said.

"Yeah, during regular hours, they try to have

168

everyone sign in. But it's pretty loose. Those of us in the East Wing are allowed visitors even when the rest of the place is locked down for the night. Those visitors do have to sign in with security. But except for Kyle's occasional girlfriends, hardly anybody takes advantage of that policy."

"I'm sure the police are checking all visitor logs," I said.

"Yeah, I heard somebody talking about that. Santiago, probably. He seems to know everything."

"Speaking of Santiago . . ." I shifted on the sofa and was rewarded with more squeaking. "I heard that more of your insulin is missing."

He sighed, clearly annoyed by the question. "So they tell me."

"You haven't checked for yourself?"

"Of course I did. As soon as they allowed me back in my room this morning. But at that point the cops had already taken all my medication away. Now I only have the cops' word on it. They did an inventory of everything they took from the apartment and made me go over it, line by line, with one of the nurses. I wish I would've known about the empty insulin containers before the cops got here; I'd have yanked them out of sight."

"You would have tampered with evidence?"

"Who says it's evidence?" His gaze was hot. "But even if it is, would I do it to protect Frances? You bet your life, I would."

A tiny voice whispered in the back of my brain: *Or protect yourself.*

"Which nurse went over the inventory with you?"

"That young girl with the pretty smile. Tara."

"Okay, so walk me through this one more time," I said. "Gus was alive Sunday morning before you and Frances left for church, right?"

"Yes. He was storming around with a bottle of scotch in one hand and a drinking glass in the other. Being belligerent, as always."

"And arguing with Frances."

"Bingo." Percy curled his lips to the side. "She couldn't have picked a worse day to mix it up with him."

"I understand he was found in bed, though. Did he usually go back to sleep in the morning?"

"Sometimes, yeah, when he wasn't feeling well. Gus had episodes—heart problems, I think—and would lie down until his dizziness passed. That was pretty normal for him."

I sat up a little straighter. "Could I take a look around his room?" I asked. "And maybe yours, too? If that isn't too much of an imposition."

"Be my guest."

"They haven't sealed his room off?"

"Nope. The police said they got everything they needed for now." Percy pointed. "That one," he said, indicating the door to my left. He followed behind as I made my way over. He was right:

There were no warning signs posted, no seal across the door, nothing to indicate any police involvement whatsoever.

"You're sure we're allowed in here?" I asked.

"The cops loaded a couple bags of Gus's belongings and carted them out. Not much, as far as I could tell. Before they left the last time, the detective in charge—a cheeky young woman, if you ask me—told us that they were finished for now and if they had any further questions for any of us, they'd be in touch."

I frowned at the knob, then remembered that every door in this facility could also be opened automatically. I stretched my sweater sleeve to cover my fist and pushed the silver plate on the wall to activate the mechanism.

Percy laughed as the door swung wide. "If you're so worried about fingerprints, you should grab a pair of latex gloves. There are boxes of them everywhere in this place."

"I'll try to remember that," I said and stepped in.

While not nearly as attractive as the apartment's living room, Gus's quarters gave off the same spacious vibe. Except for an impressive collection of heavy-framed oil paintings that took up most of the room's three pale blue walls, the place was barren. Stark. Cold. Only the wide picture window and its panoramic view of Indwell's grounds offered any sign of life.

"Let's hope they didn't take everything," Percy said as he pulled up next to me.

The hospital bed near the window had been stripped down to its forest-green mattress, and a barren IV tree stood nearby. Gus's antique highboy dresser was devoid of personality. No knickknacks, no personal items. A matching low dresser with a mirror and two contemporary armoire cabinets offered more of the same. The nightstand held a lamp and a box of facial tissues. Other than that, there was little in the room beyond a recliner and a dorm-sized refrigerator.

"Are you kidding?" I asked. "Except for the pictures on the walls, this place has been completely cleared out."

"Nah, this is normal. Exactly the way Gus liked it." Percy zoomed past me, toward the armoires. "He was a clean freak."

"So I've heard," I said.

"Don't let the cleanliness fool you, though," Percy said. "He may have been fastidious, but he was a hoarder. He's got more stuff collected in his cabinets than Kyle and I put together."

"No way," I said.

Percy tilted his chin to indicate the nearer armoire. "Open up one of those and you'll see," he said. "Gus was a master at fitting twenty things into a space built to hold two. It's all neat and tidy in there, believe me. But it's jam-packed. Kyle

172

showed me some of Gus's special hiding spots once when he wasn't around."

"I really shouldn't—"

"And just wait until you see the bathroom. Come on." He gestured for me to follow. "Put on a pair of gloves so that you won't be nervous about touching things."

The bathroom was as devoid of personality as the bedroom. The countertop was bare except for a box of purple latex gloves, an empty soap dish, and an empty toothbrush holder. Mounted on the wall above the outlet was a red plastic container meant for medical waste disposal. The shower curtain had been pulled aside but all that remained in the wide stall was a shampoo bottle and a bar of green soap.

"Did they take all his medications?" I asked.

"See for yourself."

Why not? After donning gloves, I pulled open the door to Gus's mirrored medicine cabinet. "This is pretty empty," I said as I gave the contents a quick scan.

"The police must have taken most of it."

I pushed the few remaining items around to get a better look but the shallow cabinet held little more than toothpaste, mouthwash, and dental floss.

Percy backed into the doorway to give me more room. "The guy complained whenever we left things lying around the apartment. That was one of the reasons we were lobbying to get him moved."

"You and Kyle?" I asked. "Or you and Frances?"

He gave a small shrug. "Kyle didn't seem to mind him as much as I did. Gus took a liking to the kid and shared some of his stash with him."

"What kind of stash?"

"The liquor, what else? Sometimes, when Anton visited, he and Gus would invite Kyle to join them. They'd talk for hours. I could hear them from my room."

"You weren't invited?"

"Nah." Percy made it seem as though he didn't care. "Anton liked me well enough, but Gus and I butted heads."

I opened the cabinet under the sink and crouched to look inside, happy to be wearing the gloves. They provided me freedom to pull out the cabinet's contents and examine them one by one. "Not much here," I said as I surrounded the floor around me with spare toilet paper rolls. "Gus apparently used an electric shaver." I held the device up before placing it next to my foot. "And enjoyed outdoorsy magazines." One at a time, I held up each shiny periodical, fanning its pages and shaking it. A stack of subscription cards and preprinted sale flyers—offering everything from slippers to sunglasses—tumbled to the floor.

"Nothing here," I said.

"You're thorough."

"I'm nosy." I also had a question for Percy. "Was Frances here all morning on Sunday?" I asked casually. I began to return Gus's shaving equipment, spare toilet paper, and magazines back to where I'd found them. "That is, did she arrive Sunday, or was she still here from Saturday night?"

"Are you asking me if Frances spent the night? She'd be so disappointed in you. Such a personal question."

"I'm concerned with the timing." I shut the cabinet doors and stood up. "I'm not interested in explicit details of your relationship."

"You aren't?" he asked. "Now *I'm* disappointed." His eyes crinkled up at the corners.

"You seem to think this is all so funny," I said. "But I'm worried for her. She's been a rock these past few years, but she's never had to defend herself. I don't think she's prepared for any of this."

"Frances will be fine," he said. "She didn't kill anyone and the police are focusing on her only because they're idiots who don't know what they're doing."

"Knowing something and proving it are two different things." When had I heard that before? "We need to prove that Frances didn't do it."

With a sigh, Percy said, "When Frances comes out here on the weekends, she stays in a hotel. She says it would be unseemly for her to stay with me in my room."

"What time did she get here on Sunday?"

"Seven in the morning."

"What time did the two of you leave?"

"Eight thirty-ish. And the only reason I can answer these questions so easily is because I've had practice with the detectives. When they asked me all this the first time, I had to stop and think for a while."

"And when you and Frances left the apartment, Gus was still alive, right?" I asked.

"By the time we left, he'd stopped his yammering. He was sitting on the sofa, reading the newspaper."

"Did he seem any different to you? Especially agitated? Short of breath or in pain?"

"Frances is right. You make a good detective."

When I didn't respond to his attempt at humor, he rolled his eyes. "Like I told the cops, Gus was his regular, cranky self. He said something like 'Don't hurry back on my account,' when we were leaving."

"And Kyle was at physical therapy? How long does that usually last?"

"An hour or so. But don't worry, the police covered all that with him, too. There are a couple of kids in one of the other buildings who Kyle plays video games with on Sundays. After physical therapy, he hung out with them."

"The closest building is pretty far away. And it was storming Sunday. How did he get there?"

"Shuttle."

"Did anyone else enter the apartment that morning? Before Frances showed up, I mean."

"Santiago, of course. If anyone else did, I didn't see them. But that's not saying much. When I'm in my room I don't really pay attention to what's going on in the rest of the apartment."

Wanting to get a glimpse inside the bathroom's small linen closet, I opened the door, forcing Percy to wheel backward even more. "So then if Gus *was* killed, that means someone else had to enter the apartment to do it while you were gone."

"What are you doing in my father's room?"

I spun at the unfamiliar male voice.

Before I could think twice, I peered around the linen closet door. A middle-aged man glowered down at Percy, who—for the first time since I'd met him—seemed at a loss for words.

The man's brows jumped when he saw me standing there. "And who are you?"

Chapter 17

"DAN," PERCY FINALLY MANAGED TO SAY. Strain made the word come out about two octaves too high. "When did you get in?"

"Not soon enough, it seems." He focused his attention on me. "Who are you?" he asked again. Pointing to my purple-clad hands, he added, "An investigator? When are we going to get the autopsy results? We want to start making Dad's arrangements."

The temptation to pass myself off as some sort of forensic specialist stole my ability to speak, but only for a split second. "My name is Grace Wheaton," I said. "From what I understand, the police have finished in here and have taken all they need."

Percy navigated his chair around Dan and sped back into the bedroom.

Dan was my height with an average build. He carried a paunch that made him look about five months' pregnant. Small hands, narrow shoulders, ruddy chin. He wore navy pants, a plaid short-sleeved shirt, and carried a tan windbreaker. With his brown comb-over, pale skin, and bulbous, pockmarked nose, he was as unremarkable as they came.

"That doesn't explain what you're doing here," he said, waving the windbreaker for emphasis. "My dad was a wealthy guy. He has a lot of expensive stuff in here. You better not have touched one single thing in his room—"

I cut him off with my kindest smile, hoping to nip this particular line of conversation before things got worse. "First of all, I'm very sorry about your dad. I'm sure his death came as a terrible shock. Please accept my condolences."

He shifted his weight and pursed his lips as though trying to decide what my game was.

"I'm not here to steal anything." I pressed forward, smiling, attempting to disarm. "And if the police had sealed the room, believe me, I never would have stepped in. I just thought that maybe, if I took a quick look around, I might notice something that the police overlooked."

"Something the police overlooked," he repeated, clearly unconvinced.

"I'm a friend of Percy's and Frances's," I began.

"Wait a minute. You said your name is Grace. Are you Frances's Grace?" he asked. "The one related to Bennett Marshfield?"

"That's me."

He ran a hand through his sparse hair. "Oh, okay, that explains a lot."

Banking on Dan being a fair-minded guy, I

continued, "You may have heard that the police are questioning Frances in regard to your father's death."

"I got the call last night," he said without enough inflection for me to determine whether he thought the idea of Frances being a suspect was brilliant or ridiculous. "Do the police know you're here?"

I hesitated. "Frances may have mentioned it to them."

Dan squinted. "What I'm asking is: Have the police sanctioned your little investigation here today?"

I bit my lip, then said, "No."

"Didn't think so." He stepped deeper into the bedroom and pointed toward the hallway. "Out."

Feeling like a kid caught rummaging through the teacher's desk, I slipped past him as quickly as I could. Ten feet ahead of me, Percy zoomed out the bedroom door.

"Sorry," I said. "I promise I didn't intend any harm."

"Oh sure," he said, following me out. "Then why the need for the gloves?"

Back in the man-cave living room, I peeled off the purple latex and turned to face him. "I can only imagine how bad this looks."

"Ya think?" he asked. "Indwell is giving us only a week to get the room cleared out. My brother and his wife are coming later with boxes, but I thought I'd get a head start pulling the good stuff together. Lucky I got here when I did. I *should* report you to the management."

His phrasing choice gave me hope that he might not report me—as long as I didn't aggravate him further.

"I am sorry," I said. "And I truly wouldn't want to do anything to deepen your grief."

His manner softened. "You can't just go around digging through our poor father's belongings like that. It's sacrilegious."

Back in the living room now, Percy was nowhere to be found. I returned to the uncomfortable red sofa and pointed to a nearby chair. "Why don't you have a seat?" I asked, as though I had any right to play hostess here. As he settled himself, I asked, "Have you heard anything more about what's going on?" I purposely avoided using the words *murder,* and *investigation.*

"This is all crazy business. Who would want to kill my dad?" He waved the air and gave a half laugh. "Don't answer that. Practically everybody did."

"I'm sorry to hear that."

When he scrunched up his face, he looked like an inquisitive shar-pei. "Did you know my dad?"

"I never had the pleasure." I said, wondering where Percy had gotten to.

Dan laughed again, this time with more warmth. "Hardly anybody would call it a 'pleasure.' My dad wasn't the easiest guy to get along with."

I had no idea how to run with that, so I decided to dig a little. "When did you see him last?"

"About a week ago." He made the shar-pei face again. "I was out of town. Just got home late last night."

"Out of town?" I asked, striving for casual. "Where did you go?"

"Vacation." He raised a hand, pointing vaguely northwest. "We've got a fishing cabin in the Blue Ridge Mountains."

"We?" I asked. "You and your wife?"

He seemed to think that was funny. "Nah, I'm not married anymore. The cabin belongs to our family. Harland and his wife said they might come up and join me, but they never made it."

"Was your father depressed at all?" I asked. "Melancholy or in low spirits when you saw him last?"

"You mean like—could he have killed himself? Not a chance. My dad would sooner slit somebody else's throat than let himself get hurt."

Gus sounded like a real joy to be around. "Do you know if he was started on any new medications recently? Maybe something affected his state of mind?"

"Could be, I guess."

"What kind of meds was he getting through the heparin lock?" I asked, pointing to the back of my hand. "I understand he had to have that flushed regularly. Do you know what he was receiving intravenously?"

"Not a clue."

I must have projected my surprise at his tone because he hurried to add, "I mean, I know he needed drugs for his heart. But all that medical jargon is like mishmash to me. That's why we were so glad he decided to live here. We were happy to let people who know what they're doing take care of stuff like that. We thought he'd be safe in this place."

"Your father liked living here, didn't he?"

"For the fortune my dad had to cough up every month"—Dan rubbed his thumb against his fingers—"he'd better. They should have served him prime rib every night. But yeah, he seemed to like it fine."

Before I could ask anything else, Dan continued, "I've worked my whole adult life and my best salary hasn't been half of the annual fee at this place. You ask me, it's ridiculous what they charge for a bed and three squares."

"And expert medical care," I reminded him.

He half grinned at that. "Yeah, that, too."

I heard the *whir* of Percy's wheelchair. "I see you two are getting acquainted," he said. "Sorry. Had to use the necessary."

Dan kept talking. "What I want to know," he said, "is why that idiot Santiago called the police. Don't people die here every day?"

"You agree, then, that Frances couldn't have had anything to do with your father's death?" I asked.

"She's a tough bird, that one. No offense," he said to Percy then returned his attention to me. "Nah. Why would she? Because she and my dad mixed it up sometimes? Yeah, I heard about that, but I don't buy it. This whole investigation is stupid."

His easy dismissal gave me hope. "I hope you're right and we find out that your dad died peacefully in his sleep."

"That's what I'm counting on."

"So you don't think there's anyone here who might dislike your father enough to kill him?" I remembered Anton and his contraband alcohol. "Or any regular visitors who might want to do him ill?"

Dan gave the question a moment of scrunched-face thought. "When people die, everybody is in a rush to talk about how great they were. That's nuts. If you listen to all the amazing stories, or believe all the obituaries you read, every person who ever died in the history of the world has been some kind of saint. What's up with that?"

The door to the apartment opened and Santiago walked in, carrying a small paper cup. As he joined our little group, I watched him assess the dynamic.

"Good morning," he said with a bigger grin than necessary. I blinked back my revulsion. "What a nice, cozy group we have here. Are we discussing the murder?"

"Dan and I were talking about how unlikely it is that Frances had anything to do with Gus's death," I said.

Dan regarded the younger man with unconcealed distaste. "What do you want? Back to cause more trouble?"

Santiago reacted with a look of amused surprise. "I simply pointed out a few clues, Dan," he said. "I'd expect a little gratitude."

"Gratitude?" Dan advanced toward him. Dan wasn't a large man by any standard but he had at least thirty pounds on Santiago. "Instead of my dad being buried in peace, his body's been sent out to be sliced open and taken apart. Do you have any idea what goes on in those autopsies?"

I didn't think Santiago's obnoxious grin could get worse. I was wrong.

He scoffed. "You think I've never seen an autopsy? How do you think I got my nursing degree? Mail order?"

The two men had inched closer to each other. From the look of pure loathing in Dan's eyes, I worried we'd soon have another murder investigation on our hands.

"My dad was a sick guy. We brought him here so he could live out the rest of his days in comfort. He died, just like people do every day. But, now, because of your screwup, his body is sitting on a slab in a morgue instead of being cared for properly at a funeral home."

I stepped between them to prevent further escalation. "What worries me most right now is that an innocent woman is being interrogated by police because of your accusations."

"I'm sure you believe everything Frances tells you," Santiago said with a glint in his eyes. "But I can't think of anyone else who had the means, motive, and opportunity."

Percy cut me off before I could retort. "You're looking for Kyle, I assume?"

Santiago held up the paper cup. "Time for one of his meds."

Percy tilted his head. "He took off about an hour ago."

Santiago's über upbeat demeanor took a swift nosedive. "His locator says he's here." Santiago didn't wait for a response. He stormed down the hallway toward Gus's and Kyle's rooms, muttering to himself.

"Locator?" I asked.

Percy tapped a gray bracelet-like device on his wrist. "We're supposed to keep these on all the time. There's an emergency button to press if we need to call for help. It's got some fancy GPS technology that allows the staff to find us. Indwell is a big complex and it's easy to get lost."

"And the nurses use it when they need to administer medication?" I asked.

"That, too."

"I thought that in this section, residents handled their own meds."

"Depends on what it is," Percy said. "Kyle gets a couple of narcotics. The nurses keep tight tabs on those."

"Makes sense, I guess."

Santiago returned, holding the gray locator bracelet aloft. "Found it." No more scary smile and for that, at least, I was grateful. "These things don't do any good if they get left behind."

"Does Kyle usually forget it?"

"Only when he doesn't want to be found." Santiago tucked it into the pocket of his scrubs. "Where did he go?" he asked.

"Beats me," Percy said. I didn't believe him.

"Wonderful." Santiago rolled his eyes. "This is exactly what I needed today—another game of hide-and-seek with Kyle."

I stopped him as he turned to leave. "Those locators," I said. "Do you keep a history on them? That is, can you track back to see if one of the residents was in the room with Gus Sunday morning? Anyone who shouldn't have been here?"

Santiago smiled again. I wished he hadn't. "No, sorry," he said, though it was clear he certainly wasn't sorry at all. "Instead of a Find My iPhone app, it's like a Find the Patient app. A snapshot thing. It doesn't track unless the app's engaged, and it doesn't keep a history for each person."

"Worth asking," I said.

Santiago laughed. "Yeah."

"Enough fun for today," Dan said. He headed back to his father's room. "I may as well get started sorting through Dad's belongings."

My phone rang and I reached for my purse to retrieve it. "It's Frances," I told Percy as my heart sank. How could I tell her that I was coming up empty on my investigation?

Chapter 18

AS IT TURNED OUT, FRANCES DID ALL the talking. "My lawyer thinks they're going to keep me a while longer."

"They're not arresting you, are they?" I asked.

She hesitated so long I thought I'd pass out from lack of breath.

"Autopsy results aren't in. Not the ones, at least, that could exonerate me." She spoke briefly to someone else—from the sound of it, Lily—before returning to our conversation. "She thinks I'll be here another hour at least. Wanted to let you know."

Before I could summarize my morning, she cut me off. "They're calling me back. Gotta go," she said. Then, "Idiots."

"Watch yourself," I said. "Don't answer more than you need to. And don't antagonize them."

She muttered something I couldn't make out and hung up.

"Well?" Santiago asked. "*Are* they arresting her?"

With polite derision, I said, "Of course not."

"Only a matter of time."

I wanted to smack the smug off of his face.

"Don't you need to find Kyle?" Percy asked with a glance at the little white paper cup. "Now that I think about it, he mentioned getting a haircut."

Santiago frowned. "I'll call downstairs to see if he's there."

"Good luck finding him," Percy said. The moment the nurse exited the room, he turned to me. "I can't stand that guy."

I glanced at my watch. "Is there anyone else here you think I should talk to?"

"I'm glad you met Dan instead of his brother, Harland," he whispered. "The older brother is a loose cannon."

"I would like to talk with him," I said. "Dan mentioned that he and his wife would be stopping by later."

"I'll go out with you," Percy said. "We may run into them on their way in."

As we made our way to the door, I remembered something Cathy had said. "I understand you're quite a cardplayer."

His mouth twisted into a half grin. "If we were allowed to wager with cash in this place, I'd make a killing."

Interesting choice of words. I wondered: If the man was capable of playing cards and—as Frances asserted—capable of injecting himself, could Percy have injected Gus with his insulin?

He interrupted my thoughts. "When you see

Frances, tell her I say hello, would you? She puts on that cranky exterior, but she's really a softie underneath. I bet she misses me."

"Sure, no problem." I stopped walking. "Hey, I almost forgot. Would you mind if I took a quick look at where you keep your insulin?"

He frowned up at me. "What do you think you'll find there?"

"No idea," I said with a smile to ease his obvious concern. "But Frances and I like to be thorough, remember? We prefer to see things for ourselves."

"Frances knows where I keep everything. You can ask her."

"But I know how worried you are for her and I really think I need to see the storage for myself. You don't mind, do you?" I sidestepped around him, pointing toward his bedroom. "I won't be a minute."

"You're as stubborn as she is." He worked his jaw. "Fine. But I'm coming with you."

Percy's room was, indeed, much smaller than Gus's. And where Gus had lived a cool, austere existence, Percy clearly preferred one of comfortable clutter. The floor was unobstructed enough to allow his chair wide berth, but the room's perimeter was lined with an assortment of stuff—no better word for it—all placed at a level convenient for his reach. DVDs and books were grouped in messy piles. A mini refrigerator sat in one corner near the windows. In the corner opposite, a ten-bottle wine rack. Mostly whites.

Far out of Percy's reach, the tops of his bookcases were decorated with such a variety of knickknacks, I couldn't take everything in at once. An old-fashioned metal toy fire truck. An orange lava lamp, currently cold and unlit. An arrangement of stuffed animals. Collector plates featuring characters from *Star Trek: The Next Generation*. Model starships from that, and other space-travel series, hung from the ceiling.

Next to me sat a large square laminated cabinet. Two overstuffed easy chairs flanked the cube-shaped structure. One chair was plaid, the other solid. Two motorcycle-themed blankets lay draped across the plaid one and two featuring wildlife were strewn across the other.

Percy caught me looking. "Frances likes to relax there. It's easier for me to stay in the wheelchair," he said. "But one chair by itself looked lonely. So we ordered a second."

I wondered, again, what drove Frances to spend weekends here with him. Given the little bit of history she'd shared with me, and her surly attitude toward him, I didn't understand. But perhaps I didn't need to.

I moved to the washroom. "Do you keep your insulin in here?"

"Frances says that all medications should be kept out of heat and humidity, so we store most of my regular stuff right there." He gestured with his chin.

In all the clutter, I hadn't noticed the small set of drawers tucked into the cube storage unit. Made of plastic—the kind I used in my bathroom at home to store cosmetics—the drawers were set at a perfect height for Percy's easy reach.

"May I?"

He grunted. "Not going to stop you now."

The top drawer, the smallest of the three, held over-the-counter items.

The second drawer held more of the same.

The third, and largest of the drawers, was empty. "Is this where the insulin was kept?" I asked.

"No."

Why was he being so uncooperative? "Where *was* it kept?"

He spun his chair around and gestured toward the windows with his left elbow. I followed his gaze until I understood.

"Insulin needs to be refrigerated?" I asked as I crossed the room to the small appliance. "I guess I didn't know that."

"The kind I use can be kept at room temperature for a couple of weeks with no problem. I keep one on me at all times, but we're supposed to keep the rest in there."

The fridge had been arranged so that it sat slightly off the floor. I started toward it.

"There's nothing in there anymore," Percy said. "It's empty."

I ignored his attempt to divert me. When I peered inside the cool compartment, I found a whisky bottle lying on its side, three cans of beer, a slab of Gruyère, and a squeeze bottle of ketchup.

I lifted the bottle. "Scotch?"

"Yeah. So?"

"This is the bottle Anton brought Sunday, isn't it? The one you claimed you were going to show to the police."

He shrugged. "What good would it do to give it to them? The bottle was factory sealed. I didn't want it to go to waste."

"It's not factory sealed now."

"So Kyle and I shared some. You going to rat me out?"

"What else are you hiding?" I asked.

"Nothing, I swear."

"I don't see any medication in here."

"The police took all of it. Left me nothing but this one." He snaked his fingers along the side of his leg to produce an insulin syringe.

"What happens if you need more than that?" I asked. "What if you have an emergency?"

Percy adopted a rote-verbatim tone: "Until Indwell completes its own independent investigation into the missing insulin, all patients will be required to call for help if they require emergency assistance."

"That doesn't seem like a good idea," I said.

"They tell us it's temporary. For our own good. I had to practically beg them to let me keep this one with me." After tucking his syringe back into its hiding spot, he held up the wrist bearing his locator bracelet. "You can bet I won't take this baby off until things get back to normal."

I stepped back to allow him access to the fridge. "You don't have any problem getting what you need out of there?" I asked. "I mean, if you need an item in a hurry."

With exaggerated weariness, he rolled up to the small refrigerator and reached in to demonstrate his prowess before closing the door and wheeling around to face me. "Yes, little Miss Detective," he said, "I could have removed the insulin and replaced the empties just as easily as Frances could have."

"Why are you telling me this? Did you kill Gus?"

He scoffed. "Of course not. The idea is ludicrous."

"What about Kyle?"

"He didn't do it, either."

"How can you be so sure?" I was thinking: *How do I know it wasn't you?*

"Call it gut-level certainty. Call it whatever you want. I know what I know." He did a brisk three-point turn and wheeled out of the room. "Time for you to go now."

Though unsatisfied, I followed him back into the fancy man-cave. "You know I'll have to tell Frances what you said."

"Frances knows everything I just told you. If she needed to, she'd share it with the police. Trust me."

Percy's mood had shifted and I knew our visit was at an end. He accompanied me to the door where Dan had left a couple of boxes right smack in the middle of Percy's path out.

"Nobody understands," Percy said as I pushed the first one out of his way.

I'd just bent to pick up the second box when Dan returned to the room. "What are you doing with my dad's stuff now?" he asked.

Before I had a chance to answer, the apartment door opened and a couple walked in. The man was blond and beefy. The woman short and dark, but of similar heft.

"Who are you?" the guy asked. A second later, he addressed Dan. "Geez, man. When are you going to find someone your own age?"

Chapter 19

IT TOOK A LITTLE EFFORT, BUT DAN GOT us all sorted out. Harland and his wife, Joslyn—once they understood I was not Dan's girlfriend—were clearly perplexed by my presence. "You let her into Dad's room?" Harland asked his brother. "What were you thinking?"

"She was already in there when I arrived. Snooping." Dan pointed to Percy. "Not my fault. He let her in."

Harland wore the braggadocio of a young Biff from *Back to the Future*, but physically more resembled the character's older self. In his mid- to late fifties, Harland bested me by about six inches and had to be at least double my weight. Taking a threatening step forward, he asked, "What were you looking for?" To Dan: "How do you know she didn't steal anything?"

"Yeah." Joslyn kept her thick arms folded across her bosom. "How do we know?"

Though she was probably Harland's age, Joslyn's deep-set eyes, overdue-for-a-dye black hair, and pronounced lip lines, gave her the appearance of someone much older. Her puffy cheeks glowed with high emotion.

My job here was to find something, anything, that might absolve Frances. I couldn't be intimidated by Gus's less-than-bereft family members. I took a resolute step forward, putting myself within easy reach of Harland's clenching fists.

"You don't," I said simply. "I didn't take anything, but there's really no way for you to know for sure, is there?"

My audaciousness bought me what I needed: I'd knocked them off their bullying course long enough to push back a little.

"But you also asked what I was looking for," I continued in the seconds it took him to recover. "That's a fair question. I was hoping to find something the police may have missed. They're investigating my friend Frances. I intend to prove she didn't have anything to do with your father's death."

I didn't wait for them to react. "And, as I said to Dan, please accept my sincere condolences on your loss."

Harland and Joslyn exchanged a quick glance. As though reminded that they were in mourning, their demeanor shifted. "We *are* very upset about all this," Harland said. "I'm sure you understand."

"Of course," I said magnanimously. "This is a difficult time for all of you."

"Anybody would be concerned to find a stranger rifling through their dead father's belongings."

Though she'd softened her stance, Joslyn clearly remained unmoved.

"I'm very sorry to have met you all under such unhappy circumstances, but please know that— more than anything—I want to get to the truth." Again, not giving them a chance to respond, I plunged forward. "Of course, I'm sure we'll eventually learn that your father died of natural causes."

"The police don't seem to agree with you," Joslyn said. "From what we've heard, they're convinced *his* wife"—this accompanied by an accusatory finger pointed at Percy—"had it in for my father-in-law. God rest his soul."

Harland and Dan repeated the blessing.

I bit back my knee-jerk reflex to argue. Instead, I asked, "Assuming he didn't die naturally—and I sincerely hope to find out that he did—is there anyone else who may have had motive to kill him?"

"My father-in-law was an angel," Joslyn said.

Dan shot me an I-told-you-so look.

"If Frances did this to him," Joslyn continued, "she deserves to rot in jail for the rest of her life."

Harland waved her down like one would an energetic puppy. "Don't start painting holy pictures of him just because he's dead," he said, practically echoing his brother's sentiments. "Maybe my dad wasn't the easiest guy to get along with, but he didn't deserve being drugged to death."

"I agree," I said, "and, believe me, I'll be the first to help bring the guilty party to justice. But—make no mistake—it wasn't Frances."

Joslyn started to push, asking how I could be so sure, but Harland silenced her again. "We're not going to solve it here. We have to wait for the police to sort it all out." He regarded me with interest. "What exactly did you think you'd find?"

I answered honestly. "I don't know."

Percy positioned himself next to me and elbowed my arm. "Shouldn't you be getting back to the police station?"

His insistence that I hurry along was beginning to bug me. "She said she'd be a little while longer," I reminded him. "Aren't you running late for your card game?" I stepped out of his way. "Don't let me hold you up."

Harland and Joslyn were blocking the exit. They both scuttled to one side to give Percy a clear path to the door. The look he threw me as he made his way out was not a happy one.

"See you later," I called to his back.

The moment the door eased shut behind him, I asked the question I couldn't broach with Percy in the room. "What about other people here at Indwell?" I asked. "I'm not suggesting that your father's roommates are guilty, but I don't want to overlook any possibilities."

200

Harland brightened. "If it *was* one of his roommates, then we'll have a nice lawsuit on our hands, won't we? Indwell practically forced our dad to live with these two ingrates."

I turned to see Joslyn shoot a nervous glance to the back of Harland's head.

"Indwell forced Gus to live in this apartment?" I asked her.

"Not exactly," she said.

Harland spun to face her. "What are you talking about? Once Dad saw the rooms here, compared with the other ones, there was no going back. You saw those other places. A man with his money shouldn't have to live in a one-room dump."

"That's what I mean," she said. "He didn't like the other options. They didn't exactly force him to live with Percy and Kyle. It was more like he picked living here."

"That's not how I remember it."

The four of us formed a rough semicircle outside of Gus's bedroom door. Though Dan looked eager to pop into the conversation, he remained relatively silent as Harland and Joslyn bickered.

"Your father got along well with Kyle, from what I understand," I said.

"Yeah; I didn't understand that one bit," Harland said.

Dan cleared his throat. "Me neither."

Harland jabbed Dan with his elbow. "Sometimes

felt like the old man liked that kid better than he liked us, didn't it?"

Joslyn gave the room a derisive glance. "Don't understand what the kid saw in Gus, though," she said. "Unless he was looking for a sugar daddy."

"Excuse me?" I said.

Harland waved her down again. "Don't pay her any attention. She got it into her head that Kyle befriended Dad only because he knew he was worth a lot of money." Exactly the way his brother had earlier, Harland rubbed his thumb and fingers together. "She thinks the kid wanted to get Dad to include him in the will."

"But isn't Kyle's family well-off?" I asked.

"Sure, but that doesn't mean the kid is. He depends on them for everything. According to Dad, Kyle doesn't want to live here. He wants to be out on his own."

"Is that possible?"

"Anything's possible with enough bucks," Harland said with a laugh. "Isn't that right?"

"Was there any chance of your dad doing that?" I asked. "Revising his will, I mean?"

"No way," Dan said. "Dad may have been a cranky old coot, but he was big on bloodlines. I can't tell you how many times he told us: 'Money stays in the family.' He didn't even like it much when Harland bought Joslyn a new car. Said, 'What if she divorces you, what then? She's got the car, and you got nothing.' Man, that was how many years ago? He never stopped complaining about it. Remember, Harland?"

"He was joking around," Harland said quickly, but from the look on Joslyn's face, this pronouncement came as news. "You know Dad. He said stuff."

Joslyn's cheeks reddened.

Oblivious, Dan said, "What are you talking about? Dad didn't joke around."

Before this erupted into a family squabble, I asked, "What about Anton? He seemed broken up about your father's death, but"—I shrugged— "appearances can be deceiving."

"You met Anton?" Dan asked. "When?"

"He came to visit Sunday, while the police were still here. The news seemed to come as a real shock to him," I said.

Harland slid a glance toward his father's room. "Did he have a bottle of whiskey with him? Did he leave it here?"

"He did have a bottle with him." I considered telling them that Percy had appropriated the gift for himself, but there was something about these folks that grated on my nerves. "I'm sure he took it back with him. The police weren't letting anyone into this room."

"Anton always brought the good stuff," Dan said.

Harland ran his tongue over his lower lip.

"Maybe we should look around in there. See if there's any left."

"If you find any open liquor in there, you should give it to the police. Have it tested."

"What? Now you think Anton killed him?" Harland nudged his wife. "This girl will do anything to get the heat off of Frances, won't she?"

"Yeah," Joslyn said. "Sure seems like it."

"I'm not saying that Anton did it intentionally. I'm saying that there could have been something in the liquor that interacted with your dad's medications. Have the police even considered that?"

"Nobody killed Dad," Dan said. "I wish people would stop saying that. He always said he wanted to die peacefully. He did. If it weren't for that Santiago, we'd be able to bury him peacefully, too."

"The same way you know your dad died peacefully, is the same way I know Frances could never have hurt him," I said. "Whatever we can do to help the police understand that will only help us all."

The three of them looked at one another. "I guess." Dan shifted his weight and pointed toward Gus's room. "Want to get started?" he asked Harland.

The door swung open again and Tara came in. "Oh, hello. I didn't realize you'd still be here," she said to me before turning to Dan and Harland.

"I stopped by to let you know that if you need boxes to carry your father's things out, I'd be happy to call downstairs and see if maintenance has extras. They usually do."

"That would be really nice. Thank you," Dan said.

She turned to leave, but then stopped as though remembering something. "Have you all had a chance to talk with the rest of the staff?" she asked. "I know they wanted to express sympathy."

"We saw Cathy on the way in," Harland said.

"Me, too." Dan raised a finger. "And Santiago came by earlier." He neglected to add that he'd practically chased the nurse out.

"Debbie's on lunch, but I'll let her know you're here," Tara said. "I know she'll want to see you all before you leave."

Dan gave a so-so motion with his hand. "Cleaning this room out may take a little longer than I originally thought. We may need the entire week Indwell is giving us."

"Dad had that much stuff here?" Harland asked. "Like what?"

Dan gave a half laugh. "Haven't had time to get started."

Tara seemed eager to get out and call down for those boxes. "Take however long you need. Indwell understands that this is a trying time for all of you."

"I'll join you," I said as she turned to leave. I'd

205

probably gotten as much information as I could from the Westburg family. "Thanks for talking with me," I said. "If anything occurs to you that could help the police with their investigation, please don't hesitate to let them know. And feel free to contact me, as well." I handed all three of them my business cards.

"Marshfield Manor?" Harland said as he studied the card. "That's where you work?"

"Have you ever met the owner?" Joslyn asked. "He's a billionaire, isn't he? Bennett Marshfield?"

"She's his niece," Dan said.

"Oh," Joslyn said in a completely new tone. "Oh. Pleased to meet you."

Tara looked ready to burst into laughter. "Ready to go?" she asked.

I nodded.

When the automatic door swung shut behind us, Tara turned to me with a conspiratorial grin. "Was that a sweet moment or what?" she said. "Did you see the looks on their faces? They were shocked to find out who you are."

"It's Bennett's name that impressed them. Not mine."

"Close enough. I swear, the week you and Mr. Marshfield found out you were related, Frances couldn't wait to share the news with everybody here. You'd have thought *she* was the one it was happening to. Your head must be spinning with all the changes in your life right now."

"Frances told everyone?" I pointed behind us. "Dan recognized my name right away, but Harland and Joslyn had no clue."

She rolled her eyes. "That's because Dan visits here at least three, four times a week. He may not have liked hanging out with his father, but he showed up. That's more than I can say for the two of them. I'd be surprised if they even know any of the staff members' names."

"It was nice of you to give Gus's family as much time as they needed to clear things out. I'm kind of glad, in a selfish way, to know that they'll be here a few more days. Gives me a chance to come up with more questions for them, if I need to."

"They can take all the time they want." She gave a little smile as she shrugged. "The cost for somebody to live in that apartment is more than most people make in a year. It's not like there's a waiting list."

Chapter 20

FRANCES TALKED THE ENTIRE RIDE BACK to Emberstowne. I heard about the sour smell of the interrogation room and the sassy attitude of the detectives who attempted to question her. She delivered an earful about how poorly Rosette's small-town police department was run and—though she didn't say it—I got the distinct impression that Lily Holland's presence had been the only thing that had kept Frances from being arrested and tossed into a cell by the afternoon.

Apparently, the detectives questioning Frances had tried to coax a confession by suggesting that Frances had only *accidentally* killed Gus. That, by injecting the man with insulin, she'd merely meant to make him sick.

"What kind of mealy-brained fool do they think I am?" she asked. "Like I'd admit to anything I didn't do. *Pheh.*"

"Was Lily able to get any more information? Do you know when autopsy results will be in?"

"Preliminary results are in now," Frances said. "They're waiting for word from the lab on whether Gus had unnecessary insulin floating around in there."

"When will those results come in?"

"Who knows? They didn't see fit to tell me."

It bothered me that her anger seemed different. Instead of crossing her arms, fuming, and fairly sparking the air with rage-filled fireworks, she kept her hands in her lap and fiddled with the clasp of her vinyl purse.

"What else did the detectives have to say?"

She lifted a chubby finger. "One: The only fingerprints on the empty insulin containers in Percy's room are mine." She lifted a second finger. "Two: They have a witness who swears Gus and I got into such a heated argument he was afraid we'd get violent."

"A witness? Do you mean Santiago?" I asked.

"Who else?" She gave an indignant sniff. "You ask me, he's getting his kicks out of embellishing. Makes him seem like Mr. Important. He's one of those people who lives for attention."

She'd lowered her fingers and dropped her hand back into her lap.

"Anything else?"

"According to Lily, they can't arrest me for anything. Not enough evidence. Yet. I hope to heaven Gus had a heart attack and died on his own."

"Gus's son Dan believes that's what happened."

"Too bad Dan isn't a Rosette detective. Couple of idiots. They really believe they have a homicide here." She snorted. "I can tell them a thing or two about homicides."

That was at least the second time she'd used the word *idiot* to describe them. "Tell me about them," I asked.

"Nothing like Rodriguez and Flynn, believe me. Compared to these people, our Emberstowne detectives are rocket scientists."

She took her time describing the pair of Rosette detectives, providing their names. Both female, both in their early thirties and, according to Frances, "Jumpy and yappy as excited Chihuahuas. With sharp teeth they couldn't wait to sink into my skin. Ambitious little things, eager to make a name for themselves." She shook her head. "Well, they can find themselves another chew toy."

"Did they play good cop/bad cop?"

"Pheh," she said with a humorless laugh. "Mostly they made us wait. If Lily hadn't been there, they probably would have started in sooner. We got pulled in three separate times for their prattle. In between we sat and waited. They thought they could play mind games. Like that could wear me down. Like they thought they could break me."

Staring out the window, she massaged one hand with the other.

"I'm sorry you had to go through that."

She nodded but said nothing.

I offered to drive her home rather than back to Marshfield, promising to pick her up for work the next morning. Even though the trip between the two locations wasn't a long one, she seemed far too distracted to drive herself. To my astonishment, she didn't argue.

When I pulled up in front of her tidy cottage, she gathered her purse and opened the passenger door. She'd gotten one foot out when she turned back. "I forgot to ask what you found out at Indwell today."

"We'll talk tomorrow," I said.

The spark of hopefulness in her eyes dimmed. "That means you didn't learn much."

I was sorry to disappoint her. "Tomorrow, you and I will brainstorm. Maybe I learned more than I realize."

"Maybe."

"Text me in the morning when you're ready to be picked up," I said.

"Okay." She prepared to boost herself from the car, then turned back to me again. "Don't be late."

That, at least, I could promise. "I won't."

When I arrived home, my roommates were settled in the parlor: Bruce on the sofa, Scott in one of the chairs. I got the impression that both had been staring into space before I walked in.

"What's wrong?" I asked.

"Oh, nothing," Scott said in a tone that belied his words. "Unless you count the bank pulling the rug out from under us. Then, everything is wrong."

I stripped off my jacket, dropped my purse on the floor, and sank into the other wing chair. "Where's Bootsie?" I asked.

"Cowering, most likely." Bruce rubbed his forehead. "My fault. We got in about twenty minutes ago. The minute the back door closed and I knew the neighbors couldn't hear, I let out a yell of frustration. I just had to let off some steam. Scared her, I think."

"She ran up the stairs," Scott said with a helpful point. "Haven't seen her since."

"I'm sorry," Bruce said again. "I wasn't yelling at her. But she doesn't know that."

"She'll be fine, I'm sure," I said, hoping to hear her pad down the stairs any minute. "It's you two I'm worried about. Last I heard, the bank was expediting paperwork. What's going on?"

"They've expedited things, all right," Bruce said. "Expedited us out of the running."

Before I could ask him what that meant, Scott chimed in. "As you know, the property was taken over by the bank a few years ago. That means they own it. Suddenly, even though they'd given us a verbal green light on our proposal, they're telling us they don't want to be landlords, but if we're interested they'll be happy to sell."

"Oh," I said as the weight of their words sunk in. "How can they do that? Isn't it smarter for them to lease out an abandoned building and collect rent than let it sit there doing nothing at all?"

"That's where the twist comes in," Bruce said. "There's renewed interest in the place."

Scott held up both hands. "Surprise, surprise, the bank's corporate office got wind of our intent and they decided— What were their exact words, Bruce?"

Bruce made air quotes. " 'The Granite Building would be an ideal location for a new branch.' Even better, there's so much space available they could consolidate two locations into one. Oh, happy day! A big bank on Main Street."

"The chamber of commerce would never allow that," I said. "Would they?"

Scott shrugged. "I agree that the chamber has been very careful to maintain Main Street's quaintness and they've fought off incursion attempts from fast-food chains and drugstore franchises before. I suppose that's the only hope we have to hold on to at this point."

Bruce held up a finger. "But."

"But what?"

"The bank president and two of his golf buddies are on the chamber of commerce," Scott said. "You think that might sway the decision?"

"It shouldn't."

Bruce buried his face in his hands. "Doesn't mean it won't."

Bootsie stole into the room and rubbed up against my right leg, all the while eyeing Bruce. With his head down, he didn't see her watching. Scott, staring up at the ceiling, didn't notice the little cat's arrival, either.

Bootsie looked up at me as though asking permission to leap into my lap. I sat back to give her plenty of room, but she hesitated. A second later, she bounded away, up onto the sofa next to Bruce. Startled, he sat up, then smiled.

She stepped gingerly onto his legs, then pawed herself in a circle before settling onto his lap with a huff of contentment. Bruce ran a hand along the top of her head and down her back. "I guess I'm forgiven."

"She knew you didn't mean it," I said.

We remained silent for a few seconds with familiar house sounds to keep us company.

"What's next? What can we do?" I asked.

"Besides wait?" Scott raised both arms, then rested his hands atop his head. "Nothing much."

"Are there any other properties you can look at?"

"A few, but none on Main Street," Bruce said.

"How far away?"

"One is six blocks south and four blocks east of where we are now," Scott said. "Another one is in the old section. You know—where the clock used to be."

"At one time that was a beautiful building,"

Bruce said, "but how many customers would make the trek? I'm all for bringing a blighted area back to life but we'd be the only business for blocks. Nobody will come to our place when it's that far away from the touristy stuff."

I wrinkled my nose, thinking about the town clock and the part I'd played in its destruction not all that long ago. "Unless the chamber of commerce throws more support into redeveloping that entire stretch—and finding a way to connect it to our current business district—I can't imagine it would be a good idea to locate Amethyst Cellars out there."

Bruce didn't look up from petting Bootsie. "This has been one giant disappointment after another."

"What if you bought the Granite Building outright?"

"Even if we were able to afford that size mortgage—"

"Which we can't," Scott said.

"Even if we could," Bruce continued, "no bank will be willing to lend us the money without a solid business plan. If we bought the building, we'd almost have to open a restaurant right away. We're not in a position to do that yet. We'd need to hire a consultant."

"Which requires even more money," Scott said.

"And even if we could partner with a seasoned restaurateur, where would we find one in the next couple of days? We're short of funds, we lack a solid business plan. Heck, *I* wouldn't lend us money right now."

"Our only option is to wait for our landlord to make repairs on our current building," Scott said. "And from the looks of things, he's in no hurry to get it done."

"Which means that you'll probably lose the entire summer busy season," I said. "Doesn't it?"

Scott nodded. "And who knows what the ripple effect will be? Tourists who visit every year will assume we've gone out of business. I'm sure loads of folks will cancel their wine member-ships because they'd fear we won't be able to fulfill orders."

"Which we won't be able to do until we establish a new home base," Bruce said. "Everything is back at the office, and the city will only let us in when we're escorted by safety engineers."

"Can you work from here?" I asked. "The basement is fairly empty and the temperature down there is probably good for wine."

"It's possible," Bruce said with a defeated sigh. "I suppose."

"Thanks for the suggestion, Grace," Scott said. "We may take you up on that. But right now, this new twist has zapped us of every ounce of energy we possessed. We're hitting brick wall after brick wall."

I understood. There were times in my life when I was so distraught that even good suggestions felt like monster projects. My roommates had seen me through more than one major disappointment and had given me the space I needed. I could do no less for them.

"Tomorrow." Poised to promise my best efforts, I remembered the similar words I'd offered to Frances when I'd dropped her off at home less than an hour earlier. "We'll take another look at our options tomorrow, okay?"

They both nodded and tried to smile. "Sure," Scott said.

Chapter 21

I SET OUT TO PICK UP FRANCES THE following morning about ten minutes after she texted. She lived in an older section of Emberstowne, a cramped yet tidy area featuring single-family homes on small lots, giant trees, and very little parking. I idled in the middle of her narrow street and texted that I was out front.

She didn't reply.

Less than a minute later, I was forced to move when a giant SUV couldn't get around me.

I found a small, empty spot on the far end of the next block, where I resurrected my long-neglected parallel-parking talents. Once settled, I checked my phone again only to find an error message. My text hadn't been sent.

I tried again. The message failed again.

"Great." I said aloud. "She's going to think I'm late."

I got out of the car and hurried back along the uneven sidewalk, gearing myself up for a tongue-lashing. Frances's house was a white frame home with a pitched roof, and the side entrance was situated under a striped metal awning. I trotted up the concrete steps and rang her doorbell.

"Sorry," I said the moment her door squeaked open. "I tried texting you, but it wouldn't go through."

She frowned out the screen door, which separated us. "Likely story. You just wanted to see what the inside of my house looks like."

Before I could offer even a syllable of protest, she shoved the screen door open and said, "As long as you're here you may as well come in while I get my stuff together."

My first thought upon entering was that she didn't limit her love of the color purple to her wardrobe. From the sheers covering her front windows to the area rug that took up most of her creaky wood floor to knickknacks that crammed every horizontal surface—reminding me more than a little of Percy's room—her house was a sea of plum, lilac, violet, and mauve. It smelled of sun-warmed dust mingled with old perfume. Lavender, maybe. Which, upon reflection, shouldn't have come as a surprise.

She trundled through her pint-sized living room to disappear into what had to be her bedroom, talking all the while. "I knew you wouldn't be able to resist, nosy as you are." Raising her voice, she added, "Go ahead, take a look around. Does this look like a home of a murderer?"

"As far as I'm concerned, your innocence has never been in doubt."

Even though she was out of sight, I could hear

her mumbling. "Tell that to those wet-behind-the-ears police officers."

I kept quiet and chose to meander to the very front of the house to peer out the window. "Tough to park around here," I called to her.

"Not too many early risers. Another half hour and you'd have your choice of spots, when everybody else goes to work." She emerged from her bedroom wearing a periwinkle jacket with her vinyl purse tucked under one arm. "You ready?"

Outside, she stopped and looked at the sky before locking the door. "It's supposed to rain today, isn't it?"

I peered up at the cloudless blue. "I have no idea."

She wrinkled her nose. "Smells like rain." She reopened her door, reached in, and pulled out an umbrella. "Better safe than sorry," she said. "Now I'm ready."

In my office a little while later, Frances and I sat opposite each other. "With the Mister's financial guy coming to talk to you both today, there isn't much you'll be able to get done," she said. "For me, that is."

"I've delegated most of my day-to-day work to the staff in accounting and personnel. They'll keep Marshfield running until I can get back to my responsibilities full-time. Bennett and I agree that I'm to devote all my efforts to getting your name cleared."

"Except for this meeting with Randall Cummings."

"I'm surprised he was able to reschedule on such short notice." I frowned. "To be honest, I'm a little disappointed. I'd much rather focus on you."

"That's something, I guess."

"The meeting shouldn't take long," I said. "And if Bennett hadn't insisted on it, I'd skip. But until Randall Cummings gets here, let's talk about your situation. We need to figure out what our next steps are. Does Lily have any suggestions?"

"She wants me to steer clear of the investigation."

"She's required to say that," I said. "But Rodriguez and Flynn assured me that—to the extent they're able—they're here for us." As the statement poured out of me, I remembered my phone call from Joe Bradley. I told Frances about his offer to help, adding, "I'll call him today."

"What good can he do?" Frances asked. "It's not like he's the one doing the autopsy."

"He's another expert in a field that you and I know nothing about."

"Nothing, you say?" She shifted in her seat. "With all the investigations you and I have been involved in, I'd say we know a lot."

I drew in a deep breath. "Not nearly enough, though." With a glance at the clock above the office fireplace, I pulled up my cell phone. "Let me give him a quick call now. If he has questions I can't answer, you'll be able to chime in."

"Don't know what good that will do," she said but this time with less vehemence.

Because it was early, I decided to try him at the morgue first. He picked up after two rings.

"Emberstowne Morgue, Joe Bradley." His stern tone took me aback.

I hesitated. "Good morning, Dr. Bradley. This is Grace Wheaton from Marshfield Manor. Am I interrupting you?"

"Grace, good morning," he said in a much warmer manner. "No, your call couldn't have come at a better time. My office is closed on Wednesdays and, fortunately, we've had no morgue deliveries today. I was using the quiet time to catch up on old paperwork. You're giving me a good reason to push it off again." As if suddenly understanding my hesitancy, he added, "Sorry for the impersonal greeting. The phone here at the morgue is so old it doesn't even have a display for caller ID. I never know who it could be, so I play it safe with a businesslike demeanor."

"That makes sense," I said. "I have Frances with me in my office, and I told her that you'd be willing to help answer questions we may have about the autopsy process."

"Definitely. Shoot."

Keeping an eye on Frances, who was fighting to

appear disinterested, I said, "We have no idea how long it will take to get results back from the autopsy. That is, the autopsy itself is complete, but we're waiting for an update on whether the victim—Gus—died of an insulin overdose. Any idea how long that could take?"

"He wasn't a victim," Frances grumbled. "He died of natural causes."

I ignored her to listen to what Joe had to say. "Results can take as little as a few days or as long as a few weeks, depending on how backed up the lab is or if a case is hot enough for the police to order a rush."

That wasn't much help.

"Couple of things to keep in mind, though," he said. "Your victim, Gus, wasn't diabetic, correct?"

"That's right."

"And yet several vials of insulin have gone missing at Indwell?"

"How did you know that?"

"Rodriguez called me. He doesn't have all the details, but Rosette's cops are providing updates," he said. "In any case, the pathologist will need to test for C-peptides."

"C-peptides," I repeated as I wrote it down.

"Don't worry about remembering the jargon, just know that when an insulin overdose is suspected, that's one of the tests they run to find out if insulin in the body is exogenous—meaning it came from outside the body—or endogenous, meaning that it was naturally produced."

"Rosette's coroner will do this as a matter of course?" I asked.

Frances had dropped any pretense of indifference and sat forward, straining to hear what Joe had to say. I held the phone a little away from my ear to help.

"Insulin isn't always the easiest thing to find, but because it's suspected, I'm sure the coroner took samples from Gus's body immediately. The presence of an overabundance of insulin doesn't definitively prove foul play, either."

"It doesn't?" I asked.

"Gus could have had a pancreatic tumor. If that's the case, then his body may have produced an excess of insulin. The C-peptide test will answer that."

"Okay," I said slowly. "But I assume the coroner won't be willing to share that information."

"Not until Frances is officially cleared, or formally charged, no," he said. "But if that happens, her attorney should be able to get a copy of the full report. I'd be happy to take a look at it for you."

I pulled back, sorry Frances had heard his casual mention of her being arrested. She crossed her thick arms, frowned, and turned to face the window.

"I hope it doesn't come to that," I said.

I couldn't fault Joe Bradley for dispensing information with brisk, emotionless efficiency, but it felt odd to have Frances's situation dissected with such antiseptic detachment.

"I haven't met Frances," he said. "I don't know her the way you do. I do, however, know that it's got to be tough to sit on the sidelines and wait for the police in Rosette to either make their move or call a truce. It can't be easy."

"It's not."

"But Rodriguez and Flynn are here to help. As am I. Feel free to reach out anytime you need."

I felt myself smile. Frances turned to face me just then. She made a noise of displeasure.

"I appreciate that," I said. "We both do."

When I hung up, we heard her office door open. Before I could say a word, she jumped to her feet, looking panicked.

I pointed to the clock that was just chiming nine. "It's Bennett and Randall Cummings," I said. "Right on time."

When sounds of Bennett conversing with another male drifted in, her shoulders relaxed.

I got to my feet to welcome the two men. "Who did you think it was?" I asked.

"I don't know," she said, clearly flummoxed. "I don't know anything anymore. I'll go get coffee."

With her head down, she nearly ran into Bennett as he and Randall came through the doorway, which separated the two offices.

"Whoa, Frances." Bennett caught my assistant by her shoulders as he sidestepped out of her way.

"Getting coffee," she said pushing past him and Randall, before rushing out of the room.

I made my way over to them. "Is everything okay?" Bennett asked after polite greetings.

"She's on edge," I said. "And I don't blame her a bit. Come on in."

I reclaimed the seat behind my desk as Bennett and Randall settled in across from me.

A large man with a tidy, receding hairline, Randall wore his customary dark business suit, pale dress shirt, and conservative tie. I imagined he kept a closetful of white, cream, and pale blue shirts next to a rack of navy blue and ruby red–striped ties to pair with them. Made dressing every morning a piece of cake, no doubt. I tried to picture him in less formal attire but couldn't do it. Agewise, he split the difference between Bennett and me.

"How is everything this morning, Grace?" he asked. "I understand you're ready to move forward on our transition plan. Bennett has been eager to get this process started. He's looking forward to you taking over."

I held up my hands. "I know I'm repeating myself, but you need to understand that I'm not pushing for control of Bennett's finances."

"*Our* finances," Bennett corrected.

"I know." Randall beamed. "Bennett and I have

worked together for many years and I'd like to believe he and I understand each other. Let's take it one step at a time. And if, at any point, you have a question, stop me. I'm happy to take as much time as we need."

I sat back, not quite sure what to expect.

"This is a big step for you," Randall continued. "My job is to make the transition as smooth and painless as it can be. You and I have worked together a couple of other times, Grace. I think that even though we have a lot of paperwork ahead of us, it won't be too arduous a process."

There was something about this man's high energy that always improved my mood. "I'm sure it won't be."

"Good." He slapped his hands together, rubbed them, then said, "You ready to begin?"

"Almost," I said.

That surprised them. "Bennett," I began, "I have an idea I've been meaning to discuss with you." Shooting an apologetic smile at the adviser, I explained, "With all that's been going on here recently, Bennett and I haven't had a moment alone."

Randall slapped his hands on his knees. "I'll give you privacy."

"No, no," I said before he could get up. "This involves finances. And I'd like your opinion on this, too." Turning to Bennett again, I said, "I haven't brought this up with Scott or Bruce yet, but I was considering helping them out. Financially, I mean. Would you be okay with that?"

"Would I be okay with that?" He seemed genuinely surprised by the question. "Gracie, this is exactly what I'm talking about. I've told you before that I want you to feel comfortable with your newfound affluence. And the best way to achieve that is to start making investment decisions on your own. We learn not only from our successes, but from our mistakes as well. Isn't that right, Randall?"

Scratching the side of his face, the jolly man frowned. "I need to understand what sort of financial help you're considering. What will the money be used for?"

I explained Bruce and Scott's predicament and how their hopes of renting the Granite Building had been dashed. "The bank owns the property and, right now, it seems as though they intend to use it to open a new branch. If Bruce and Scott were able to buy the building outright, however, they'd be able to expand on their own timeline."

"Do your roommates have experience running a restaurant?" Randall asked. "You realize that that's one of the most difficult businesses to launch successfully."

"They've never launched a restaurant before but both have managed high-end establishments in the past. That kind of expansion is a goal they'd hoped to work toward eventually. The building issues they're facing now happen to be speeding up their timeline."

Randall pushed out his bottom lip. "How much of an investment are we talking about?"

"That's the part I don't know. I can find out."

"Hang on." Randall drew out his phone and began tapping into it. "The Granite Building, right?"

"Right."

Within moments he'd pulled up whatever information he needed. "Here we go," he said. "Round numbers, this is probably what the bank's asking price would be." Turning the device to face me, and then Bennett, he showed us the number.

"That's a lot of money," I said.

"For a building in that location, it's fair." Bennett pulled in a deep breath. "They'd also need working capital to make improvements."

"Do you think lending money to friends is a mistake?" I asked.

"Let me make one point clear." Randall held up a finger. "Unless you're buying the building outright yourself and offering them a mortgage, you can't lend them the money to buy the building."

"I can't?"

"Borrowed funds cannot be used as a down payment to secure a mortgage." He shook his head. "You can gift them the money, but there are all sorts of tax consequences to that and I don't recommend it. You can own the building yourself and be their landlord. Or you can form a partnership or corporation with them and—assuming the business turns a profit eventually—reap the benefits of a sound investment."

"We're getting ahead of ourselves here," Bennett said. He offered me an indulgent smile. "There are no absolute right answers. What works for one person could result in miserable failure for another. Right now, what I want most is to watch you spread your wings and fly on your own. Make your best decision. Take some risk. Don't worry about what Randall or I think." He wagged a finger at me. "Mind you, if you want to tear down one wing of the mansion to rebuild it as a waterpark, I'd prefer to discuss the matter before the wrecking crews show up."

"Never." I laughed. "I wouldn't harm a single brick."

Bennett sobered. "Unless you must," he said. "Change is a part of life. It's how we survive and how we grow. You've taught me that. Innovation, development, and improvement are impossible if we refuse to evolve."

Over the past few years, I had suggested a number of modernizations—elevating our gift shop souvenirs, expanding choices in the Birdcage Room, and upgrading security—most of which had turned out to be tremendous enhancements. I thought about my recent idea to reclaim some of the office space and restore rooms to their former glory. Worth discussing, but not right now. "I'll keep that in mind."

"Talk with your roommates," Randall said. "If you decide to go forward with this venture, I'll help you come up with a business plan."

"Thanks," I said. "I appreciate that."

"We're going to be here for a while, aren't we?" I asked.

Randall patted the portfolio. "This is only the beginning," he said with a mischievous grin. "I've got a whole wall of files like this one back at the office."

I felt myself blanch.

"But don't worry," he hurried to assure me. "This one is the most important, the most intricate. Once these corporate documents are modified, the rest will be easy. A lot of signatures, sure, but not so many decisions. This one's the master account. The one that rules them all."

"With that *Lord of the Rings* reference, I'm really getting worried."

"Don't be. Let's start with the basics." Grin firmly in place, he opened the portfolio's blue cardboard cover and turned it to face me. "Will you confirm your information?"

"Sure." Even though I'd provided my vital statistics to Randall weeks earlier, I read over the listing of my full name, address, birth date, and social security number to confirm accuracy. While I went over the data, Frances came in with a tray laden with a plate of pastries, coffee, and three cups and saucers that trembled softly against one another as she laid the spread on the far edge of my desk. My first thought was: *Only three cups?* Frances always included a setting for herself when she brought in treats. But this time was different; we weren't discussing Marshfield Estates—the property. We were discussing Marshfield family matters. She couldn't be part of the conversation.

Her hands shook as she placed the first cup in front of me. "You know what, Frances?" I asked. "I can do this."

At first, she flashed a hot glare. Any other day, she may have quipped that my offer to help was a lame attempt to get rid of her. Today, however, her indignant expression fell away almost immediately. "I'll get back to my office," she said quietly. "In case Lily calls with an update."

"Let me know if you hear any news," I said.

Without a word, she nodded and left the room. My heart broke for her when she quietly shut the door between our offices.

Even Bennett winced.

"She never does that," I said. To Randall, I explained, "Frances is notorious for eavesdropping."

Bennett stared after her. "Why can't we be done with this nonsense already? The poor woman." When he turned to me again, he shook his head. "Frances may not be the warmest member of the staff, but even at her prickliest, she doesn't deserve this."

I wished I could skip this meeting with Randall and get back to Indwell. Whatever the answers were, they were there. I didn't know how I'd uncover the truth behind Gus's death, but I knew that sitting here signing papers wasn't going to do it.

"All the information is correct," I said to Randall.

"I'm relieved to hear it." As he turned to the portfolio's next page, he grinned again. "Because I've used that data to prefill the forms we need you to sign today."

Randall went through each document, one by one, explaining what it meant and why it was necessary. "I'll provide you with copies of each," he said. "Digital copies, if you prefer."

"I do," I said.

We'd gotten through about five sections of the massive portfolio when scuffling sounds from Frances's office stopped me mid-signature.

"What's going on in there?" I got to my feet.

Both men followed me to the door. "Is your assistant all right?" Randall asked.

"I don't know—"

Though muffled slightly by the heavy wooden door between our offices, Frances's exclamation, "You wouldn't dare!" shot me into action.

I bolted into her office, not knowing what to expect.

Her neck red, her face flushed, Frances stood, shifting her attention between two women, who were advancing on her position, coming at her from either side of the desk. Behind them, near the door, Flynn leaned back, hand cupping his chin. Next to him, Rodriguez mopped his face with a handkerchief.

"Miz Wheaton." The older detective's relief was palpable. "We could use your help."

Chapter 22

"WHAT'S GOING ON IN HERE?" I ASKED.

Frances, Flynn, and Rodriguez began talking at once. I tuned them out. In the split second I had to assess the two women flanking Frances's desk—noting their brisk impatience and the hip-level bulge beneath each of their blazers—I knew they must be Rosette's detectives.

And one heartsick beat later, it dawned on me why they were here.

"Stop," I said. And to my surprise, all chatter ceased.

As I crossed the room, Bennett spoke in low tones, directing Randall out. "Please wait for me in the break room down the hall," he said, gesturing vaguely.

Randall didn't argue.

I skirted past the shorter of the two detectives to take a position next to Frances. Heat and fear rolled off of her. "Are you okay?" I asked.

She didn't make eye contact. "For now."

Behind everyone, Bennett raised a hand, catching my attention. He mimed making a phone call. A second later, he was gone.

"My name is Grace Wheaton," I said to the two

women. "I'm in charge of Marshfield Manor. May I see some identification from both of you?"

They exchanged an amused glance. "Sure," said the one nearest Frances. Big-boned with wide features and skin the same color as her pale hair, she flipped her badge case open. "My name's Madigan," she said as I read along. "And Nieman over there is my partner. Detectives from Rosette. We have a warrant for Frances Sliwa's arrest."

Though I knew my efforts were largely futile, I held out my hand. "May I see the warrant?"

Nieman was shorter than Madigan with a thick torso and dark, wiry hair. The abundance of charcoal liner she'd applied made her eyes look like shiny outlined pebbles.

While Madigan reached for papers from her back pocket, I lasered my attention on Rodriguez and Flynn. "You couldn't have given us the courtesy of a heads-up?"

"Not our call," Flynn snapped, but he shot a look of contempt at Madigan as he did so.

Rodriguez ran the handkerchief across his forehead again, then swiped the back of his neck. "Grace, I'm sorry. It's not our case."

I took the papers from Madigan without thanking her. Frances edged close. Her shoulder grazed my arm as I read.

"Did you examine this warrant?" I asked Rodriguez.

He nodded, looking miserable. "Yeah. Every-thing's in order."

"There was nothing we could do," Flynn said. "These two didn't even want us along, but our chief insisted."

I swallowed fear as I studied the document, though I had no idea what I was looking for. I squinted at the name on the bottom. "Who signed this warrant?"

Madigan answered, "Judge Madigan."

"Judge *Madigan?*" I repeated. "That's your name."

"Irrelevant."

Madigan reached, but I pulled away. "Any relation to you?"

"What difference does it make?"

When I continued to refuse to return the warrant, Madigan said, "My father."

"You don't think there's a little conflict of interest here?" I asked.

"Facts are facts." Madigan snatched the docu-ment back from me. "The judge wouldn't have issued the warrant without probable cause. You want to challenge that, be my guest. But right now this warrant is valid and I have a duty to bring Frances Sliwa in."

I could feel Frances tremble. "I don't want to go," she said hoarsely. "Can I refuse?"

The thought of Frances being put through jail intake procedures made my stomach quake. "This isn't right," I said.

Madigan shook her head. "Preliminary tox results are in. Our victim could have died of an insulin overdose."

"*Could* have?" I asked, jumping on the qualifier. "That's not exactly definitive. You're still waiting for final results, then?"

"Preliminary findings are not inconsistent with an insulin overdose."

"And you're arresting Frances on that?"

"We have the warrant." Madigan's patience with me was gone. "Please step away from the suspect."

Frances gripped my forearm with both hands.

When Madigan took a step closer, I noticed that Bennett had returned to the room. I could tell he was trying to signal me, but my focus was on the detective three feet away.

"Listen, hang on," I said. "The autopsy. What about that?"

"Ms. Wheaton, please step out of the way. You're making this more difficult than it needs to be."

"What about defensive wounds?" I asked. "If Frances really did kill Gus, how come he didn't fight back?" I pointed to my assistant, who was clutching me close, like a terrified toddler. "Frances has no bruises, no scratches, nothing. Do you really think she could have injected Gus without him noticing? Could someone inject *you* without your knowledge?"

"He could have been asleep," Nieman said.

"You think he wouldn't wake up when a

needle's jammed into his thigh?" With my free hand I pantomimed, repeatedly slamming my fist against my leg. "And wait—if the killer used four vials, that means four punctures, doesn't it?"

Madigan had dead eyes. "Ma'am, we could take you in for obstruction of justice. Please step aside."

Frances tightened her grip. These two cops would have to arrest me before I'd let them take her into custody.

"Where were they?" I asked.

Madigan and Nieman exchanged a glance. Nieman took a step forward.

"Stop, right there, both of you," I said in a voice that came from somewhere primal and deep.

They stopped.

"Answer me. Where were the puncture wounds on Gus's body?" I still held out hope that the man had injected himself. "How many were there?"

Nieman sent her partner a puzzled look.

I pounced on what I hoped was a crack of doubt in the shorter detective's certainty. "Were the puncture marks between Gus's toes?" I asked. "Do you think maybe he did it himself and tried to hide the evidence?"

"Ms. Sliwa's attorney will be given a copy of the autopsy report," Madigan said. "We have no reason, nor inclination, to discuss the matter with you. Now, for the last time, please step aside."

She started for me as the office door opened.

"Hold on one minute." Lily Holland stormed

into the room, arms high and outstretched. "Ms. Sliwa is my client. She's not going anywhere until I say she is."

Madigan huffed with impatience. Nieman seemed relieved.

"Thank goodness I was on my way here." Out of breath, Lily strode past them, coming to stand behind the desk with Frances and me. I would have stepped away and returned to Bennett's side, but Frances held fast.

Lily faced Madigan and held out a hand. "Let's see the warrant."

"How many times do we have to go through this?" Madigan asked as she handed over the document again.

Even though I knew everyone in the room could probably hear me, I whispered to alert Lily to the fact that Madigan and the judge were related to one another.

Lily scanned the text quickly. "You call this probable cause?" she asked without looking up. She made several wordless expressions of distaste before handing the warrant back to Madigan. "How did you ever get a judge to sign off with so little substance?"

"We're here to arrest Ms. Sliwa," Madigan said. "Not to debate the process."

Lily scoffed. "We'll see." To Frances, she said, "It looks as though you and I will be taking a quick trip to Rosette today."

Frances's fingers dug deeper into my arm. "I didn't do it."

Lily turned a finger toward herself, making direct eye contact with Frances. "Keep your attention on me. Let me handle everything. You were advised of your rights, I assume?"

Frances nodded.

"Don't say a word." She waited for Frances to acknowledge her. "Good. Not a single word. Let me do my job." She placed an arm around my assistant's shoulders. "It's time to go now. But don't despair. This shouldn't take long."

Lily's gaze settled on Frances's hands, still clamped around my arm.

"I'll come with you," I said.

Before Lily could reply, Frances shook her head. Snapping out of her terror—or at least faking that she had—she let go of my arm. "No," she said. "You won't."

Lily waved a finger. "Not a word, remember?"

Frances gave an indignant head waggle before pointing to the two Rosette cops.

Lily understood. "Detectives, could you please step outside the office for a moment? I need to consult with my client."

Madigan flexed her jaw. The two women trotted out. Flynn and Rodriguez remained inside, by the door with Bennett.

As soon as Rosette's cops were gone, I said, "Frances, I can't let you go there alone."

Lily cleared her throat. "She won't be alone."

"You know what I mean." Facing Frances again, I went on, "There's no way I'm staying here."

"No." Frances shook her head. "Lily has the legal part covered." She jammed a finger into my shoulder. "I need you to clear this whole mess up. You have to go back out there and find out what really happened at Indwell."

Bennett came around the desk to join our small group. He took Frances's hands in his. "You're right. Grace will be able to get more done at Indwell." With an offhand glance over his shoulder, he asked, "And the rest of us here will do our best to clear your name, too. Right, Detectives?"

Rodriguez answered right away. "We'll help wherever we can."

Flynn rolled his eyes. "Yeah."

"Lily will take good care of you. And she'll keep us updated." Bennett squeezed Frances's hands. "You will never be alone. We're behind you completely."

"And the sooner we end this 'Kumbaya' moment, the quicker we can get started, right?" Flynn asked.

Frances turned to me. "Tooney's helping, right?"

"We're all behind you, Frances," I said. "I promise we'll get this cleared up soon."

Chapter 23

BEFORE THEY LEFT, I PULLED LILY ASIDE and put in a quick request. She nodded, then joined Rodriguez and Flynn as they escorted Frances away. The moment they were gone, I picked up the office phone.

"Are you calling Mr. Tooney?" Bennett asked.

I nodded. "I need to bring him up to date."

Our favorite investigator picked up immediately. We spoke briefly. After securing his promise to double down on his investigative efforts, I pulled out my cell phone and searched my contacts.

Bennett, who had paced Frances's office while Tooney and I talked, stopped to regard me quizzically. "Who are you calling now?"

"Dr. Bradley. Emberstowne's coroner. I spoke with him earlier." I explained that Rodriguez had put us in touch and told him about the coroner's gracious offer to help.

"Is that why you asked Lily to get you a copy of the autopsy?" Bennett asked. "Do you think this Dr. Bradley can find something Rosette's coroner missed?"

"I have no idea, but the sooner he has all the

information, the better our chances." The phone number I'd dialed earlier went straight to voice mail. I remembered him saying that his office was closed today and that no new bodies had shown up at the morgue this morning.

Biting my lip and hoping I wasn't intruding too terribly on his personal time, I dialed his cell. When he still hadn't answered after the third ring, I curbed my disappointment and waited for the tone, resigning to leaving a message.

A second later, he surprised me by picking up. "Hello?" he asked with far more discomposure than I would have expected. "Hello? Grace? Are you there?"

The low-level shushing sound in the background after the delayed pickup made me wonder if he was busy in a lab somewhere and I'd interrupted his work.

"Yes, I'm sorry. Did I call at a bad time?"

"No." He chuckled. "I'm driving a new car this morning and you're my first call on this hands-free setup. The controls are placed differently and I got confused. Took me way too long to figure out the right button to answer." He waited a beat before asking, "What's up?"

In a rush, I told him about Frances's arrest and how she'd asked me to go back to Indwell to dig for more information. "I've asked her lawyer, Lily Holland, to get a copy of Gus's autopsy report to you as soon as possible. She needs your e-mail or a fax number. I wanted to call you to give you a heads-up."

Bennett stepped close to whisper. "Let me do something to help. If Lily sends the report here, I can bring a copy to him."

I nodded.

Joe's jovial tone shifted to one of deep concern. "That's not a problem. Do you have Lily Holland's number handy? I'll get in touch with her immediately."

"Just a second," I said. "I'll get it for you."

As I brought the phone forward to search for the lawyer's number in my contacts, Joe's voice rose. "Hold on before you do that," he called. "Grace?"

Clapping the device back to my ear, I said, "Yes?"

"Let me pull over. I haven't figured out a hands-free way to record information yet. I'm about a mile from the exit. I'll call you right back."

When we hung up, Bennett asked me if I'd like him to accompany me to Indwell.

A sudden realization hit. "Randall Cummings," I said. "I'd forgotten all about him."

Bennett clapped a hand to his forehead. "The poor man is probably still waiting for me in the break room."

"Why don't you work with Randall?" I asked. "I'll manage Indwell on my own."

Bennett's expression told me he was torn. "Are you sure?"

As much as I would have appreciated being able to discuss things on the ride out, I nodded. "I'll be fine. You go ahead."

He gave a terse smile. "I'll collect any documents he needs you to sign. We can go over them later."

"Thanks, Bennett."

We locked eyes for a long moment, reading each other's mind. "Poor Frances," I finally said.

"Indeed."

When my cell phone rang, Bennett left.

Joe didn't waste time with niceties when I answered. As soon as he took down Lily Holland's number he asked, "How soon are you taking off for Rosette?"

"I'm leaving now."

"I can swing by and pick you up. We can get a hard copy of the report from Lily at the police department while we're out there."

"But . . . it's all the way out in Rosette." Taken aback by the offer, I stumbled over my words. "That is, I'd love to get a copy of the autopsy report, but I hadn't planned on stopping by the police department. I'm going directly to Indwell, the assisted-living facility."

"What do you plan to do there?"

"I don't know exactly," I said honestly. "I guess I planned to ask more questions, poke around a bit more. See if anything new comes to light."

"Before I called you back, Detective Rodriguez called me. Fortunately, this time, I was quicker to answer. In any case, he suggested I go out there with you."

"He did?"

"I know I'm new to Emberstowne, but Detective Rodriguez and his partner have told me a lot about you—and Frances, of course—and all your past investigations. I'm happy to offer assistance."

"That's very kind, but—"

"I know it will come as no surprise that Detective Rodriguez is concerned for both of you. This one hits close to home. His hands are tied because Rosette is out of his jurisdiction."

"He said all that?"

"He did. He thinks that having an Emberstowne official on hand—even if it's just a coroner— could prove helpful." When I was slow to respond, he added, "Unless you think I'm over-stepping."

"No, of course not," I said automatically. "But what about an emergency? What if you get called back? Should we drive separately?"

"That's the benefit of being part of a medical group and not on my own. One of my partners is on call today and will handle any emergencies that arise. If, for some reason, she needs to reach me, she has my cell."

"Then, yes, absolutely." I gave him directions to

meet me in the guard's lot just inside the front gates. "How soon can you be here?" I asked.

"I'm not far. I'll be there in five."

THE LAST TIME I'D SEEN JOE BRADLEY— in fact, the only time I'd seen Joe Bradley—had been several months ago in my snow-covered yard. Back then, he'd been wearing a knit cap and a heavy jacket. Although he'd seemed personable enough, his reason for being on my property was to examine a murder victim, and we'd spent no more than thirty seconds getting acquainted. I wondered if I'd even recognize him.

As soon as the shuttle driver dropped me off about a hundred feet inside the main gate, I started across the short garden walkway to the guard's lot, scanning the area for the silver sedan he'd described. Just as I spotted the car, it began to drizzle. Frances had been right to grab an umbrella, I thought. Too bad the police had made her leave it behind.

By the time Joe got out of the car and met me halfway, the drops were coming down heavier and faster.

We shook hands quickly in the middle of the tiny parking lot before hurrying back to his car. He was as tall as I remembered with wavy hair and eyes that crinkled into slits when he smiled. He walked with a slight limp and had a five o'clock shadow even though it was still before noon. One corner of his mouth curled up higher than the other, and his nose was a tiny bit big. But his eyes were bright, his smile warm. It surprised me to realize I felt immediately at ease.

"I'd say it's nice to see you again, Grace," he said, "but both times we've met it's been under less than desirable circumstances."

"Then let's hope we're able to put an end to these meetings," I said. "I truly appreciate your offer to come with me. I'm just not sure what you or I will be able to do for Frances."

"Maybe nothing," he agreed. "But it certainly can't hurt to try."

When we were both safely in the car, the rain began coming down in handfuls. "Wow. Perfect timing," I said.

Frowning, he pulled out of the lot and turned on his lights and wipers. "Let's hope it passes over us soon." He turned to me. "Seat belt?"

I was already buckling myself in. "Got it." I inhaled deeply. "New-car smell. Gotta love it."

"Yeah." He gave a quick sniff. "You're right."

As we cleared Marshfield's front gate, I said, "I noticed you've ditched your cane."

"Good memory." His eyes clouded. "But the cane's in the backseat. I'm in the process of weaning myself."

I was tempted to ask about the injury he'd alluded to during our first meeting but decided against it. If he wanted me to know, he'd tell me.

"Do you need directions to Indwell?"

He shook his head. "I've been out there a number of times to visit patients."

"I didn't realize your practice reached out that far."

Even though he smiled, he looked sad. "It doesn't. I used to live in a small town a little northeast of Rosette. I keep in contact with some of my patients there. You develop a relationship with people, you know? You see the same patients for years, you get to know them and their families." He shrugged. "Can't give that up."

"I'm surprised you moved to Emberstowne, then. Why the change?" I asked.

"Long story. Ask me again sometime."

"Fair enough," I said, and turned my thoughts to Frances. I hoped she was holding up. Although Lily Holland seemed to be a formidable advocate, Frances must be panicked right now.

We rode for a few minutes in silence. Joe was a steady driver, assertive though not aggressive.

"Should we start by picking up the report at the police station?" I asked. "Or would you rather we do that on the way back?"

"I spoke with Frances's attorney," he said. "She'll let me know when it's ready. Today sometime, for sure."

"That's good."

He made a so-so motion with his head.

"What aren't you telling me?" I asked.

"Nothing really," he said. "It's just a sense. She sounded very frustrated."

I pinched the bridge of my nose.

"I'm sorry," Joe said.

"Not your fault," I replied without looking up.

He didn't say anything for a little bit. When he did, it was to ask me to tell him more about Frances. "What's she like?" he asked. "I've never met her in person, but Detective Rodriguez seems to hold her in high regard."

"How to explain Frances?" I asked rhetorically. "She's worked at Marshfield for at least forty years. When I started working there—a little more than three years ago—she made it clear that she didn't like me even a little bit."

"You're kidding me," Joe said with a start. "From the way Detective Rodriguez describes the two of you, I assumed you were best friends."

Despite myself, I laughed. "Frances would cringe to hear you say that."

"I can't imagine anyone but a close friend doing as much as you are to help her."

"No, you misunderstand. She and I are friends; she simply doesn't like to acknowledge the fact."

"Why not?"

"It's impossible to explain until you meet her. No, that's not accurate, either. She's impossible to understand until you really get to know her. I think that when I started at Marshfield she saw me as a threat and worried I'd usurp her position there."

"You have," he said. "In the most profound way possible."

"That's true. But even before the world knew I was a Marshfield by blood, she'd begun to warm up a little. She likes to have her efforts appreciated."

"I take it you do," he said. "Appreciate her, that is."

"It's impossible not to." Now that I was putting my relationship with Frances into actual words, they came easily. "In truth, she's amazing. I've never met anyone so driven and determined. And yet, everything she's ever done—everything I'm aware of, at least—has been for someone else. She's tirelessly loyal to Bennett and has become increasingly protective of me. And now with this situation at Indwell, caring for an ex-husband who left her for another woman—" I frowned out the windshield. "Makes me wonder if she ever does anything for herself."

Joe remained silent as I gave myself a moment to digest what I'd just said.

"All she wants," I finally finished, "is to be valued."

Joe shot me a quick glance. "Isn't that what we all want?"

I smiled. "The thing is, even though I've known her for more than three years, I don't know much about her personally. Until this murder investigation blew up and Bennett and I were called to Indwell, we had no idea where Frances went every weekend."

"She works five days a week at Marshfield then spends every weekend at Indwell?"

"With few exceptions over the past ten years, yes. That's my understanding."

"Wow. That doesn't leave time for much of a personal life. I wonder why all the secrecy?"

Frances's fear of her gossipy friends finding out was not my story to share. I shrugged. "Frances is a very private person."

"Detective Rodriguez is convinced that Frances had nothing to do with the Indwell victim's death."

"Gus," I supplied. "The deceased patient's name was Gus. No, she couldn't have."

"I've worked with the Emberstowne police on a couple of matters and I've gotten to know Detective Rodriguez. I'll be honest, if it weren't for his insistence I contact you, I probably wouldn't be here today. He and his partner are really worked up about your assistant's involvement here."

"Really? Even Flynn?" I asked.

"I'll admit Flynn seems a little less willing to stick his neck out on her behalf, but he's been pushing me, too. Their hands are tied with regard to the investigation and they believe I may have more of an in with Rosette's authorities." Before I could say anything, he hurried to add, "But, I can't insert myself into the official investigation. I won't try to influence anyone involved in this case. I'm here simply as an advocate for the truth."

"Makes sense," I said. "Until you have a chance to form your own judgment, you're dependent on Rodriguez's and Flynn's assurances that Frances is innocent."

"And yours."

"And mine," I agreed. "But you don't really know me either, do you?"

"Not yet," he said as he merged onto the expressway. "But we've got time. Right now, how about you bring me up to date on who's who in this investigation?"

Chapter 24

BY THE TIME I FINISHED DESCRIBING THE nurses, aides, Indwell residents, and family members I'd met in the course of my inquiries, we'd arrived at our destination. Joe's questions and requests for clarification: "Wait, which one of Gus's sons is that again?" helped pass the time quickly.

The moment we stepped through the facility's front doors, Cathy looked up. Her instant alertness and the high-wattage beam on her shiny, pink face told me that she'd already gotten word of Frances's arrest.

Had it only been three days since this nightmare began? Those three days had given the police sufficient time to build a strong enough case against Frances to warrant an arrest. By contrast, how much had I accomplished in my attempt to clear her name? Nothing. Nothing at all.

Cathy fidgeted in her swivel seat. She raised her hand, beckoning us closer. "Grace, over here."

Joe touched my arm, stopping me. "Are you okay?" he asked.

I nodded, even though "okay" was a stretch. 'Whenever Frances and I have helped the police solve a murder, she and I have done it together. And neither of us has ever been so personally involved."

I thought about the most recent skirmish with my sister and decided that didn't count.

"But I'm sure your experiences with Frances have taught you a lot. I'm the newbie here. Show me the ropes."

"Don't patronize me." I knew he was trying to make me feel better, but there was no way I'd allow such an exaggeration to slide. "You're telling me that you—a coroner—have never been involved in a homicide before?"

"I'm not patronizing. I'm telling the truth. Of course I've been involved in homicides as a forensic expert. But as an investigator?" He shook his head slowly. "They really don't let us out of the lab, you know. It's not like on TV."

Despite myself, I smiled. "Not at all like on TV."

"Come on. Show me how it's done."

While we'd been talking near the door, another aide—clipboard in hand—had approached Cathy with a question. With a vehement shake of her blond head, Cathy had shushed her colleague, making no effort to disguise the fact that she was straining to listen in on my conversation with Joe.

Now, as we resumed our trek to the reception desk, Cathy leaned forward, eyes bright, gesturing again for us to hurry. Her colleague, obviously weary of being ignored, walked away.

"I didn't think I'd see you here again, Grace," Cathy said. "Not after they arrested Frances and all, I mean. I wonder what took them so long." Her dismissive *tsk*ing reminded me, briefly, of Frances. But there was too much eager-terrier frenzy in Cathy's delivery to compare it with that of my acerbic assistant. Eyebrows arched, she gave Joe a curious once-over. "Who are you?" She cocked her head toward me. "Boyfriend?"

Joe shot me an amused glance.

"No," I said.

I signed us both in on the visitor's sheet, purposely scribbling so that Cathy wouldn't be able to make out Joe's last name. There were probably several hundred Joe Bradleys in the United States, but only one who served as coroner in Emberstowne. The less this zealous assistant knew about him, the better.

"Do you know if Percy is in his apartment?" I asked. "We'd like to talk with him."

Clearly disappointed by our unwillingness to chat, she frowned. "Don't they say that once you get past the forty-eight-hour mark after a murder, the police never find the killer?"

"Plenty of cases have been solved long after the crime was committed."

"That's not what they say on TV."

Shooting an exasperated glance to Joe, I

stopped myself from explaining further. From the first time I'd met her, I'd suspected Cathy was a sound-bite person. Feed her a tidbit of information she could sink her teeth into and—true or not—she'd gleefully bark it to the world.

"Percy," I repeated. "Do you happen to know where he is?"

Cathy studied my companion again and I got the fleeting impression she intended to barter: Percy's whereabouts for Joe's identity. But a moment later, she relented. "Gus's family is taking forever to clean out his room," she said as though that were an answer. "Percy's sticking around while they're there. He's afraid they might steal some of his stuff."

"He actually said that?" I asked.

Cathy rolled her eyes. "No. But I can tell."

I pointed. "We'll head down there now."

"You might want to suggest to Frances that she plead guilty. I heard that judges are way more lenient if you show remorse." Though delivered with a guileless smile, her comment took me aback. "I'll bet she could even get a minimum sentence if she tells them it was a crime of passion. I'd hate to see her spend the next twenty years in jail. She's so old she'd probably die in there, wouldn't she?"

My hands fisted and twitched as I resisted the terrific temptation to reach across the desk and strangle Cathy into silence. Instead, I said,

"Frances is innocent and the sooner everyone here realizes that, the sooner we'll find out what really happened to Gus."

"Good luck with that."

I bit the insides of my cheeks.

Cathy twisted the visitor sign-in sheet to read it. "Nice to meet you, Mr. . . . um . . . Braddock."

I turned to Joe. "Let's go."

Two nurses I didn't recognize sat behind the small desk down the left corridor of the East Wing. Our presence didn't seem to concern them so I didn't bother trekking over to introduce myself. The door to Percy's apartment was wide open. I peered inside, saw no one, and knocked on the jamb. "Hello?"

When no one answered my hail, I shrugged. "Let's hope they don't mind us barging in."

We'd gotten about four steps into the apartment when Harland emerged from Gus's room. He had his left arm wrapped around a lidded banker's box and his right around the base of a table lamp whose shade smashed against the side of his face.

"Hey," he said when he spotted me. "I heard they arrested your friend."

"Bad news travels fast around here," I said.

"To my mind, it's good news. The best." Harland flicked a dismissive glance at Joe before addressing me again. "The detective told us they got her cold." With a contemptuous glare, he added, "You can't just go around murdering people and expect to get away with it."

A shrill voice came from the depths of the corridor. "Who are you talking to? They better have sent somebody to help us carry all this."

One second later, Joslyn rounded the corner to stand behind her husband. "Oh," she said, clearly disappointed. She had her hair pulled tightly off her face, which was shiny with exertion. "It's only you."

Out of the corner of my eye, I could see Joe taking it all in.

"I realize this is a difficult time for your family," I said to them. "But if someone did kill your dad, Harland, the police are wasting their time interrogating Frances. She didn't do it."

Joslyn rolled her eyes. "Yeah, then who did?"

"I don't know," I answered honestly. "Maybe no one did. And we have to consider the possibility that Gus may have taken his own life."

"Nope. No way," Harland tried to punctuate his words with a hand gesture, but the box and lamp in his arms prevented more than a vague body swing. "Dad took out a big insurance policy some years back. There's a suicide rider. He told us about it. If he'd have killed himself, that big premium payment he made would be lost. He'd never let that happen."

"Then maybe," I began, rattled by this new

260

information, "he really did die of natural causes, after all."

"Or maybe somebody—like your friend Frances—killed him because he was a cranky old man who made her life miserable," Harland said.

"What do you want here, anyway?" Joslyn asked.

"I have a few more questions for Percy."

"Why? You think maybe he did it?" Harland asked.

The last thing I wanted to do was set the hounds on yet another innocent suspect, but the truth was I didn't know Percy. "I'm exploring every option." I decided to take a chance—to appeal to their sense of fair play. "Even though I've known the two of you only a short time, I know you're not looking to convict an innocent person. I know that what you really want is for the guilty party to be brought to justice. Right?"

"Yeah," Harland said halfheartedly. "Sure."

Joslyn made a face. "You're trying to make us feel bad for Frances. But the cops think she killed my father-in-law, and I don't know of anybody else who could've done him in like that."

Joe cleared his throat. "You wouldn't happen to have received your father's autopsy report, have you?"

Still gripping both cumbersome items, Harland shifted his weight. A fine line of sweat had begun to form along his hairline. "Not yet. Why do you ask?"

"I'd love to have a look at the findings." Joe gave a disarming smile. "Call it professional curiosity. I'm a family physician by day but I like to dabble in the world of forensic pathology."

"You're a doctor?" Joslyn perked up. "There's a million of them roaming around this place and I can't get a straight answer from any of them." She turned around and twisted her arm to indicate an area just above the small of her back. Talking over her left shoulder, she said, "I've had a pain, right there, for about three months. Hurts every time I take out the garbage. And now moving all this junk is making it worse. I want more painkillers but my goofy doctor is making me go for physical therapy before he'll prescribe more. That's crazy. What do you think?"

Joe scratched the side of his face. "I'd never second-guess a colleague without doing a full exam on a patient." Cutting off Joslyn before she could offer to submit to one on the spot, he added, "I think what you're really asking is if you ought to get a second opinion. That, I can support."

Turning back to face the group, she nodded with gusto. "All right." She elbowed her husband. "Hear that? I should find a different doctor who'll prescribe me some powerful pills."

That wasn't at all what Joe had suggested, but there was no point in correcting her.

Changing subjects, I said, "It looks like you have a big project ahead of you, so we'll leave you to it."

"Do you know they expect us to clean this place after we clear everything out?" Joslyn asked. "If it isn't sparkling and pristine, they said they'll add another fee to the final charges."

Harland again shifted his unwieldy bundles. "My brother's coming to help out later, but at the rate we're going, it'll be two months before we have Dad's room cleared out."

Eager to be away from the sweaty, unpleasant people, I smiled. "Thanks for the update. If you see Percy, please let him know we're looking for him."

"Yeah, sure," Harland said.

As we made our way to the door, Joslyn called to our backs. "Tell them I want to talk to somebody in charge. We shouldn't have to cart all this junk out of here by ourselves. It's inhumane."

The moment we left the apartment, I blew out a breath.

"Wow." Joe hiked a thumb toward the closed door behind us. "So that's the grieving family? Any chance either of those two killed Gus?"

"Don't I wish," I said. Then, a split second later: "Wait, that didn't come out right."

Joe chuckled. "No worries. I get it."

"I've been trying to get a straight answer about who was here to visit Gus the morning of his death. Harland and Joslyn hadn't visited that day, or even the night before. So, no. They aren't likely suspects at this point."

"Is there any chance they may have made it in without being seen?"

"Anything is possible, I suppose. Hang on— there's Percy." I spotted him talking with Santiago down by the nurses' station. The two men were in such deep discussion they didn't notice our approach until we were right on top of them.

"Percy," I said, "we were looking for you."

"And I've been trying to get in touch with Frances. What's going on?" Percy's voice growled an octave lower than usual. "Santiago said that the police arrested her. They didn't, did they?"

Before I could answer, Santiago chimed in. "I've got a friend who works at the PD. Told me the cops drove all the way out to Emberstowne this morning to pick her up." The young man eased backward to lean against the desk and favored me with a grin that I wanted to punch off his face. "I understand you were there for the fireworks. Am I right?"

Flexing my hands, I battled a desperate urge to deck this guy right here, right now, in front of everyone. I'd bet they'd applaud. "Hardly fireworks." I worked so hard to maintain an impassive expression, my cheeks hurt. "Frances has nothing to hide. She's happy to cooperate with the authorities."

Santiago lifted his chin. "Hey, look who's here."

Hands in his pockets, Dan loitered outside his father's apartment door, stopping to view the framed artwork on display in the hallway as though seeing the pieces for the first time. He radiated the air of a man en route to a commitment who wanted to be anywhere but where he was.

Flashing us a quick grin, Santiago boosted himself from his perch. "I wonder if *he's* heard about the arrest yet," he said.

What was wrong with this guy? How could someone so cheered by others' misfortunes have settled on a career in nursing? It was mind-numbing. Speechless, I turned to Joe, who shot me a commiserating "I can't believe this" look.

I leaned close and pointed to the new arrival. "Dan. The missing brother."

"He isn't dressed for hard labor," Joe whispered back.

He wasn't. Where Harland and Joslyn had been blue-jeaned and T-shirted, Dan wore dark slacks, a long-sleeved dress shirt, and a conservative tie. He held a jacket thrown over his shoulder.

Raising his hand, Santiago signaled Dan to join us.

Dan acknowledged Santiago's greeting but didn't look particularly pleased at the prospect of swinging by to chat. As luck would have it, however, Debbie emerged from another patient room just then, nearly bumping into him.

They were too far away for us to overhear their conversation, but their brief interaction threw Santiago into a tizzy. "Why should she get to share all the good gossip?"

"Gossip?" Percy twisted his chair to confront Santiago head-on. "That's my wife you're talking about."

"Uh-huh," Santiago said. "And she'd be the first one to appreciate how juicy all this is. Don't tell me she wouldn't."

Percy sucked in his cheeks. His upper body rose and his eyes glittered. "If I could get out of this chair, you low-life scum, the police would have another murder to investigate—but this time there would be zero doubt who did it."

Unfazed, Santiago glanced over to Joe and then to me and found no sympathy. "If we're done here, I suppose I ought to check on a few residents." His smile was as cold as his tone.

Before leaving, he tapped his chin, then brought his face low, close to Percy's. "I'm betting you haven't taken your anxiety medicine today, have you?" Without waiting for an answer, he said, "I think we may need to discuss upping your dosage. All this misplaced anger isn't healthy." Straightening himself, he pivoted and walked away.

Percy wheeled to position himself closer to me.

"Imbecile," he said loud enough for Santiago to hear. "I don't know how that guy keeps his job. We all complain about him. Nobody listens."

Picking up on that, I asked, "Did Gus complain about Santiago?"

"Sure, yeah." Percy didn't seem to catch the reason for my interest. "Like I said, we all did."

"And you told me Gus was wealthy." I glanced over to make sure Dan and Debbie weren't close enough to overhear. "Rich enough for Indwell's administration to pay attention to his concerns?"

Percy's eyes lit up. "Are you suggesting that Santiago may have had a motive? To shut Gus up so that Santiago didn't lose his job?"

"It's a stretch," I admitted. "That's a pretty drastic measure. Way out of proportion. What do you know about Santiago? Is there anything in his personal life that suggests violent tendencies?"

Joe leaned in. "If you know where he worked before coming to Indwell, I could make discreet inquiries. I have a network of colleagues scattered all over the country. You never know."

"I don't." Percy's mouth set in a line. "I've always tried to avoid him myself. But I can find out." He gave a brisk nod and said, "I'll do my best," before wheeling away.

"You'd do that?" I asked Joe. "That's incredibly generous of you."

"Not so generous. Curiosity is getting the better of me." He gave a sheepish grin. "Something isn't right here. Now I'm intrigued and I want answers." He lowered his voice as Debbie and Dan made their way toward us. "Is this what it's like all the time?" he asked, "I mean, is this how you've gotten involved in so many investigations before?"

"Yep," I said. "This is exactly what it's like."

Chapter 25

AFTER CALLING DAN AND DEBBIE OVER and making quick introductions, I learned that Dan had heard about Frances's arrest before he'd left home this morning. All of Santiago's aggravation was for naught.

"Harland and Joslyn will be glad to see you," I said with a vague gesture toward the apartment.

"They're here cleaning again?" Dan ran a hand through his hair. "What is up with those two?"

"I don't understand," I said. "If you didn't come to help, then why are you here?"

Dan cough-laughed. "I don't know. I felt compelled to stop by. Does that make me a weirdo?" He turned to Debbie. "Is that normal? People coming back even after their parents are gone?"

"Perfectly understandable," Debbie said solemnly. "Everybody grieves in their own way."

"I thought I'd take a look around my dad's room again before you guys rent it out to someone else." He shrugged. "But if Harland and Joslyn are here, it might be smarter to sneak out before they see me."

"Then you'd better get going." Debbie tapped her watch. "They're bound to catch you."

"Ever since Dad died, they've been fanatical about his possessions," he said. "They think he hid money in there. No way." Again, he turned to Debbie. "You guys made it clear that we weren't supposed to let him keep valuables in his room."

"Very true," she said. "Indwell can't be responsible for lost items. Your dad signed a contract to that effect before he moved in."

"Exactly. So there's nothing in there for me to worry about, right?"

She shrugged with a look that said, "What am I supposed to say to that?"

For a man eager to make a clean getaway, Dan seemed reluctant to leave our little group.

"What are they doing with all of your father's stuff?" Joe asked.

Dan didn't seem to mind the fact that a complete stranger had posed the question. "They want to go through it all next week, piece by piece, at Harland's house to see if there's anything we want to keep as a memento."

"I imagine you'll find some lovely surprises," Debbie said.

Dan nodded. "I guess I'll come back another time."

I was itching to broach the Santiago-as-the-killer idea to Dan, but reluctant to do so in front of Debbie. Although I got the distinct impression she and Santiago weren't friends, they *were* coworkers, and who knew what sort of an allegiance existed between them.

"Joe and I plan to stop by the Rosette police department on our way back to Marshfield," I said to Dan. "We'll walk you out."

He and I fell into step together. Next to me, Joe kept pace.

"You look like you came straight from work," I said as we made our way toward Indwell's lobby. "What do you do for a living?"

"Until recently, I was a high school social studies teacher. Not working right now, though," Dan said. "Burned out a few years back, but I stuck with it until my pension kicked in."

"Aren't you a little young for a pension?"

"Ha," he said. "No, I'm not, but thanks. I took the earliest exit they offered. I just got to a point in my life where I realized my best days were behind me and if I didn't stop to smell the roses now, I never would." He shrugged. "Maybe a couple of years off will inspire me to return to the classroom. In the meantime, I can always sub."

"How long have you been out?" Joe asked.

"This is my first semester as a free man," he said with a chuckle. "I took that trip to celebrate, but wound up coming back to all this." He waved vaguely over his shoulder. "I'm starting to feel guilty about that."

"You do? Why?" I asked.

271

"I don't know." He gave a one-shoulder shrug. "Maybe if I hadn't gone away, my dad would still be alive."

"You think you could have prevented his death?"

"Sounds silly, doesn't it?" he asked. "But I can't help it. Did they tell you I used to visit him all the time here? Three times a week, at least. Never missed. Until I went on vacation."

Another aide had replaced Cathy at the front desk so we were spared making small talk with the nosy woman.

"What kind of relationship did your father have with Santiago?" I asked.

"That crazy nurse who called the police and got this whole mess started?"

"Yes, him. Did he and your father get along?"

"Why? You have reason to think *he* could have killed Dad?"

"I heard that your dad had registered a few complaints. Maybe Santiago was afraid of losing his job."

Dan tilted his head one way then another as though examining the question from different angles. "I don't think so. That wouldn't make any sense. If he did it, then why would he call the police? Why wouldn't he just report a regular death?"

That was the one argument I had no answer for. "I know I'm grasping at straws but maybe he thought that calling the police would deflect suspicion. That by reporting an alleged murder, he would come across as the innocent informant."

"I guess." He seemed unconvinced. "I'll tell you this much: I wish he would have kept his mouth shut."

"I do, too," I said. "That's only because I know Frances has been unfairly accused. But what if someone did murder your dad? Wouldn't you want that person brought to justice?"

"At this point, I just want it done. Nobody killed our dad, and this is all a ridiculous waste of time."

"So you don't believe Frances is guilty?" Joe asked.

"No," Dan said with a dismissive swipe. "But it's not like I can march down to the police department and demand they release her. They're not going to listen to me."

"If you thought of anything—any evidence or information that could help clear Frances—you would tell the police though, right?"

"There's nothing for me to tell," he said. "Maybe if I'd been here, I'd know more." He shook his head. "But I wasn't. I don't know anything."

Debbie came hurrying toward us, waving. "Dan!" When she reached us, she said, "I'm glad I caught you before you left. Harland and Joslyn are carting boxes out via one of the side entrances. I didn't mention that you were here.

Harland found this and asked me to give it to you if you happened to show up later today."

The item in question was a small leather box—the kind expensive pen and pencil sets arrived in. She placed it into Dan's palm.

"What is it?" Joe asked.

The wells of Dan's eyes turned bright red. He stared down at the box and gingerly opened its hinged lid. Inside—sure enough—was a fancy silver pen.

"Harland said that this one doesn't count as one of your picks," Debbie said. "He said it belonged to you already."

Still staring down at the pen, Dan nodded. He cleared his throat. "Yeah." His voice cracked. "I bought this for Dad with my first paycheck. Thought he chucked it years ago. Didn't realize he kept it." Snapping it shut, he tucked it into his pants pocket and wiped at his face with the back of his hand.

I locked eyes with Debbie, who looked like a kid that had mistakenly done something terribly wrong. "I'm sorry," she said. "I thought it would give you comfort."

Dan shook his head. "Makes it worse."

"We'd better get going," I said.

Composure regained, Dan cleared his throat again and smiled at me. "You take it easy," he said as he swung his sport coat on. "Good luck to your friend Frances. Maybe she'll be released soon."

"Thanks. I hope your day improves," I said.

"Say hi to your girlfriend for us," Debbie said.

He shook his head. "What?"

"You're all dressed up," she said. "I assume you have a hot date tonight."

I warped back to Harland's comment when I'd first met him, when he'd assumed I was Dan's girlfriend.

My brain immediately jumped into high gear. If Dan had a girlfriend, could she have overdosed Gus with insulin? I had no idea what sort of motive the woman could have or even if she'd visited Gus while Dan was away. I was mulling ways to pose that question delicately when Debbie came in with an assist.

"We've been hearing about this girlfriend of his for months," she said with a wink. "But he refuses to bring her around. I'm starting to wonder if the woman really exists."

"She exists, all right," he said. "And no, no hot date. She's been giving me the cold shoulder lately."

"Sorry to hear that," I said.

"You'd think with all I've had to deal with this week, she'd be a little nicer. A little more sympathetic. She doesn't understand why I can't give her all the attention she wants."

"Why don't you bring her with you next time?" Debbie asked. "We can all tell her what a great guy you are."

"Yeah, right." He cough-laughed again. "You have to understand," he said, even though we didn't, "there was no way I could let my dad know about her. The old man never liked any of the women I brought around for him to meet. Including my ex-wife. He never liked anyone Harland dated, either."

"Not even Joslyn?" I asked.

"He *hated* her," Dan said. "I'm surprised Joslyn didn't start dancing a jig when we got the word that he was gone."

The more I learned about Gus, the wider the suspect pool grew.

Chapter 26

WHEN JOE AND I LEFT INDWELL, I CALLED Rosette's police department to let Frances and Lily know we were on our way. A man answered the phone.

"They're not here," he said.

"Where did they go?"

"Now how would I know that?"

I tried to press him to find out if Frances had been incarcerated, or if Lily had been able to arrange for her release, but he refused to share information. When I hung up, I frowned. "So much for small-town friendliness."

"Where do you think they are?" Joe asked.

"I'll try Frances first," I said as I dialed. "I'm sure it'll go to voice mail, but—"

She answered on the first ring. "Took you long enough."

"You're out?" I said, barely able to mask the exuberant catch in my voice. "What happened? Where are you?"

"I'll tell you more when we get back," she said. "The Mister came through with the cash for my bail, thank goodness. Kept me from having to spend the night in a stinking jail cell."

"I'm on my way back to Marshfield," I said. "I don't have any solid clues but I do have a few ideas I'd like to discuss with you. We need to put our heads together."

"Hang on." She pulled away from the phone. When she returned, she said, "Lily wants you to know that she has that extra copy of the autopsy report. Right now I'm going to close my eyes a bit while Lily drives back. See you at Marshfield."

"She's out?" Joe asked when I hung up.

"Yes, and she sounds exhausted. Not that I can blame her."

He drove in silence for a little while. "I overheard her say that they're bringing the autopsy report with them."

"Do you mind coming up to my office when we get back?" I asked. "I know it's another stop."

"I'm looking forward to getting a look at that report. Wouldn't miss it."

He merged onto the interstate.

"I really appreciate your help." I stared out the window. Now that the rain had finally let up, I focused on the puffy-white clouds drifting in sharp contrast against the piercing blue sky.

"There has to be more to the story. Right now nothing makes sense."

"Something does," I said. "We just can't see it yet."

"That's true."

"I need to clear the clutter and let my brain work

on the puzzle in the background while I do something else. This situation with Frances has taken all my attention." Even my roommates' financial troubles with Amethyst Cellars had taken a backseat.

"What better way to relax than a car ride?" he asked. "What else can we talk about?"

I hesitated then asked, "Why do you use a cane?"

His brows jumped. He didn't look at me, but his expression darkened. "You're very direct."

"If you don't want to talk about it, just say so. No worries."

He frowned at the street ahead, merged into the middle lane, then said, "I was in a car accident, a bad one. Got T-boned by a drunk driver in the middle of an intersection. It took me more than a year to get back on my feet, and it's taking even longer than that to lose the cane."

"You didn't seem to need it today."

"I have good days and bad ones. Today's one of the better ones."

"I'm sorry to hear about the accident. Was anyone else hurt in the crash?"

"Yes." He turned to me. "Let's change the subject, okay?"

"I'm sorry," I said.

"Not your fault. But let's keep the rest for another day."

We traveled another mile or so before I spoke

again. "Is there anything you'd like to talk about?"

He gave a wry smile. "Now that you mention it, there is. As long as you don't mind my being direct this time."

"Not at all."

"There's a lot of talk around Emberstowne about you."

"So you've mentioned."

"I want to ask you about a couple of things." He slid a glance at me, as though judging my reaction.

"Go on."

"The big news, of course, is that you and Bennett Marshfield recently discovered that you're related to each other."

"It's been the talk of the town since we got the test results. I'd hoped to keep it quiet."

"That's sort of what I was getting at." He turned to look at me again, briefly. "You don't seem at all affected by your newfound wealth. You seem down-to-earth and not the least bit impressed with yourself."

I laughed out loud. A genuine, from-the-belly laugh. The first time I'd done so in days. "I don't know how to take that," I said, still smiling. "Is it a compliment or am I somehow falling down in my chi-chi-pooh-pooh role?"

He laughed now, too. "That's exactly what I'm talking about. It seems to me that discovering you're the heir to such a vast fortune would make you look at life differently."

"I don't want to look at life differently."

"And I wish I'd never gotten T-boned," he said. "But that doesn't make the reality go away. Surely life has changed for you. I imagine family, friends, and even strangers have approached you for a handout since the news hit."

"I have very little family," I said carefully. "So far, they're unaware. I hope to keep it that way."

When he shot me a quizzical look, I shrugged. "Long story. I will admit that I get a lot of donation requests. They pour into Marshfield Manor by the thousands. They used to come to Bennett's attention. Now a lot of them come to me. I've had to hire a young woman to sort through and help weed out the money grabbers from the honest requests. But otherwise, no, not much has changed." I turned to him. "But like I said, I don't want it to."

"Most people probably wouldn't share that attitude. They'd be out taking trips, buying cars, living the high life."

I tapped my fingernails along the armrest. "That's one of the reasons why I held off taking the DNA test for so long. I knew the truth in my heart and that was enough. I didn't need the world to know. All I care about is that Bennett and I are family. I didn't want anyone to think I loved him for his money."

"You held off testing?"

"For a few years," I said, staring out the windshield. "But it was so important to Bennett that I finally relented. And here we are."

"Wow," he said. He completed a lane change then shot me another glance. "Most people in your shoes would be giddy with glee. Don't get me wrong; I find your attitude fascinating and refreshing. But I have to ask: What's holding you back?"

I thought about Liza again, and how that chapter of my life was not yet completely written. "You know what?" I said. "Let's save that part of the story for another day, too."

BENNETT, FRANCES, AND LILY WERE gathered in my office when Joe and I arrived. Except for the purple pouches that puffed beneath her eyes, Frances's face was devoid of color. I made quick introductions. It seemed I was doing that a lot lately.

"Pleased to meet you, Frances," Joe said.

"So you're that new coroner Grace has been talking about." After shaking hands with him she rubbed her palm against the side of her pant leg. "Can't say I'm happy to meet you."

"I get that a lot," Joe said. "Completely understandable."

"Good job spotting the judge's name on that warrant, Grace," Lily said. "Seems father and daughter are both a little trigger-happy: The officer to make her first homicide arrest and Judge Madigan to bolster his daughter's career."

"So it's bogus?"

"We didn't get that lucky." Lily shook her head. "The warrant may have been issued in haste, but it's still valid."

Frances turned to me. "When we showed up in court, Lily put the screws to that guy like you wouldn't believe. He still set my bail way too high." She took a moment to beam at Bennett. "But like I told you, the Mister put up the cash to get me released. Thank goodness."

"The police weren't happy about it," Lily said, "but with help from a Rosette colleague, we were able to offer a strong argument for release. Thank goodness for small-town politics."

"How long until Frances needs to be back in court?" I asked.

Lily named a date two weeks in the future as she pulled a file from her briefcase. "Here you go." She handed Joe a copy of the autopsy report. "It isn't complete, of course, because it doesn't include final toxicology findings. My legal team will go over this tomorrow, but if you come up with any 'Aha!' moments, I'd be happy to hear them."

"Thanks." Joe began paging through. "Did they give you an estimate as to when the tox results will be in?"

"They've put a rush on the lab, but I'm guessing we may not have a final answer before we go back to court for Frances's next hearing."

Joe continued to flip through the papers.

"Thank you, Dr. Bradley," she said. "Again, please contact me if you find anything of interest."

He glanced up at the obvious dismissal. "Yes, sure," he said. "I guess I'll take off now."

I walked him out of the offices into the corridor. "Sorry," I said. "She's a little brusque."

"Part of the job description. Don't worry about it."

"I can't thank you enough for all your help," I said. "This has been a long day for you. I've eaten up all your time off. I'll bet you can't wait to get home."

"Honestly, it's been enlightening," he said. "It may sound weird, but I enjoyed myself." He held the report aloft. "And as an added bonus, I have this absorbing reading ahead of me tonight."

Chapter 27

"HELLO?" I CALLED AS I STEPPED THROUGH our back door that evening. The kitchen lights were off and although sunlight slicing through the back window provided enough illumination for me to see, the room felt more than empty, as though all the life had been sucked out of it. There were cleaning supplies strewn all over the table and cardboard boxes piled on each of the chairs.

"Bruce? Scott?" I called a little louder.

I heard the soft padding of Bootsie's paws down the stairs before she bounded into the room to greet me. "How are you, baby?" I asked as I dropped my purse on the table and stooped to pick her up. "Where is everyone?"

She opened her mouth and yawned. Not much of an answer.

A second later, I heard scuffling from the basement. "That you, Grace? We're down here."

As I opened the door to head down, Bootsie twisted out of my hold. Jumping to the floor, she made her way over to her food and water bowls, turning to give me a sleepy-eyed "Go on without me" look.

Bruce and Scott waited for me at the bottom of

the stairs. Clad in dirty jeans and sweat-stained T-shirts, they wore identical expressions of frustration. "You're just in time," Scott said as I made my way down.

"For what?"

"For the grand reopening of Amethyst Cellars," Bruce said. "*In* the cellar. What could be more appropriate?" When he gestured me forward, I noticed his hands were covered in grime.

Crates and boxes—dozens of them—were lined up about shoulder height along the far wall. I recognized wine cases among the varied sizes and shapes. And I couldn't miss the bloodred wine staining most of the cardboard before me.

Set in front of the boxes were fragments of furniture. Or at least that's what they looked like to me. Amethyst Cellars's cherrywood cabinetry—spotlighted and shiny—always looked so rich and elegant. Here, broken into components under harsh fluorescent light, the red-colored wood looked scuffed, old, and forlorn.

"This is only half of it," Scott said. "There's more upstairs in the living room and parlor. We don't have it in us to carry the rest down here tonight."

"You guys have been moving everything here yourselves?" I asked.

"We had no choice," Bruce said. "If we didn't get it out today, we risked losing our inventory when the contractors came in. Building inspectors are forcing our landlord to gut the place before putting it back together. Anything left there after five o'clock this afternoon gets tossed."

"But none of this was your fault."

"Tell that to the inspectors," Scott said. "Their job is to ensure safety. They don't care about stuff."

"Have you eaten?" I asked.

Bruce waved to indicate a pile of fast-food papers and bags. "We brought in burgers about an hour ago. Sorry we didn't think to order anything for you."

"Don't worry about it," I said.

"But it gets worse," Scott said.

"How can it?" I shook my head. "Forget I said that. What do you mean?"

"The landlord is already warning us that with all the money he's putting in to restoring the building, he's going to have to raise our rent."

"That's ridiculous."

Bruce made his way over to one of the battered cases on the floor. He opened the purple-spattered cardboard flaps of one marked "Rioja" and pulled out a bottle, hefting it one-handed. "Can't sell this." He turned the bottle so its label faced me. Streaked with red, it looked as though it had been caught in a rain shower of wine. "May as well drink it. We deserve it after the long day we've had, don't we, Scott?"

At the dismay on my face, Scott said, "At least

half the bottles are stained like that. Some worse. We may eventually be able to offer customers a demolition discount, but that plan is a long way off."

"How many bottles did you lose completely?" I asked.

Bruce shrugged. "I have a guess. Do you?"

"Broken bottles?" Scott nodded. "I think we lost at least eight cases."

Bruce shook his head. "More like twelve."

Scott's shoulders drooped.

"Insurance will cover some of the loss, at least." Bruce was still holding the bottle of Rioja. "And on that happy note, let's go upstairs and celebrate that we didn't lose more."

I followed them as they trudged into the kitchen. Their despair was absolute, their misery complete. They had hopes, dreams, and plans, but no way to implement any of it. But even as my heart broke for them, I felt a tingle of anticipation.

When we got to the top of the stairs, Scott turned the kitchen lights on and Bruce handed me the bottle. "Care to do the honors, Grace? I can't wait to get out of these filthy clothes, and I'll bet Scott feels the same way."

"Sure." I moved to the drawer where we kept the corkscrew.

"I need a shower," Scott said. "Maybe two."

They sounded so utterly dejected and yet my excitement continued to build. I couldn't wait for them to come back down. Spinning, I caught them as they crossed the threshold to the dining room. "Wait."

They stopped in their tracks.

"What's wrong?" Scott asked.

"We didn't ask you how everything went with Frances today," Bruce said. "I'm so sorry. We've been so busy that I completely forgot. Have the Rosette detectives finally seen the light and dropped charges?"

"No." I raised a hand to my forehead. I couldn't believe how much had transpired today. "Frances was arrested," I said. "This morning."

Bruce reached out to grab the doorjamb as though to steady himself. "And you let us go on and on about our problems? How is she? Where is she?"

Scott's mouth had dropped open. "No." He drew the word out. "No, that can't be."

"It's okay," I said, talking quickly now. "No, wait. It's not okay. But at least she's been released. Bennett covered her bail."

"Thank heavens for Bennett," Bruce said.

"But charges are still pending?" Scott asked.

"They are. And we can't let our guard down for a moment. Bennett, Tooney, and I—along with Joe Bradley, the coroner—are doing our very best to ensure those charges are dismissed. And soon."

"I'm so sorry," Bruce said. "Is there anything we can do to help?"

"Yes, there is," I said. "I know you want to get cleaned up but this can't wait. Would you both please have a seat?"

As they moved the boxes, cleaning supplies, and assorted detritus, I opened the bottle of wine and pulled three glasses from the shelf.

"You know we'll do whatever we can," Scott said.

"I know that. And I'm counting on you both."

I placed the glasses on the table and began to pour.

"The suspense is too much," Bruce said. "Forget the wine. Just tell us already."

"The wine is part of it." They shot confused expressions at me and at each other. "I have two favors to ask."

When all three glasses were poured, I set the bottle on the table and sat down. "Okay, the first favor involves one of the people in Gus's life who sort of works in your line of business. A man named Anton Holcroft."

"The restaurateur?" Bruce asked.

"You know him?"

Scott's jaw dropped again. "This 'Gus' Frances is accused of killing—the victim. Are you talking about Gustave Westburg?"

My turn to look surprised. "How do you know these people?"

"We don't," Bruce said. "But we've heard of

them. They owned a slew of restaurants along the coast. Hugely successful."

"They made a killing together," Scott said.

Bruce frowned. "Scott!"

"Oh, sorry. Bad choice of words."

"How did I never hear of them before?" I asked.

Scott shrugged. "Probably because you aren't in the business."

"And because they sold out their holdings about ten years ago. Well before you moved down here." Bruce tapped the table. "What do you need us to do?"

I gave a little laugh. "I was going to ask you to do some homework on Anton for me. I'd like to know what kind of man he is, what makes him tick. I met him only once and my impression was that he was truly broken up by the news of Gus's death, but that could have been an act."

Bruce and Scott exchanged a glance across the table. "We *could* contact him under the guise of looking to hire a consultant," Bruce said. "I mean, we would love to work with Anton Holcroft if we could, so that isn't much of a stretch. The fact that we have no money to actually hire him is beside the point."

"And that's where we come to the other favor."

The two waited expectantly.

"I want to buy the Granite Building," I said. "And provide you whatever funds you need to make it operational."

They exploded with questions and surprised exclamations.

"Grace, what?"

"No, we can't let you do that."

"That's too much money. Not a chance."

I waited for them to jabber themselves into silence.

Bruce finally said, "That's extraordinarily generous of you, but we told you before—we won't take a handout."

"But that's the beauty of this. It isn't a hand-out." Excited, I sat up straighter, as the idea I'd broached to Bennett gained momentum in my heart. "Not if we're partners."

The two men looked at each other then at me. The room remained silent for about a count of five.

"What are you talking about, Grace?" Scott asked, speaking slowly. "What do you mean by 'partners'?"

Mounting enthusiasm warmed me. I leaned forward, elbows on the kitchen table. "The Granite Building is still available for sale, isn't it?"

"As far as we know," Scott said. "But remember, the bank wants to put up a new branch in that location."

"But the chamber of commerce would have to approve that. Which they may not choose to do if there's a better option."

"True," Scott said. "But that's a long shot."

"Not if we offer to buy it outright. No mortgage. The bank walks away with a nice profit on their foreclosure and you have a new home for Amethyst Cellars."

"You would do that for us?" Bruce asked.

"I've been thinking about this for some time, but I needed to discuss it with Bennett's financial guy before I mentioned it to you."

"You talked this over with Bennett's financial guy?" Scott asked.

"He said that I could either hold the mortgage myself or partner with you two." I waited a beat. "I'd rather be your partner than your landlord."

The two of them sat in shocked silence.

I cleared my throat to recapture their attention. "I wouldn't want to push myself in as a managing partner, though. More a silent investor. You two have built something special here, and I'm not savvy enough about the wine or restaurant business to have an informed opinion. You won't have to consult me on every decision, but I do want to invest enough to get you started in the new location."

"But, but"—Scott's brow furrowed as my proposal sunk in—"we can't ask you to do that."

"You're not asking me. I'm offering." My words came faster. "With the funds Bennett has made available to me, I can do this."

"Grace, wait." Scott held up both hands as

though to ward me off. "We haven't developed a business plan yet. We haven't ordered an inspection on the building. It may not be up to code, and repairs could cost you more than the investment is worth. This may not be a sound financial decision."

"I'm not investing in a building," I said. "I'm investing in *you*. I have no doubt that you'll examine every detail before moving forward. That you'll do whatever homework you feel is necessary." I made eye contact with each of them in turn. "Trust me, I *want* to do this. Bennett has encouraged me to invest in ventures I believe in. And I believe in you."

This time when they exchanged glances, there was something in their eyes that hadn't been there five minutes earlier: hope.

"This is too generous of you," Bruce said.

I grinned. "Not generous at all. I've seen what you two are capable of. I expect us all to turn a tidy profit."

Spontaneously, we stretched our hands out across the table and grasped tightly. "We make an awesome team, don't we?" I asked.

Bruce's eyes were red-rimmed and glassy. "We do."

My cell phone rang, interrupting our warm moment of togetherness.

"Thank you, Grace. Thank you, so very much." Scott's voice was thick with emotion. He smiled and cleared his throat. "Tomorrow morning, we'll go talk to the bank."

"Good. Keep me updated," I said as I released their hands and reached for my phone. "It's the coroner," I said when I saw the caller ID. "I hope it's good news."

Chapter 28

I TOOK THE CALL IN THE PARLOR AND realized the boys hadn't been kidding. There were boxes everywhere. Bootsie wandered between them, jumping from level to level as though scaling cardboard mountains. No wonder she hadn't wanted to make the trek to the basement. Our main level had been turned into a kitty playground.

Joe sounded eager, excited. "Where are you?"

"Home, why?"

"I've been going over this autopsy report and I'd like to talk with you about it. I'm in my office right now. Am I calling too late?"

"No, not at all." Instinctively, I glanced at the clock. Seven thirty. I couldn't remember the last time I'd eaten. This was the day that wouldn't end. "Did you find something that could help Frances?"

"I don't know. Maybe. Is there somewhere we can meet? I don't want to be rude and invite myself over, but—"

"And I don't usually make the excuse that my house is a mess, but Bruce and Scott literally emptied out Amethyst Cellars into our living space today and I don't have a single free chair I could offer you."

He made a small noise of disappointment.

"Would you mind if we met at Hugo's?" I asked him. "I'm starving."

"Not many people would be willing to discuss an autopsy report over dinner." He laughed quietly. "How soon?"

"It takes me about ten minutes to walk there."

"Ten minutes it is."

HUGO'S WAS A POPULAR RESTAURANT, but because it wasn't a weekend and the town wasn't yet in high season, I had no trouble snagging a table in the back where Joe and I could converse freely without fear of being overheard.

I seated myself with my back to the wall. Less than two minutes later, the hostess pointed Joe in the direction of my table. He carried a manila folder in one hand and waved to me with the other. No cane tonight either, apparently. And his limp was barely noticeable.

"This place has a nice vibe." Giving Hugo's a quick once-over, he lowered himself into the chair to my right and placed the folder on the table in front of him. "Have you ordered?"

"Not yet," I said.

"Do you mind if I hit you with a couple of questions while we wait?"

I liked the way he got straight to business. "Please."

He opened the folder to the autopsy report, where two preprinted line drawings of the male human form took up most of the first page. One drawing was to document findings on the body when viewed faceup, the other, facedown. Handwritten notes were scribbled around both outlines.

"First of all, the coroner who performed the autopsy did not indicate the presence of any unexplained skin punctures. Reading through her notes, I've been able to determine that she did, indeed, perform a thorough examination."

"That's great news," I said. "Insulin is typically injected into the thighs, abdomen, or buttocks, right?"

He nodded but didn't smile.

"So that means Gus didn't die of an insulin overdose?"

"Not necessarily."

"But if there aren't any puncture wounds—"

"Hang on, look right here."

Just then, a waitress arrived at our table. Joe shut the folder as she introduced herself. I could barely wait for her to get through her welcoming spiel.

"Can I bring you something to drink while you look at the menus?" she asked.

"I'm ready to order. I'll have a cheeseburger

and fries, please," I said. "And I'm fine with water to drink." When Joe glanced over, I could tell he sensed my impatience. I shrugged.

He nodded. "Same for me."

As soon as she was gone again, he reopened the folder and positioned it between us. He pointed to the facedown human outline. "The coroner who performed the autopsy noted the presence of a heparin lock on the back of Gus's left hand."

"That's what started the whole investigation," I said.

"What do you mean?"

"When Santiago found Gus dead, it was because he'd gone in there to flush Gus's heparin lock."

Joe sat forward, eyes glinting. "I hadn't heard that detail before."

"Is it significant?"

"Does Frances have any medical training?"

"Not that I'm aware of."

He sat back, tapping a finger against the page. "If Gus died of insulin poisoning, I'd wager he received the dose through his heparin lock."

"Meaning Frances is still a suspect."

"Technically, yes, but if she had no medical training, then she probably wouldn't know she had that option." He gave an exaggerated shrug. "And unless Gus was an incredibly sound sleeper, I highly doubt the man would allow a nonmedical person to inject him with anything."

When our burger platters arrived, Joe shut the

file again and moved it to the side. Our waitress asked typical, polite questions and then, to my relief, took off again promptly.

"Keep in mind"—Joe pinched three fries and used them for emphasis—"we still don't know whether Gus received *any* insulin. This discussion may be moot. But, for the sake of argument, let's say he did."

"If he did, are you saying that one of the nurses injected him?"

"Again, not necessarily." Joe lifted his burger with both hands. "Anyone who wears a heparin lock for a while knows how they work."

I lifted my burger off the plate. "Meaning Gus could have injected himself."

Mouth full, he nodded vigorously. A few seconds of chewing later, he added, "Let's hope Gus died a natural, peaceful death. But even if he didn't, I think there's enough to cast doubt on Frances being the killer."

We spent the rest of dinner discussing the case and tossing ideas back and forth. Joe ate at a more leisurely pace than I did and still had half his food left by the time I'd polished off my burger and consumed every fry.

"You weren't kidding about being hungry," he said as the waitress slipped the empty plate out from under me.

"It's been an incredibly long day," I said. "I'll be glad to see the end of it."

The waitress placed the bill on the table between us.

He reached for it. "Then I won't keep you."

I laid my hand on the little leather folder first. "My treat," I said. "It's the least I can do for all your help." When he hesitated, I added, "I insist."

"Well then, thank you."

As he withdrew, I noticed a faint tan line on the ring finger of his left hand. Worse, he caught me noticing.

"Maybe we can do this again sometime," he said, breaking the awkward moment. I was grateful to him for lessening my embarrassment. A corner of his mouth curled up. "Without an autopsy report to analyze."

I'd enjoyed our time together—both at Indwell today and here at dinner. Though I barely knew him, Joe Bradley already felt like an old friend. "I'd like that."

BENNETT HAD URGED FRANCES TO STAY home and take care of herself while the storm of her suspicion raged, but—true to form—she showed up at work the next morning, right on time.

"I feel safer here," she explained when I asked her. "If the cops come for me again, at least one of you will know about it. If they cart me away when I'm home alone, who knows how long it would be before somebody notices I've gone missing."

"Speaking of Bennett," I said. "He's due here any minute. He wants to hear what Tooney has come up with."

"Have you told the Mister about what your coroner friend said?" she asked.

"Not yet. Have you called Lily Holland to tell her?"

She nodded. "She said it's good information, but we'll need more if we expect to get charges dropped."

"Let's hope Tooney has what we need."

She snorted. "I'm not holding out hope. If all this was about you, he'd have had you declared innocent before the cops had left Indwell the first time. But this is for me, so I can't expect him to care."

"Not true," I said.

The door to Frances's office opened and Tooney walked in.

"See?" she said. "If he wanted to come into your office, he'd knock first."

Distraught, Tooney asked, "I was supposed to knock?"

"Come on in," I said, pointing to the seat next to mine. "I can't wait to hear what you've come up with."

A second later, Bennett strode in. "How are things today?" he asked. "Were you able to sleep, Frances? Is there anything you need?"

"I'm fine."

I got up to pull a chair from my office into Frances's.

"I can get it, Gracie," Bennett said.

When we were all settled around Frances's desk, I held out a hand. "Mr. Tooney, we are all ears."

His cheeks pinkened. "I hope some of this helps." He pulled out a notebook from his pocket. "I've been shadowing each of the people Frances named, one at a time. A few of them live pretty close together, so I've been able to develop an efficient route that takes me past their homes when I know they're off work. I had to learn their routines pretty quick, you understand. And I've been able to discreetly ask questions and follow them around enough to make some educated guesses about how they spend their free time."

Frances tightened her crossed arms and made a face.

"Great," I said. "Go on."

"Starting with Gus's family: Harland and his wife have been looking at new cars. Expensive ones."

Frances made a noise.

"How expensive?" I asked.

"Considering they live in a modest house in an old neighborhood and both drive fifteen-year-old clunkers, I'd say very. He seems to favor a black Mercedes while she's eyeing a green Jaguar." He shrugged. "I can't say for certain, but they sure act like people who expect to be coming into money soon."

"That's not surprising," Frances said. "Gus was rich. I'm sure both sons stand to inherit a big chunk of change."

Tooney waited for her to finish. "Dan, the younger son, eats out every night at the same restaurant a few miles outside Rosette." Before I could ask, he anticipated my question. "Vern's Steak House. Popular with locals. He may be considering a move to Florida. I can't decide if the brochures he's left behind at the restaurant indicate that he's planning a move or he's just dreaming."

This sort of information wasn't much help. I could feel Frances's frustration grow. "What about Indwell's staff? Did you learn anything valuable about them?"

"Tara was off work yesterday. She spent all her time with her fiancé—which she usually does."

"Knew that," Frances said.

"Santiago puts in extra hours as often as he can."

"Knew that, too."

Tooney frowned. "He lives alone and binge-watches zombie and vampire TV shows." He cocked an eyebrow and added, "He attends Gamblers Anonymous meetings twice a week after work."

"So?" Frances fidgeted.

"Debbie is divorced and lives with her mother. Cathy loves her dachshunds more than she loves her husband, I think. She buys a lot—and I do mean a lot—of stuff via mail order."

"What kind of stuff?" Frances asked.

"No way for me to know," he said. "Boxes pile up on her front stoop every day. I'm surprised she can fit anything more into her house."

Frances twisted her mouth to one side and looked away. "I knew I couldn't count on your help."

"Hang on, Frances," I said. "Maybe the reason why Tooney hasn't been able to dig up any dirt on these people is because there isn't any dirt to find. It still hasn't been proven that Gus died of insulin poisoning."

"Doesn't seem to matter to the cops though, does it?"

I drew in a deep breath. "Let's focus on the positive, shall we?" I turned to Bennett and Tooney. "Joe and I were discussing the autopsy report last night. He came up with an interesting observation."

"Joe?" Tooney asked. "Are you talking about the coroner, Dr. Bradley?"

"Exactly," I said. "He didn't know Gus had a heparin lock." I tapped the back of my left hand. "If Gus died of insulin poisoning, the vials could have been injected via that port. It stands to reason that he either did it himself or one of the nurses did it under the guise of a routine flush."

Tooney's soft face crumpled in on itself as he pondered that. "I don't know if I buy him injecting himself," he said slowly.

"What, you think Gus would have let me inject him?" Frances asked in a huff. "That man and I never got within ten feet of each other. We shared a mutual loathing."

"What's troubling you, Mr. Tooney?" Bennett asked.

"The way I see it, these insulin vials are like rounds of ammunition. If you fire a semi-automatic, spent shell casings are going to fly out with each shot. Most criminals—or people, at least, who know about forensic evidence—will pick up their spent shell casings and remove them from the crime scene so detectives have less evidence to work with."

"I see where you're going," I said. "If Gus dosed himself, why pick up all but one syringe cap?"

Bennett sat forward. "Could Gus have become too disoriented to notice the one on the floor?"

Tooney frowned. "But he would've had to have disposed of the rest of them somewhere, right?"

"Right," I said. "The cops searched through Gus's wastebaskets. Nothing there."

"So then whoever dosed him took the vials and their caps out of the room," Tooney said. "But whoever it was missed one."

"The one that Santiago found rolling around on the floor," Frances said. "Nosy creep."

"I'm sure that's why one vial is completely missing," I said. "Once the killer realized that a cap had gone astray, he or she couldn't return the obviously used vial to Percy's refrigerator."

"The killer probably never anticipated Santiago's involvement," Bennett said.

Tooney nodded. "Exactly. Which means—"

"That Santiago is probably not our killer," Bennett said.

I wrinkled my nose. This wasn't new news.

Frances bristled. "How does any of this help me? It doesn't, does it?" She pointed a finger at Tooney. "You go ahead—keep eliminating other suspects. Why not? It's not like the Mister pays your salary or anything. I'm sure that's exactly how he wants his money spent—helping total strangers stay out of trouble."

Bennett and I exchanged a glance. Though we both understood that Frances was disappointed by Tooney's information—or rather, lack thereof—I wanted to keep her spirits up. "Sometimes we have to take a step back before we take a step forward." My words felt as lame as they sounded.

"For me, a step back means being locked up behind bars. No, thank you." She stared Tooney down. "I only just met the new coroner and he's done more for me than you ever have," she said. "Thanks for nothing."

My office phone rang. Frances glanced at the display on her console. "It's the front desk," she said and picked up.

Her brows danced high on her forehead, but all she said was, "Yes, fine. She'll be right down, I'm sure. Yes. Got it."

When she hung up, she glared at Tooney. "Did you forget Anton?" she asked.

"Anton?" Tooney said. "No, Grace—"

"You remember Gus's best friend, don't you? Or wasn't he on your list of people to investigate?" she asked him. Before he had a chance to respond, she turned to me. "He's here. Wants to talk with you."

"He's here? Now?"

"In the flesh."

"Okay, I'll go talk with him." This was unexpected. "But before I do, you need to know that Tooney didn't follow Anton because I asked Bruce and Scott to investigate him."

"You did? What were you thinking?"

"They're in the same line of business," I said. "Doesn't matter now. But don't blame Tooney, okay? Why does Anton want to talk with me?"

"No idea." She shook her head. "They're showing him to the Birdcage Room right now. He'll wait for you there."

Tooney shuffled to his feet. "I'll keep at it. I'll keep shadowing these people. I promise I'll come up with something, Frances."

I got up to accompany him out. "I'll be back as soon as I can."

As Tooney and I made our way downstairs, I said, "Frances is going through a rough time. On a good day, she's brittle and ornery. With all that's going on, she's having a tough time holding it together. She needs to lash out. I'm sorry you took the brunt of it."

"She has every right to be angry," he said. "I should have found something to help her by now."

Chapter 29

WHEN I ARRIVED AT THE BIRDCAGE, I scanned the sea of small tables where a smattering of guests conversed quietly, sipping morning beverages and enjoying house-made pastries while mellow music drifted through the air. It took me a moment, but I finally spotted Anton. Hands clasped behind his back, the thickset man stood silhouetted against the curved, two-story grid of windows that gave the room its name.

Sensing my approach, perhaps, he turned as I reached him.

"Nice to see you again, Anton," I said. "What brings you to Marshfield this morning?"

His face broke into a wide smile. "You are a vision." Spreading his arms to encompass the surroundings, he said, "A perfect jewel in a magnificent setting." Before I had a chance to react, he grabbed my shoulders and kissed me on each cheek. "Thank you for agreeing to meet with me."

I hadn't realized we were on such comfortable terms. Taking a step back, I indicated one of the nearby empty tables. "Please, join me."

The moment we sat, one of the Birdcage

waitresses came by. The young woman attempted to hand us menus, but Anton said he didn't care to order. "Nothing for either of us, then," I said. The moment she was gone, I turned to him. "I confess I'm curious as to the reason for your visit today."

Much like the posture he'd assumed Sunday after learning of Gus's death, Anton sat hunched, leaning hard on the table, hands clamped in front of him. His face was etched with lines. "Frances did not kill my friend. She should never have been arrested. The police are making a mistake by investigating her."

"We know that," I said gently. I hoped Anton's visit today wasn't merely to express solidarity. "But lacking concrete evidence that proves otherwise, the police seem all too willing to prosecute."

He continued to stare at his clenched hands.

"You wouldn't have any information that could help exonerate Frances, would you?" I asked.

He rubbed his thick thumbs together several times before answering. "That is why I am here." Finally looking up long enough to make brief eye contact, he said, "What I have isn't evidence, but it is insight."

I tugged my chair closer to the tiny table. "Go on."

"I have struggled in my heart with whether to say anything or not, but I find I must." He flicked another glance up at me. His bloodshot eyes

311

were heavy-lidded; shiny, capillary-speckled bags pouched beneath them. "I have no proof, only speculation."

"Tell me," I said.

He worked his lips much the same way he'd worked his thumbs a moment earlier. "I have known Gus most of my adult life," he began. "And so I have known his sons ever since they were children."

I sat up straighter.

"Gus was hard on them both, to be sure. He was not a cruel man, but neither was he kind. The boys avoided him, always. Their mother didn't help matters. When she divorced Gus, she worked hard to turn the boys against him. Not that it took much effort on her part. By then they were adults who had already embarked on their own lives."

"Where is she now?"

"She died some years ago. Although the boys were bereft, they weren't stupid. They recognized that their elderly wealthy father had become ill and that their obligatory visits and birthday phone calls probably weren't enough to ensure them an inheritance. So they attempted to reconcile with Gus, telling him that the only reason they stayed away was for their mother's sake. They promised they'd become real sons to him now that she was gone."

"You know this?" I asked.

"I watched it happen."

"And did they?" I asked. "Become real sons to Gus?"

"Gus was a very smart man," Anton said. "He saw through their charade. He knew what they were after."

"And you believe one—or both—of them may have killed Gus?" I asked. "But why? If he was as ill as you say, why not maintain the happy family illusion and wait for their father's inevitable demise?"

"Because they believed—mistakenly—that every penny spent at Indwell was that much less they'd inherit."

Though I remembered both Harland's and Dan's complaints about the cost of housing Gus at Indwell, I picked up on Anton's word choice. "Mistakenly?"

"Gus took out a life insurance policy several years ago."

"The two-million-dollar policy?"

"That's the one. Harland and Dan are beneficiaries."

"So I understand," I said. "However—and not to be so cold about it—why wouldn't they simply wait for Gus to die a natural death?"

"Because Gus took out that policy only to appease them. They wanted a look at Gus's will; they were afraid he'd written them out." Another bloodshot glance to ensure I was paying attention.

"He had. That's what I'm here to tell you. Gus left everything to me."

I felt my jaw drop. "Wait." I attempted to process what he'd just revealed. "You?"

He nodded sadly. "I found out myself only yesterday. Gus added a codicil, or whatever it's called, explaining his reasoning. He said he knew his sons were money-grubbers. The only reason he waxed poetic about keeping the fortune in the family and made certain they both knew about the insurance policy, was to fool them into believing he would leave his entire estate to them. To stop them from constantly bothering him about his money. And it worked."

"Are you telling me that the sons inherit nothing?"

"They are still entitled to the proceeds from that insurance policy. And Gus bequeathed a token amount for both. My friend believed that would be enough to keep them quiet, to prevent them from challenging my claim."

"But this means—"

"It means, first of all, that I had motive." He brought his gaze back up to meet mine and held firm. "Even though I didn't know the terms of the will until yesterday, the fact that Gus's death is being investigated as a homicide changes everything. The boys could argue that their father was planning to change his will again—this time to include them—but before he could, I killed him."

"But you said that they didn't know the terms of the will, either."

"They still don't. They will soon enough. That doesn't mean they won't try."

I studied the dull face across the table. Could I be staring into the eyes of Gus's killer right now?

"You see why I struggled about telling you all this," he said. "As soon as the police learn the details of the will—which will happen by the end of the week, I'm told—I'll become suspect number one."

"What do you expect from me?"

"I've done homework on you," he said. "You have a reputation for finding the truth. I wanted to help you by giving you my story. The truth as I see it."

To help? I wondered. *Or to throw me off?*

"Two more things," he said, holding up a corresponding number of fingers. He grimaced, then made a very obvious assessment of the room to ensure no one could hear. He lowered his voice. "The day before Gus died, I brought him a . . . gift."

"What kind of gift?"

He glanced around the room again, then whispered, "A bottle of alcohol. In a jar with no label."

"Illegal moonshine?"

His whole body jerked. "How do you know about such things?"

315

I shook my head, reluctant to share details about a guest at Marshfield who had been murdered using the high-octane alcohol. "I have my sources."

Anton allowed a small grin. "The good news is that Gus loved the stuff. He thought it was hilarious whenever I was able to sneak it in under the nurses' noses. I brought a new supply about once a month. We barely made a dent in the newest bottle. Just had a couple of shots, then hid it in his armoire."

"What's the bad news?"

"It's missing."

"From Gus's room?"

Anton nodded. "I talked with Harland and Joslyn. They haven't seen it. Neither has Dan. They said they looked through both armoires and it wasn't there."

"Maybe the police confiscated it."

"That's what I'm afraid of. If they open the jar and figure out what it is, they'll be after me in a heartbeat."

Maybe they should be, I thought. But what I said was, "I can understand your concern."

"I know you're working with Frances's attorney. Do you think there's any way you could ask her if they found a jar of clear liquid about this size in Gus's room?" He positioned his hands to indicate. "Not knowing is killing me."

A faint memory tickled my brain. "You said he hid it in the armoire?"

"Yes," he brightened. "Have you seen it?"

"No, sorry." Though Percy had talked about sharing scotch with Kyle, he'd never mentioned anything about illegal moonshine. "But I'll make some discreet inquiries."

"I'd appreciate that."

"You said two things. What else?" I asked.

He pulled in a deep breath and blew it out. "Harland is deep in debt."

"How do you know this?"

"Gus took a great deal of pride in his business acumen. Harland has no such talent. He and Joslyn have overspent and under saved. They're facing retirement with nothing to show for it. Harland couldn't bring himself to admit his failings to Gus. And, to be fair, Gus would have ridiculed him mercilessly. Several months ago, Harland came to me and asked to borrow a significant sum."

"You gave it to him?"

Anton spread his hands. "I've known them since they were boys, remember? Harland promised that when his day came, he would pay it all back, with interest."

I thought about Tooney's report that Harland and his wife had been pricing expensive cars. "And Harland now believes his day is here?"

"I assume he does. But it isn't," Anton said. 'Now that I've seen the will."

"He's still entitled to half of that two-million-dollar policy."

"True," Anton said. "But compared to the value of the estate, that's pocket change." He glanced around the Birdcage. The place was beginning to fill up. "I've taken too much of your time," he said as he got to his feet. "I'm sorry."

"You've given me a lot to think about." We made our way toward the mansion's front doors. "Harland and Dan aren't going to be happy when they get the news."

"They'll come gunning for me, make no mistake. That's another reason why I wanted to share this with you. Harland and Dan may try to pin Gus's murder on me in the hopes of nullifying the will."

"And you wouldn't like that at all, would you?"

He caught the unspoken accusation in my words. "I'm a very wealthy man in my own right. I don't need Gus's money, and I honestly don't even want it. When my friend first fell ill, he declined rapidly. I was sure we would lose him. But after he moved into Indwell, he rallied. Gus was a grumpy guy. Maybe the fact that he had more people there to torment gave him a reason to wake up every morning." Anton chuckled. "Indwell is expensive, but it was worth every penny. If Gus had run out of money, I would have gladly shared my fortune to keep my friend happy and alive."

Despite myself, I was moved by Anton's impassioned speech.

"Remember," he said, "Harland believed his father's money was being wasted at Indwell. I'm not convinced Harland or Dan killed Gus, but if one of them did, I suspect it was because they sought to halt the financial bleed."

Before we parted at the front door, Anton grasped my shoulders and again followed with a quick kiss to each cheek. "You are a good friend to Frances. And now to Percy." He winked at me. "I only hope I have been some small help."

I waved as he made his way down the front stairs to board the estate shuttle. The minute he was gone, I dragged my cell phone from my pocket. As I crossed Marshfield's stately first floor, I dialed Bruce. His phone went directly to voice mail. "Hey, on second thought," I said in a message, "don't bother investigating Anton Holcroft for me, okay?" I debated a split second, then added, "Let me rephrase that: I'd rather you *not* contact Anton Holcroft at all."

I hung up and made my way to the staff stairway, then dialed Scott's phone. It, too, went straight to voice mail. "I'm sure I'm being overly cautious here, but humor me, okay? I'd prefer it if you and Bruce do *not* get in contact with Anton Holcroft. At all. Something has come up. I'll explain when I can. Call me."

Chapter 30

I WAITED UNTIL I WAS BACK UPSTAIRS TO place a third phone call. Frances followed me into my office. "What did Anton want? Who are you calling?"

I held up a finger as the call connected. Voice mail, yet again. At least this time I knew why I wasn't getting through. We were right in the middle of his office hours. "Joe," I began after the beep, "was there anything in Gus's autopsy report about his blood alcohol levels? Could ingesting liquor—specifically a high-alcohol-content liquor—have caused his death?"

Part of me wanted to refer to our meet-up at Hugo's the night before, but with Frances squinting at me, listening in, I thought better of it. "No rush. I know you're busy. Call me when you can."

"The Mister had to leave for a meeting." Frances nodded at the phone still in my hand. "But what's up with the alcohol? Don't tell me we've got another Dr. Keay situation here."

"Funny you should say that," I said as I dropped into my chair. "Anton apparently kept Gus supplied with illegal moonshine."

"That's what he came here to tell you?"

"There's more," I said. "Have a seat."

I shared most of what Anton had told me, including his revelation about Gus's will and Harland's financial difficulties. What I didn't share was my plan to corner Percy about the missing moonshine. I had a sneaking suspicion he knew exactly where that jar was.

JOE RETURNED MY CALL LATER THAT afternoon. "What's up?" he asked when I answered. "Why the questions about alcohol?"

I told him.

Almost as soon as I started explaining, Frances came into my office to listen in, making no secret of her eavesdropping. She leaned forward to stage-whisper, "Ask him if it could kill Gus the way it killed Dr. Keay."

I shook my head. We already knew the answer to that. Of course it could.

"First of all, the direct answer to your question is no," Joe said. "I didn't note the victim's blood alcohol level. I wasn't looking for that. I'll do so as soon as I can."

"I know it's a long shot," I said.

"Maybe Anton added a little something to the moonshine," Frances stage-whispered again, this time louder. "Maybe that's why he wants you to find the jar. Because he poisoned Gus."

The same thought had occurred to me when

Anton had first mentioned the moonshine, but I hadn't wanted to get Frances's hopes up.

"Ask him," Frances said none too quietly.

Joe gave a soft laugh. "Tell her I can hear every word she says. And, of course there's a chance Anton slipped Gus a deadly cocktail. But we won't know for sure until the screening is complete."

Frances inched closer, insinuating herself into our conversation. "If only we knew where that jar was," she said. "We could have it tested ourselves."

"The police may be testing it even as we speak," I said.

"I think we would have heard about it by now." She narrowed her eyes at me.

"I agree with Frances," Joe said. "It's either still at Indwell, or one of the sons has it stashed away."

We talked a little longer and when we hung up, Frances was still glaring. "You know where the jar is, don't you?"

I still had no intention of telling her my plan to corner Percy. "I don't know anything."

"But you have an idea."

"All I have is a hunch," I said. "I'll zip out to Indwell tomorrow and see what turns up."

"*Hmph,*" she said.

FOR THE SECOND DAY IN A ROW, THE house was silent when I arrived home after work even though both my roommates' cars were in the driveway. After greeting Bootsie, I opened the basement door and called down, "Guys?" No answer. "Bruce? Scott?"

Turning on lights as I moved through the house, I stood at the bottom of the stairs that led up to the bedroom level and called my roommates' names again.

Back in the kitchen, I searched around for a note. Finding none, I pulled out my cell phone and dialed.

Scott answered on the first ring. "Is that you, Grace?" he asked. His words were slurred. "Where are you?"

"Home," I said. "Where are you? Where's Bruce?"

"He's here. We're both here."

"Are you drunk?"

"Nah," he said. "Okay, maybe a little bit. Your friend Anton is a great guy." I could tell he pulled the phone away from his ear. I could picture him holding it out. "You want to talk to Grace?"

In the background, Anton demurred. "I already have bothered her too much today."

They were with Anton? Right now?

I called Scott's name twice before he returned to the phone. "Where are you?" I asked.

He hung up.

Hands shaking, I dialed Bruce. "Hey, Grace," he said sounding a lot less tipsy than his partner had. "What, did Scott cut you off?"

"Didn't you get my message?" I asked.

"Message?" he asked.

It didn't matter. "Where are you?"

"Hugo's," he said.

I breathed my relief.

"We spent just about the entire afternoon here with Anton," Bruce went on. "He says he'd be happy to help us set up the restaurant. Can you believe it? He's bought lots of property before and knows everything about converting places into restaurants. And he likes us. I think we're going to work really well together. Isn't that great?"

"Yeah," I said through clenched teeth. "When are you coming home?"

"We were just about to leave. Anton said he'd drive us back."

"No," I shouted. "I'll come get you."

"You don't have to do that, Grace," Bruce said.

"I want to drive past the Granite Building and take a look at it on the way back. It will be so much better if you two are with me. Plus, if you've all been drinking, he shouldn't be driving."

"He's got a driver, I think, but okay." I could practically see him shrug. "Grace is coming to get us," he said away from the phone.

"I'm leaving right now," I said. "Don't move until I get there."

Bruce laughed. "You're acting really strange tonight, Grace."

"Yeah," I said. "Just stay there, okay?"

I picked them up outside of Hugo's without incident. Anton, they said, was still inside, buying rounds for other patrons and making new friends.

"I thought you wanted to drive past the Granite Building," Bruce said when I took the turn that led home.

"Another time, maybe," I said. "My nerves are shot tonight."

"Why?" he asked.

From the backseat, Scott held up his phone. "Hey, I got a missed call from you this morning, Grace. What did you need?"

I shook my head. "Let me get you both home. We'll talk about it tomorrow."

Bruce grinned and nodded, looking like a cheery bobble-head. "Thanks for the idea about contacting Anton. As soon as he found out we were your roommates, he couldn't do enough for us."

I rubbed my forehead. Anton's visit to Marshfield this morning may have been as innocent as he'd claimed. But I'd suffered too many close calls in the past to take chances.

"Can't wait until we get to hang out with him again," Scott said as he played my voice mail message on speakerphone.

The two men stared at me when my directive was complete. "Why didn't you want us to meet him today?" Bruce asked. "What happened?"

Scott leaned forward. "You sound really upset."

Both hands gripping the steering wheel, I made the final, tight turn onto our driveway. "I'm sure he's a wonderful resource but until this business at Indwell is settled, I'd like you both to stay clear of him."

I threw the car into Park.

"Okay?" I asked.

Bruce studied me. "Yeah. Okay."

"Scott?" I asked.

He sat back and wrinkled his nose. "Am I going to remember this tomorrow?"

"I'll remind you," I said.

Chapter 31

I DID, INDEED, REMIND BRUCE AND SCOTT the next morning about avoiding Anton. I mentioned my concerns more than once because, even though both men were up early enough to join me for coffee, I had my doubts that Scott was fully awake.

"It was a good night last night," he said. With both hands wrapped around his mug, he stared out across the quiet kitchen as though reliving the evening.

"I don't understand what's got you worried," Bruce said after I'd explained a second time Anton's visit to Marshfield. "Nothing he told you makes him seem particularly guilty. Besides, he doesn't strike me as the murderous type."

"They never do," I said solemnly. "I know I'm overreacting and, the truth is, I don't believe Anton killed Gus, either. But we've all been involved in too many close calls over the years to take chances."

Scott zoned back in. "That's true."

"If he calls, put him off for a few days, all right? At least until the final lab results come in and we find out, once and for all, if Gus died a natural death."

"You got it, Grace," Bruce said. "But what about you? Are you being careful?"

I nodded. "I asked Tooney to find me whatever he can on Anton. In the meantime, I need to talk with Percy. I think he may be able to shed light on the whereabouts of that moonshine. I'd like to know what else he may be hiding."

THE DRIVE TO INDWELL SEEMED TO BE getting shorter with each visit. Maybe because, after so many trips in so few days, I no longer needed to pay close attention to road signs.

When I knocked at Percy and Kyle's apartment and received no answer, I headed for the nurses' station down the hall. Maybe, if I asked nicely, they'd use Percy's locator bracelet to find out where he was.

A nurse I'd never met before, dressed in typical staff scrubs, was in such close consultation with Debbie and Cathy that none of the three noticed my approach. They were all huddled around a trifold brochure laid open on the desk. When Debbie pointed, the unfamiliar nurse gave a gasp of surprise. Cathy grinned, as though she'd scored the exact reaction she'd expected.

When I cleared my throat, all three looked up.

"Hi." I pointed over my shoulder. "Do any of you happen to know where Percy is right now?"

Cathy patted the unfamiliar nurse's arm. "That's Grace. Frances's friend."

Debbie seemed puzzled. "We heard Frances was released on bail," she said. "We didn't expect to see you."

"Just following up on a new development."

"Oh?" Debbie's interest was clearly piqued. "What happened?"

I wasn't about to mention Anton's moonshine to staff members. "Nothing major."

The nurse asked, "Did you really solve a bunch of murders in Emberstowne? Is that why you're here? Because you're trying to solve Gus's murder now?"

Put on the spot, I demurred. "I'm only here to help."

She flicked a glance down at the trifold brochure. "Wait until you see what they found in Gus's room today."

"What is it?" I turned my head in an attempt to read the brochure upside down. "Who found it? Harland and Joslyn?"

"We found it," Cathy said, snatching the paper up from the desk. "Harland and Joslyn hadn't gotten to cleaning the bathroom yet." Waving the brochure near my face, she said, "You're going to love this. Frances is going to love this. It's the answer to her prayers." Grinning at Debbie, she added, "I only wish Santiago was here today. I'd love to see the look on his face when we show it to him."

My patience was thinner than the flimsy sheet Cathy flapped between us. "I give," I said. "What is it?"

A chime dinged softly behind Debbie. She turned to silence it. "Mrs. Anderson's occupational therapist will be here in five minutes." She focused on the other nurse. "Would you please get her ready?"

Looking disappointed to be kicked out of the conversation, the woman scuttled away.

"What did you find?" I asked again.

"Take a look," Cathy said with more than a little pride. "Won't Santiago be disappointed."

She handed me the trifold brochure. It wasn't the sort of glossy, high-quality handout used to promote everything from day trips to home security systems. This looked more like it had been downloaded from the Internet and produced on an ordinary inkjet printer.

The lack of weight and professionalism wasn't what drew my attention most, however. What made me gasp a little was the crisp blue title on the front of the fold-out page: *Your Life, Your Decision. A Helpful Guide to Death When You Choose.*

"What is this?" I didn't really expect an answer. From its bullet-point list offering links to assisted-suicide centers in Oregon, to the gentle words of support for the patient who prefers to "chart his or her own course through the end of life," I could tell precisely what it was.

Cathy and Debbie didn't say a word as I flipped the printout back and forth. "You say you found this in Gus's room?"

"Today," Cathy said.

"It looks as though Gus may have committed suicide after all," Debbie said. "I never would have expected that of him." She held up both hands and shrugged. "But we never really know what another person is thinking, do we?"

I listened only absentmindedly. "How did Harland and Joslyn miss this?" I asked.

"Like I said," Cathy said, "they hadn't finished clearing out the bathroom yet."

"Cathy called the police," Debbie said. "They're coming by to pick it up."

"I'm sure they'll dust it for fingerprints," I said, disappointed in myself for touching it without thinking. "Unfortunately, our prints will be all over it."

"They can dust paper for fingerprints?" Debbie asked.

"Definitely," I said. "I wish I would have thought of that sooner." Pinching the upper right corner, I asked, "Could you make a copy for me?"

Cathy's eyes widened. "What do you plan to do with it?"

"I'll read it over," I said. "This feels odd. I want a chance to study it."

As Cathy turned away to make the requested copy, Debbie's attention was drawn to something behind me. Her face registered surprise. "Dan," she called.

I glanced up to see him on a purposeful path to his father's former apartment. He wore a vexed expression and carried a small, empty cardboard box in one hand.

"Dan," she called again as she waved him over, "come see what we found in your father's room."

Dan halted midstride, then trotted over. "What's going on?" he asked, looking as surprised by my presence as Cathy and Debbie had been. "Nice to see you again, Grace."

"You're here to clean out more of your father's things?" I directed my gaze to the box.

"Yeah," he said. "We still have a long way to go."

"Wait until you see this," Cathy said.

She started to hand him the folded sheet.

"Give him the copy," I said. "Put the original in a plastic bag until the police get here."

She rolled her eyes but acquiesced, handing him the reproduction.

Agitated, probably by my directive, Dan grabbed the proffered sheet with both hands. "What is this?"

"Good news," Cathy said. Her brow furrowed. "Or maybe not good news. I guess it depends on your perspective. Your dad had it in his room. Hidden in the bathroom."

It didn't take long for Dan to grasp the obvious.

"This is ridiculous. My father didn't commit suicide."

Cathy seemed pleased as punch. "That probably doesn't help with your dad's insurance policy, does it? But at least he wasn't murdered."

Dan pulled in his lips.

"This isn't proof," I said.

"But it could help Frances," Debbie said. "Maybe even enough to get the charges dropped."

"Who found this?" I asked.

Cathy raised a tiny pink hand. "Me and Debbie. We found it together."

"You found it together?" Dan asked.

Debbie shrugged. "The administration wanted us to assess how much longer we thought you and your family might need to clear the room out. Cathy and I went in to take a look around."

Dan kept turning the paper over and over as though he couldn't believe what it said. "This looks like it was printed from a computer," he said. "My dad didn't use computers."

"Maybe he had someone print it for him? Maybe Kyle did it?" Cathy said helpfully. "That kid is always messing with technology."

Dan frowned.

"Where did you find it?" I asked. "Would you mind showing me?"

Another chime sounded. Debbie silenced it. "I have to take care of a patient."

"I'll show you," Cathy said. "Follow me."

Dan and I fell into step behind her, and I was surprised that she didn't bother knocking before entering the apartment. She did, however, call out, "Yoo-hoo, anyone here?" before allowing us in. "Percy and Kyle must be out," she said with a careless shrug. "Not surprising."

"Any idea where Percy could be?" I asked. "I have a couple of questions for him."

Cathy wrinkled her nose. "Either playing cards in the Sun Gallery or out at one of the other buildings. Flirting with the ladies, most likely."

"He does that?"

She laughed. "He's a hoot, that one."

As we followed Cathy into Gus's room, Dan asked, "What kind of questions do you have for Percy? Does it have to do with my dad's death?"

"A couple of tangential issues," I answered vaguely. "Probably nothing. I hope to find out for sure today."

I got the impression Dan intended to press the issue. I shook my head with a pointed look at Cathy. She missed the silent interchange entirely. He gave a quick nod.

Cathy led us into Gus's bathroom. "It was in here," she said, tapping the cabinet beneath the sink. She crouched in front of the vanity doors and opened them. "Right there."

She pointed to the stack of toilet paper I'd sorted through on Monday. I knelt down next to her and peered in. "Where, exactly?" I asked.

She picked up the two top rolls of toilet paper and rested her hand on the two that remained. "In between these rolls," she said. "Like he was trying to hide it so nobody would notice."

"You're sure?" I asked.

"I saw it myself. I'm the one who found it," she said with a hint of defensiveness. "Of course I'm sure."

"This doesn't seem at all like something my dad would look into," Dan said again. His tone had taken on a quality that suggested stating something enough times would somehow make it true.

As we returned to Gus's bedroom, Cathy's pager went off. She took a look at its display. "Oops, gotta run," she said. "One of our patients is going home today. Almost forgot." Pointing at Dan, she said, "You can stay, because you're still cleaning out your dad's room." She waved her extended finger at me. "But you have to go. I can't allow you in here unsupervised when the residents aren't home."

"I'd like to stay a minute and talk with Dan," I said.

He startled. "You do?"

"You have to take responsibility for her, then," Cathy said. "Do you?"

"Grace? Are you in there? Debbie said you were looking for me."

Percy. Perfect timing. "In here," I called.

335

Cathy grinned. "I guess it's okay for you to stay now."

"Give me a minute," Percy shouted when she was gone. "I need to go to my room."

Dan wore a guarded expression. "What did you want to talk with me about?"

"That pamphlet you're holding."

"My dad didn't commit suicide." The paper made *whoppy* noises as he shook it. "This is wrong."

"Someone put it there," I said. "After your father died."

His mouth opened. Then closed. "How do you know that?" He tilted his head. "Do you know *who* put it there?"

"No idea," I said. "That's what I wanted to talk with you about. If your father committed suicide, his insurance policy is invalid, right?"

"He didn't commit suicide. Not my dad." He shook the paper again. "How do you know someone put this here?"

"Remember when you caught me looking around in your father's bathroom on Monday?"

He rubbed his shar-pei face looking like a man who had lost all patience. "I remember."

"I had already gone through that cabinet," I said. "I emptied its entire contents onto the floor and poked through it all before replacing it. I'd planned to do the same thing with his linen closet but you walked in and interrupted me before I could get started."

"Are you saying that this pamphlet wasn't there?" he asked.

"That's exactly what I'm saying."

He blinked several times as he digested that information. "What do you suppose is going on?" he asked.

"I see two possibilities," I said. "Either someone wants to invalidate your insurance claim, or someone wants the police to believe Gus wasn't murdered."

At that moment, Percy rolled in. "Why were you looking for me?" he asked. "How's Frances? Is she coming out to see me tomorrow? Do you know?"

Dan looked like someone who'd been smacked upside the head with a two-by-four. I decided to give him time to process my theories before I asked him about likely pamphlet-planting suspects. But I had my own suspicions in that matter.

"Percy," I said. "Just the man I'm looking for."

He narrowed his eyes. "I don't like the sound of that."

"Do you remember when Dan caught me digging through his father's toiletries on Monday?" I asked as I pointed toward the bathroom. "Of course you do. The minute Dan showed up, you scurried back in here."

"What of it?"

I waited.

Percy squirmed in his wheelchair.

"Where is it, Percy?" I asked.

Next to me, Dan looked utterly befuddled.

Percy raised his chin defiantly. "Where's what?"

"You know what I'm looking for," I said. "Gus's moonshine. The jar Anton brought him last week."

Obviously dumbfounded, Dan pointed at Percy. "He has it?" To Percy: "*You* have it?"

Percy's mouth twitched and he looked away.

Dan started to pace again. "Anton's been bugging me and Harland about that." Still holding the brochure copy, he raised both hands to hold his head. "I don't know what's going on around here anymore. Everybody's got secrets."

"What difference does it make?" Percy asked me. "Gus didn't need it anymore."

"Where is it?" I asked again. "In your room? That's why you didn't want me following you in there on Monday, isn't it? While Dan cornered me in here, you were busy hiding it in your room, weren't you?"

"I guess I can't pull anything over on you, Miss Detective."

"Let's go," I said. "Show me where it is."

We followed Percy across the man-cave and into his bedroom. Although he groused mightily, he led us to a pile of books on a shelf next to his refrigerator. The jar of moonshine was tucked behind the small stack.

"Why?" I asked.

The jar's contents sloshed as he heaved it onto the windowsill. "Why shouldn't I take it? Kyle and I both had to put up with having Gus as a roommate, but he always invited Kyle—never me—to share his stash. I deserved some, too."

The jar appeared to be three-quarters full. "How much have you had?"

"Only one shot a night since Monday."

"Any ill effects?" I asked. "Any unexplained reactions?"

"Worried about me, are you?" A corner of Percy's mouth quirked up. "Nah, I'm fine. Same as always."

"How did the police miss this?" I asked.

"Beats me," Percy said. "I heard this was their first homicide. They've probably got a lot to learn."

Dan stared up at the ceiling. "I don't know what to make of this."

"What's with him?" Percy asked.

I stepped closer to Dan and slid the pamphlet out of his hand. Dan regarded me curiously, but didn't stop me.

I dropped the paper onto Percy's lap. "Now tell me about this."

He edged his hand close to the edge of the page, tapping to straighten it. Squinting down at it, he asked, "What are you talking about? What is this?"

"Cathy found this in Gus's bathroom."

I gave him a moment to absorb its meaning. When he finished, he used the side of his hand to shove it away, as though wanting to distance himself from it. "Gus wouldn't have even entertained the idea of assisted suicide. Not for a minute. Besides, this looks like it was printed off a computer. Gus didn't use computers."

"I don't believe Gus left it there," I said. "It wasn't there on Monday when I went through the cabinet."

"So why are you showing it to me?"

"Why did you leave it in Gus's bathroom cabinet?"

Percy's reaction—surprised confusion—seemed genuine. "I've never seen that paper before."

"Really?" Although I believed him, I decided to press to be certain. "You didn't think that planting seeds of doubt by making the police believe Gus had considered suicide would help take the heat off Frances?"

Sudden comprehension dawned, suffusing his face with stunned delight. "It could, couldn't it?" he said. "Wish I'd thought of it. But no, sorry to say. I didn't."

I took it back. "If you didn't plant it there, who did?"

We both turned to Dan.

"Do you have any ideas?" I asked.

He shook his head. "I'm fresh out of them."

Chapter 32

AS I PREPARED TO LEAVE THE APARTMENT, I hoisted my purse onto my shoulder and tied my spring jacket around its straps. I'd wrapped one of Percy's hand towels around the jar of moonshine so as not to add my fingerprints to whatever evidence lingered there, and tucked the toweled burden into the crook of my elbow.

I'd gotten as far as the man-cave with my parcels when the apartment door opened and Debbie walked in. With her were the two detectives, Nieman and Madigan. Madigan held the clear plastic bag containing the trifold brochure.

"Oh good, you found Percy," Debbie said to me before turning to Dan. "I was about to show these two officers where Cathy and I found your father's brochure."

"My father didn't commit suicide," Dan said to the two detectives. "Ask Grace here. She'll tell you." He nudged my arm. "Tell them what you told me. That this paper was planted in his room."

Madigan blew out an exasperated sigh. "What now, Ms. Wheaton?"

As I explained the situation, Nieman took notes.

"Could you have missed it when you were here Monday?" Madigan asked.

"Not a chance," I said. "I took that cabinet's contents out and put each item back one at a time. It wasn't there."

"Why were you going through Mr. Westburg's belongings?" Nieman asked.

I hesitated. "I thought I'd see if anything had been overlooked."

"You mean by us?" Madigan asked.

"Or the evidence techs. Whoever searched Gus's room."

"That would be us," she said.

"Doesn't matter why she was in there," Nieman said. "What matters is that she says this paper wasn't there Monday. Would you swear to that?" she asked me.

"Absolutely."

Madigan frowned. "I don't get you. This is the first inkling we have that Mr. Westburg may have contemplated suicide. If he did, then your friend Frances is off the hook. Why volunteer information that can't help her?"

"Because it's the truth," I said. "And the more truth we all have, the quicker we'll find out how Gus really died." Before Madigan could dismiss me, I said, "And then there's this." I held up the towel-wrapped jar of moonshine.

The two detectives exchanged a look.

"Care to explain?" Madigan asked.

I did, finishing with "Now that we've recovered it, I assume you'll want to take it to the lab to have the contents tested for poison."

Nieman scratched the side of her head. "Are you saying we missed this when we removed items from the victim's room on Sunday?"

"Apparently so."

Madigan glared at Percy. "Does the term 'tampering with evidence' mean anything to you?"

Percy looked away.

I handed the jar to Nieman. "I'm sure Percy will be happy to cooperate with your department if it means getting to the truth. Right, Percy?"

He didn't answer.

"Even if we do find reason to suspect that Anton Holcroft killed the victim, the fact that this jar was removed from the room could hinder our investigation," Madigan said. "There's a thing called chain of custody that applies to evidence."

I knew that, but I also knew that this revelation had the potential to help Frances's case. A lot.

Madigan worked her jaw. "You," she said to me, while pointing to the red sofa, "wait here." Turning to Debbie, she said, "You show me where this paper was found."

I sat on the red sofa, dropping my jacket and purse next to me. Percy pulled up and sat to my left. Dan stared after the nurse and cops as they disappeared into his father's room.

"I don't know anything anymore," he said. "I just don't know."

Percy stared at his hands in his lap.

A few minutes later, the threesome emerged. "Okay, now your turn," Madigan said to me. Turning to Percy, she added, "You, too. Show me where you hid this."

"What difference would that make?"

"We like to be thorough, okay?" Madigan said.

She and Nieman followed us into Percy's room, where he dutifully pointed out his hidey-hole. "Right there," he said. "I had it behind those books."

Madigan expanded a telescoping baton and used the narrow end to explore the area for a couple of minutes. She may have been seeking to appear official, but she came across as petty and desperate. Nieman stared over her partner's shoulder.

"Finding lots of clues in there, Officer?" Percy taunted.

With tiny taps, Madigan continued to poke around. "What else did you take from Gus's room?" she asked without looking up.

"Nothing," Percy said. He turned to me with accusation in his eyes. "What did you tell her?"

I held both hands up. "All I knew about was the moonshine," I said. *And the factory-sealed scotch,* I thought. But that had been taken from Anton directly, not from Gus. "Why, is there more?"

Percy glared at me.

Nieman turned to face him. "Fess up now and I'll consider overlooking your infraction."

"You think I could have managed to sneak out more than one jar?" He held up fingers that resembled crooked twigs. "With these hands?"

"You could have gone through Gus's room before I got here," I said.

His glare intensified. "You're not helping matters."

"I'm trying to help Frances."

"Fine," he said. "The truth is, I'd completely forgotten about the moonshine until Grace asked to see Gus's room. When we were in there, I remembered it and thought that—if the opportunity arose—I'd grab it. The opportunity did arise and I took it." He stared up at Madigan. "That's the truth. You want to handcuff me and wheel me in on charges, have at it. I've got nothing else to tell you."

The detectives must have believed him, because they exchanged an uneasy glance. Madigan gave a brisk nod. "Let's go," she said.

Debbie and Dan were waiting for us in the man-cave. He still held on to the copy of the assisted-suicide brochure.

"May I see that a moment?" I asked.

"This? Why? You said yourself that my dad couldn't have put it there."

"That's actually the copy Grace asked us to

make." Debbie winked at me as she tugged the paper out of Dan's hands. "I'll go make another copy for you, okay?"

"Thank you," I said.

After she left, the police asked a few more questions, then—apparently satisfied—took off themselves. Debbie returned moments later. "Here you go," she said as she handed one copy of the brochure to me and another to Dan. "I made one for our files, too. Just in case."

Dan didn't thank her. "I'm not happy about this. Not happy at all."

Percy shrugged. "I'm probably in trouble."

"Let's worry about that later," I said as I grabbed my things. "Right now I'm thrilled to be able to tell Frances that there are two interesting developments that can help point the police in the right direction."

"Away from her," Percy said.

"Exactly." I nodded. "I was hoping Gus died a natural death. Right now, it's looking more and more as though someone murdered him. With any luck, today's developments will put the police solidly on the guilty party's trail."

I RETURNED TO MARSHFIELD IN A TRIUM- phant mood. Even though we were no closer to figuring out what had truly happened to Gus, I believed we were a lot closer to clearing Frances's name. After alerting Lily Holland and sharing the updates with our homicide detectives, Frances, Bennett, and I gathered in my office for the last half hour of the workday before we took off for the weekend.

"I knew you'd find evidence to help me," Frances said. Turning to Bennett, she added, "Of course, it took her a little longer because I wasn't able to help, but we knew she'd come through eventually, didn't we?"

"Let's not celebrate yet," I said, though I was finding it hard to tamp down my own good cheer. "The police won't back off their interest in you until there's something more substantial to work with than a planted pamphlet and a renegade jar of moonshine."

"But it may be enough for Lily to work with," Bennett said.

"It may."

"Good. Then that's settled." Frances crossed her arms.

"What is?" Bennett asked.

"I'm visiting Percy tomorrow."

"Going back to Indwell?" I asked, aghast. "No. Not a good idea. Didn't Lily tell you to stay away from the place until you were completely cleared?"

"She *encouraged* me to stay away from Indwell. She didn't forbid me to go."

"I don't think it's a good idea, Frances," Bennett said. "Let's give Grace and the police a little more time."

"With very few exceptions, I always visit Percy on weekends. Tomorrow is Saturday, and I refuse to stay locked up in my own house because some toddler detectives think they have a case against me."

"I wouldn't risk it," I said.

"Good thing I'm not letting you decide then, isn't it?" she said. "I'm convinced that we're on the right track now. And I refuse to miss my weekend visit."

Bennett and I exchanged helpless glances.

"It comes down to this," Frances said. "I've got nothing to worry about, do I? And yet, I've been cowering back here at Marshfield like I'm scared they'll find out the truth. Well, I know the truth. I'm innocent. And it's about time I start acting like it."

When I opened my mouth to protest further, she pointed at me. "Not another word. Tomorrow I'm going to Indwell."

Bennett pinched his lips together.

"Fine," I said. "Then I'm going with you."

She blinked, clearly surprised. A second later, she shook her head. "I plan to stay at a nearby hotel and not come back to Emberstowne until Sunday. You have to let me go on my own."

"Until this is over, not a chance," I said. "I'll pack a bag."

Chapter 33

FRANCES HAD A FEW ERRANDS TO RUN Saturday, so I picked her up a little after noon. "I made reservations for both of us at the hotel," she said when she got in. "Not that Rosette is a hotbed of entertainment or anything, but you never know when some local event fills a place up. I didn't want to risk you being shut out." She faked a shudder. "Or, heaven forbid, we have to share a room."

When we got to Indwell, a new face greeted us at the lobby desk. "Cathy's not in today, I take it?" I asked her.

The young woman, barely out of her teens, smiled up at us. "She called in sick. Did you need her for something?"

"No, thank you," I said. "We're fine."

"Who are you here to visit?" she asked with a glance at the registry where Frances was signing us in.

"Percy Sliwa."

"Do you know the way?"

Frances snorted and rolled her eyes.

"We do, thanks," I said.

349

We knocked at Percy's apartment. He called out, "Be right there."

When the door swung open, I watched his expression shift from relief at seeing Frances to dismay at my presence, to resignation that manifested itself into a tepid smile.

"Good to see you," he said, rolling to accompany Frances as she made her way in. "I wasn't sure you'd be willing to come out this weekend."

"When has anyone been able to stop me from what I want to do?" she asked.

"True enough." He slid me a sideways glance. "Although I didn't expect a chaperone."

"Hmph," Frances said. "Turns out when Grace sets her mind to do something, there's no talking her out of it. She's a lot like me that way."

If he intended to protest my presence further, he held back. "I suppose she told you about the moonshine too, did she?"

Frances positioned herself in front of her ex-husband, feet set shoulder-width apart, fists at her hips, peering at him over the tops of her half-moon glasses. "What else do you have in your room that you shouldn't have?" she asked.

"Not a thing."

"Oh, really," she asked without budging. "So you won't mind me doing a little spring cleaning in there today, will you?"

Kyle emerged from his room just then. "Hey, cool. Fireworks." He grinned up at me. "How ya doing, Grace?" he asked. Before I could answer, he zipped past me to join Frances. "What was it like in jail? Did you get strip-searched?"

"Certainly not," she said, her cheeks flaming red. "What is wrong with you?"

He smiled again. "We get bored here all day doing nothing. Gus's murder and your arrest are the most exciting things that have happened here in forever. I heard about that assisted-suicide brochure. Any idea who put it in Gus's room?"

"Did you?" I asked.

"Ha!" Kyle seemed amused by the idea. "No, but I wish I'd thought of it. People are going nuts about it. That's all everybody talked about yesterday."

"I imagine," I said. "Who's here today? I know Cathy called in sick."

"Did she?" He twisted his head from side to side. "I know Santiago's here; I've seen him. I think it's Debbie's day off. Maybe Tara's, too."

"Did any of them have anything of interest to share about the brochure?" I asked. "Was there discussion as to who may have planted it in Gus's room?"

He shook his head. "Not that I can remember. They had a lot to say about that moonshine, though. Debbie thinks the police will probably arrest Anton next."

"Speaking of the moonshine," Frances said to

351

Percy, "your friend here is trying to distract me, but I'm not falling for it. What else do you have in your room? Or should Grace and I head in there now to have a look?"

"Sorry, bro. I tried," Kyle said as he headed away. He hit the metal panel on the wall and turned back to us as the door swung open. "Don't miss me too much while I'm gone, okay?"

"Yeah, sure." Percy dragged his attention back to us when his roommate was gone. "It's beautiful outside today, Frannie. Want to go for a walk?" With a glance at me, he added, "You can come, too."

Frances sidestepped his wheelchair and made a beeline for his room.

"Okay, okay," Percy said as he zoomed after her. "I give."

Curious as to what would happen next, I followed. Percy's room was as cluttered as it had been the last time I was here. The only difference between that visit and now was Frances's glowering presence in the room's center. "Well?" she asked. "Where is it? Or should I start digging on my own?"

Percy took his sweet time. I hadn't realized what an unpleasant sight a pouting man could be. He rolled to the cabinet opposite his refrigerator and leaned forward to open its right-hand door. I got the distinct impression he was exaggerating the difficulty accessing his storage spaces, but every time Frances attempted to assist, he snapped a refusal.

"Have a seat," she said to me. "This may take a while."

She claimed the easy chair with the wildlife afghan, while I settled myself in the one with the motorcycle-themed throws. We talked a little about the case, about Marshfield, anything to pass the time. All the while, she watched Percy's movements with such attentiveness I wondered if she was making a mental log of his hiding spots to remember later.

By the time he'd completed his slow-motion collecting, Percy had amassed seven airline-sized bottles of liquor. One by one, he painstakingly transferred them from his lap to Frances's. Three vodkas, four gins.

"That's all of it," he announced with a measure of pride. "Happy now?"

Frances picked up each of the bottles in turn, examining them. "And not one of them have been opened yet," she said.

"See?" he said sounding like a plaintive four-year-old. "I haven't been pushing any limits at all."

"Imagine that." She gathered all seven bottles as she got to her feet. "Hold on to these, will you?" she asked as she placed them in my lap. "I have a feeling he may have missed a spot or two."

Percy's silent pout morphed into an all-out

whine. "Wait, no. Frances, come on. You know I didn't—"

Too late. She removed a small stack of books from atop a shoe box that sat on a waist-high shelf near the windows. Lifting the shoe box, she shook it. Even sitting across the room, I could hear the sloshing liquid inside. She replaced the box on the shelf, lifted the lid, and smiled beatifically at Percy. "Oh, look what I found here." She hoisted a bottle of gin and swirled it around. About half its contents were still intact. "Haven't been pushing your limits at all, have you?"

She placed the bottle on the floor next to me and returned to digging.

By the time Frances finished searching the room, she'd amassed three half-full bottles of vodka, two of gin, and two unopened bottles of anisette, all of which she piled up around my chair.

"How many of these did you take from Gus's room?" I asked.

Percy didn't answer me.

"We have to give these to the police, Frances."

"Hello in there?"

The three of us turned to face Santiago in the doorway. He held a blue-capped syringe aloft. "I'm looking for Kyle—again—it's time for one of his special meds." Before any of us could answer, he noticed the mountain of liquor at my feet. "Well, what do we have here?"

"I didn't take these from Gus," Percy said. "He gave them to Kyle but his parents get all worked up if they find liquor in his room. They think alcohol is the work of the devil. So he keeps it in here."

"You really expect us to believe that?" I asked.

"It's the truth."

"Kyle's not here?" Santiago asked. "His locator bracelet says . . ." The nurse shook his head. "That kid. He left it here again, didn't he?"

At that moment, my cell phone rang. Bruce. I left the little bottles on my chair and stepped out into the man-cave to take the call.

"Grace, good news," he said when I picked up. "The bank says they'll have preliminary paperwork ready for us next week. Would you be able to swing by their offices Monday morning to sign a few documents?"

"Absolutely," I said. "What time?"

"We can make it whatever time is convenient for you. The documents they're requiring are basically you promising to fund the purchase of the Granite Building if the inspection goes through. Because Scott and I can't afford the purchase on our own, the bank won't move forward without proof that you're committed to this venture."

"I'll be there. Can we do it early on Monday? Maybe about eight in the morning? I can stop at the bank on my way to work."

"Perfect, I'll set it up. How are things going with Frances?" he asked.

I turned as she, Percy, and Santiago emerged from Percy's room. Frances carried five of the liquor bottles. She deposited them on the floor near the sofa and returned to Percy's room for the rest.

"Interesting," I said.

"Got it. You can't talk."

Frances stacked the two unopened bottles next to the first five, then went back for the seven little airline versions.

"That's right. See you when I get home tomorrow," I said.

As I ended the call, the apartment door opened, and Kyle rolled in. He spotted Santiago at the same moment the nurse spotted him. "There you are," Santiago said with an exultant grin.

"I was just coming back for my locator bracelet," Kyle said, fooling no one.

"Sure you were." Santiago raised the syringe he carried. "Don't worry—this won't hurt a bit."

"Liar," Kyle said.

Frances returned. From the clinking sounds coming from her purse, I knew she'd stuffed all the small bottles inside.

After donning purple latex gloves from a box on the wall, Santiago approached Kyle. He grimaced.

I don't know why I chose to watch, but I did. Santiago rolled up Kyle's sleeve, ripped open a sanitizing wipe, and cleaned the young man's upper arm. "If Kyle here would agree to wear a heparin lock," Santiago said, "we could administer these injections without any pain whatsoever."

"Stick me all you like, I refuse to wear one of those things. They get in the way when I'm playing video games."

Santiago held Kyle's skin taut with one hand and brought the still-capped syringe up with his other. Using his teeth, he yanked the blue cap off the top of the syringe and plunged the needle into Kyle's smooth arm.

Kyle clenched his eyes.

Two seconds later, it was done. Santiago removed the needle. "There, that wasn't so bad, was it?" As he spoke, the blue cap tumbled from its perch between his teeth. Santiago swooped to pick it up.

I turned to Frances whose brows had jumped high on her head. She'd seen it, too.

"What?" Percy asked.

"Nothing," we said in unison.

"What is up with you two?" Santiago asked as he bandaged Kyle's arm and rolled his sleeve back down.

"Not a thing," I said.

Frances stood staring, eyes wide. I knew exactly what she was thinking.

Santiago shrugged and pointed. "What do you plan to do with all that liquor you found?"

Kyle noticed the pile on the floor. "They found my liquor?"

Frances regained her composure. "Yes, we did," she said. "And we're getting rid of it."

Santiago made a *tsk*ing noise. "And now that Gus is gone, good luck replenishing your stash, boys," he said. "Nice job, ladies."

"You won't really get rid of it all, will you?" Kyle asked. Like Percy had earlier, he sounded like a whiny toddler. "My parents don't understand. I may be disabled, but I'm an adult. I have every right to drink in the privacy of my own home."

Santiago had deposited the used syringe in the medical waste box on the wall and began stripping off his latex gloves. "The only reason we go through Kyle's room searching for contraband is because his parents demand it. There's no medical reason Kyle can't enjoy a drink now and then. In moderation, that is. But because his parents are the ones paying the bills, we have to do what they say. Of course, if Percy keeps all this in his room, then Kyle's parents will have nothing to complain about, will they?" He gave one of his scary giant grins. "I won't tell if you won't."

"Frannie, honey," Percy said. "You can't be so hard-hearted. Leave us the open bottles, will you? I promise I won't overdo. Kyle promises, too, don't you, Kyle?"

"I know my limits," Kyle said. "I don't get

drunk. I just want to feel like a normal person. Don't take that away from me."

"I don't know," she said, but I could tell she was wavering.

"You can take those two unopened bottles," Percy said. "Gus loved anisette, but neither Kyle nor I can stand the stuff."

"Then why did you keep it?" I asked.

Percy shrugged. "Any port in a storm, you know? If we ran out of the good stuff, we'd still have that, at least." Turning his pleading face toward Frances, he said, "If it makes you feel better, take it away. But leave us the open stuff. We're adults, Frances. Disabled maybe, but still adults. Don't treat us like children."

Shaking her head, she began pulling the tiny bottles from her purse, lining them up on a side table. "Fine," she said. "But if I find out that either of you is misbehaving . . ."

Percy and Kyle shared a conspiratorial grin. "You won't."

"You two can put these away, then," she said. "Back in your little secret hiding places."

Kyle zoomed over to the table and began placing the small bottles in his lap, one at a time. "Thanks, Frances. You're all right."

Santiago held both hands over his eyes. "I'm not seeing any of this," he said. When he uncovered his eyes, he winked. "By the way, it's almost dinnertime. I assume you ladies will be joining these two." A moment later, he was gone.

"You hear that, Kyle?" Percy shouted. "Time to strap on the feed bag."

"Yeah, yeah."

Frances handed me one of the bottles of anisette. "I can fit one in my purse, can you fit this one?" she asked. "I don't want to be seen carrying these out of Indwell. Who knows what the staff would report to the police then."

I wasn't sure this was the best idea she'd ever had, but I desperately wanted to leave—I needed to talk with Frances, away from Indwell. I shoved the bottle into my cavernous purse. "Are you ready to go?" I asked.

"Yes," she said.

"But you usually stay and have dinner with me on Saturday nights," Percy said.

Frances patted his shoulder. "Not tonight. Grace and I have a few things to discuss."

"Like what?" he asked. "It has to do with Kyle's injection, doesn't it? I saw the look that passed between you two. What was that about?"

Before Frances could answer, I interrupted. "We'll tell you later," I said. "Right now we need to make a few phone calls."

"You can't do that after dinner?"

"We'll be back later," I said. "Come on, Frances. Let's go."

She didn't need urging. "We'll be back later," she repeated.

Chapter 34

"WE NEED TO CALL LILY HOLLAND," I SAID as Frances and I hurried out to the car.

"She told me that they checked the syringes and caps for fingerprints," she said. "But she never mentioned testing for DNA."

The moment we'd seen Santiago pull the syringe cap off with his teeth, the proverbial lightbulb had switched on over both of our heads. If someone had injected Gus's heparin lock with insulin, there was a good chance he or she had used the same method Santiago had. Although the killer may have taken the precaution of donning gloves before doing the deed, he or she may have never considered the possibility that saliva—and therefore DNA—had transferred to the caps.

I pulled up my phone and dialed.

"Lily," I said when the lawyer answered. "This is Grace Wheaton. I'm here with Frances at Indwell."

"She went to Indwell? I asked her not to."

"Yes, I understand. But that's not important right now."

"Does she realize how—"

"Lily," I said firmly to grab her attention. "We

need to know if the insulin syringe caps—from the empty vials found in Percy's room—are being tested for DNA."

"Not that I'm aware of. Why would they?"

I explained what we'd witnessed when Santiago gave Kyle his injection. "Whoever killed Gus—if anyone did—may have handled the syringe the same way. There could be DNA trace evidence on those syringe caps."

"Hmm," she said. I could tell she was taking notes. "I'll check with the Rosette police to see if they've ordered DNA tests. If not, I'll request them myself."

"This could be exactly the break we're looking for." I could barely contain my glee.

"Could be. But don't get your hopes up. They could also come up completely clear. Remember, my job isn't to find the guilty party. My job is to exonerate Frances."

"With any luck, we can manage both at the same time."

"Yes, well," she said with far less exuberance than I'd hoped for. "I'll be in touch. In the meantime, please ask Frances to steer clear of Indwell."

"She plans to come back tonight," I said. "And probably tomorrow morning as well."

Lily let out an aggrieved sigh. "You'll be with her?"

"Every minute."

"Keep her out of trouble."

Frances had heard every word. "She expects *you* to keep *me* out of trouble?" she asked when I hung up. "I never encountered so much trouble until you arrived in Emberstowne. *Hmph.*"

I debated, then called Joe, reasoning that he might be interested in this new development. He didn't answer but then again, it was Saturday evening. I supposed he might be out. On a date, perhaps. I didn't leave a message.

"What are you frowning about?" Frances asked when I hung up.

"I'm not frowning," I lied. "I'm starting to get hungry. That affects my mood."

"Hmph," she said. "Let's check into the hotel and then grab a bite before we come back."

"Let me call Tooney first."

He answered on the first ring. "What's up, Grace?" he asked in a very quiet voice.

"Can you talk?" I asked.

"I can listen."

When I told him our DNA theory, he gave a low whistle. "That's excellent," he said. "Good thinking."

"Where are you?" I asked. "I know you were planning to follow Anton today."

"Yes. I'm still here. Our friend is in a meeting."

"Anyone I know?"

"Two people. A couple."

"Harland and Joslyn?"

"Bingo."

"Where are you? Can you tell me that?"

"Sorry, I won't be able to make it over tonight," he said conversationally. "Having dinner at a place about fifty miles away."

"Got it. You're able to hear what they're talking about?"

"Some. I'll get back to you later."

"Thanks, Tooney," I said.

When I got off the phone, I grinned. "I finally feel as though we're making headway." I pulled out of Indwell's parking lot and started out the long driveway. "Do you mind if we grab dinner before we check in? I wasn't kidding about being hungry."

"Suit yourself." She rattled off the names of several restaurants in town.

"That one," I said. "Vern's Steak House."

"It isn't much of a steakhouse," she said. "More like a diner that offers steak as an option."

"Tooney mentioned that one. He said that Dan eats there almost every night. Maybe we'll run into him."

"Oh?" she asked with a suggestive eyebrow waggle. "Dan's a single guy and you're hoping to accidentally—on purpose—run into him?"

"Yeah, right," I said. "Where is this place?"

"Take a left out of the front gate," she said. "Why *do* you want to run into him, if I may ask?"

"There was something odd in his manner yesterday. When he came in and found out about that assisted-suicide brochure, he reacted peculiarly."

"How so?"

"I can't put my finger on it, but I'd almost have to say that he took the news personally."

"Maybe it *was* personal," Frances said. "Make another right at the third stoplight."

"Personal as in: Someone wants Dan to lose out on his share of two million dollars, you mean?"

"Why would anyone care?"

"Why, indeed? But that absolves Harland and Joslyn, because suicide would leave them high and dry, too," I said.

"Who dislikes Dan or Harland enough to want to cause them trouble?"

"I haven't detected any animosity from the staff members," I said. "I honestly believe that whoever killed Gus is the one who planted the brochure. The killer probably got scared and hoped to convince the police to drop the case."

"It won't help anybody now, not after you've told everyone that the brochure was planted."

I took the turn at the third stoplight. "If someone did kill Gus, they've gotten sloppy."

"Being scared of getting caught will do that to you." She pointed. "Right there. Vern's Steak House."

"You're right," I said as I slowed to pull into the adjacent parking lot. "It looks like a converted franchise restaurant."

An instrumental rendition of a '70s disco tune greeted us as we pulled open the restaurant's glass doors. We made our way past a proud showcase of plastic pastries, stopping at the waist-high PLEASE WAIT TO BE SEATED sign. The diminutive hostess couldn't have been older than seventeen. "Two?" she asked as she grabbed napkins and flatware from a gray bin. "Booth or a table?"

"Booth, please," I said.

The busy restaurant was set up like a large inverted L. The hostess led us to a window booth in the first section, which overlooked and ran parallel to the main street. The second section veered off at a right angle to my left. From where I sat, I could see only about a quarter of the tables there. As soon as we were left alone with our menus, I told Frances that I'd wanted to zip over to the ladies' room to have a look around. "Maybe Dan's seated in the back section," I said.

"And if he is, you plan on casually striking up a conversation?"

"Why not?" I asked.

"He's one of the few people who's insisted from the start that his father died naturally," she said. "I suppose that's something."

"Yes, but I'm telling you that his reaction yesterday was off. I'd like the chance to talk with him about it away from Indwell. He may feel less intimidated and be more likely to open up."

Frances opened her menu. "Suit yourself."

I scooched sideways out of the booth and made my way across the restaurant, scanning the tables of both sections as I headed for the washroom. There was a waitstaff station positioned in the center of the gateway between the two rooms. Two waitresses—both in their mid-thirties, I guessed—stood there. The first one, inputting an order into the restaurant's computer terminal, had short, shiny hair that was so black it looked blue. She pointedly ignored her colleague, who was merrily chatting and complaining as she combined coffee from three glass carafes into a fourth.

As I made my way around them, I stopped short.

"Are you okay?" the computer inputter asked when I grabbed the edge of the wait station.

Dan—his profile was unmistakable—sat with his back to the washroom wall. I opened my mouth but hesitated before answering. It wasn't his presence that had startled me into silence. It was that of his companion.

Seated facing my direction, Debbie leaned in close to him, staring intently at him from the side. Her lips were moving, very quickly.

"Yes," I said. "I'm . . . yes. Fine."

Instinctively, I ducked sideways behind the wait station's shoulder-high shelf. Lined with bright ketchup and mustard bottles, it provided enough cover for me to study the couple's interactions unseen. With his hands fisted inside one another atop the table before him, Dan shook his head. Debbie leaned closer, spoke faster. They were too far, there was too much chatter and clanking, too much synthesized music piping in to hear a word they were saying.

"Someone you know?" the coffee-pouring waitress asked me. She wore her chestnut hair in a long ponytail down her back and grinned at me with uneven teeth.

Before I could answer, the blue-black-haired waitress sidled up. "Who are you more surprised to see? Him or her?"

"He's a regular here, isn't he?" I asked. "Dan, I mean."

The two women exchanged a look.

"I'm not his girlfriend," I said in answer to their unspoken curiosity. "I have zero interest in him romantically. I know he's a regular," I said again. "But have you ever seen her before?"

"Never saw this one." The waitress holding the coffeepot shook her head, making her ponytail swing from side to side. "He gets lots of women. Don't know why he brings them here, though, unless he's cheap."

"I got the impression this one wasn't invited. He seemed surprised when she followed him in," the second waitress said. "The man's a player, for sure."

"How does he do it?" the first one asked. "Is he rich or something?"

"You'd never guess it by the way he tips," the other one said.

Still talking earnestly, Debbie laid a hand on Dan's. He shook her off. When she sat back, stunned, they both shot surreptitious glances around the room. I ducked deeper behind the shelves.

"Did they see me?" I asked the short-haired waitress.

She shook her head. "I don't think so." Wrinkling her nose, she added, "But it looks like they're ready to order. I should get over there."

"I'll be right back," I said. When I got to Frances, I didn't sit down.

"What took you so long?" she asked.

A thousand ideas were rushing through my head at once and I didn't care to voice any of them here. "We need to go," I said.

Our waitress, the ponytailed woman, had dropped off waters. "Let me guess, you two won't be dining with us tonight."

"What's going on?" Frances asked.

"I'll explain in the car. Go on out," I said, handing her the keys. "I'll be right behind you."

She grumbled but complied.

"I'm sorry," I said to the ponytailed waitress.

"No problem. This is the most excitement we've had here in weeks. I wish you'd tell me what's going on, though. Is that older woman his wife? Is he cheating on her?"

"Something like that," I said. "Do you mind if I sneak back to the station over there for one more look?"

"Be my guest."

I returned to my perch to watch.

As soon as they handed their menus to their waitress, Debbie inched her chair even closer to Dan's and began talking again. Whatever she was saying to him made him angry. I watched it build from the tightness of his brow to the flexing of his jaw. When she ran a hand down his upper arm, he flinched as though burned. Her gaze sharpened and her voice rose just as one instrumental tune ended and seconds before the next one began. "We don't have any choice. It's our only chance."

Dan rubbed his temples, then gazed out at some middle distance, much the way he had right after the assisted-suicide brochure had been found. I was convinced I wouldn't learn anything more and was about to walk away, when he sat up as though shocked. He pointed.

Belatedly, I realized that with his back to the wall, he had a completely unobstructed view through the windows of the parking lot. The two of them had been engrossed in conversation earlier and must have missed our arrival. Now, however, he'd taken to staring away; he must have spotted Frances. Any doubt that he had seen her diminished when Debbie stared out at the same point and her cheeks grew red. She glanced around the restaurant again and, this time, I ducked away for good.

Outside, it took all my willpower to not look back through the restaurant's windows to see if Dan and Debbie were watching. I had no doubt they were, but I couldn't let them know I'd seen them. With pained nonchalance, I climbed into the driver's seat. Frances continued to grumble about not knowing what was going on. "I thought you were hungry," she said.

I threw the car into reverse and pulled away slowly, trying not to look anything but casual and unconcerned. If the waitresses told them of our behavior, Frances and I could be in trouble. I hoped they wouldn't.

Right now all I wanted to do was put as much space between us and them as possible. "Who knows what hotel you stay at when you visit Percy?" I asked.

"What do you mean 'Who knows?' I don't understand."

"I mean, is your hotel choice common knowledge? If Indwell had to get in touch with you over the weekend, would they know where you were staying?"

She shook her head. "I don't always stay at the same place. But even if I did, there's no reason for anyone to know which hotel I'm at. If they need to call, they can get me on my cell phone."

"And you're sure you never mentioned your hotel casually?" I asked. "To anyone?"

"Yes, I'm sure. It's nobody's business where I stay, is it?"

"Okay, good." I strove to get my heart rate down to a manageable level. "But before we head out there, let's drive around a little bit."

She noticed me checking the rearview mirror. "You think we're being followed? What happened back at the restaurant?"

I told Frances what I'd observed. "I'm sure I'm overreacting," I said as I took a circuitous route around Rosette, studying every car that followed us for more than a block or two.

"You think those two are in cahoots?" she asked.

"I don't know. I don't know what to think." I pulled off the road when I spied a fast-food drive-thru. "Let's grab something fast and get to the hotel. We have a few more phone calls ahead of us."

Chapter 35

FRANCES'S HOTEL—THE *SUNSET VIEW*— turned out to be one of those single-story, sprawling structures on the outskirts of town, constructed back when the word *motel* conjured up visions of happy families traversing the country in wood-paneled station wagons.

Although our dinner delay and time spent driving around to shake an imaginary tail meant that we'd already missed the inn's titular view this evening, there was enough waning light to appreciate the motor court's tidy appearance.

Horseshoe-shaped, red-bricked, and gray-roofed, the Sunset View seemed to be striving for an early-American motif. Fifteen identical picture windows trimmed in colonial blue, and fifteen identical white six-panel doors were arranged in precise intervals around the central parking lot.

We parked in front of the glass-enclosed main office, which sat to the structure's far right. An illuminated yellow sign blinked OFFICE, in case there was any doubt. With potted indoor greenery lining its perimeter and one bright spot of orange moving about inside, it reminded me of a fish tank with a sole occupant.

When I opened the bell-jangling glass door, the musty motel scent hit me with a wave of vacation nostalgia, making me remember my parents and their attempts to show us the country. A hunched-over older man in a bright orange shirt glanced up expectantly.

Frances stepped to the desk. "We have reservations for two rooms."

The bowed man on the other side of the counter blinked at us from behind round, rimless glasses. I would bet he was the motel's original owner and had lived here nonstop ever since. "Sliwa?" he asked in a voice so vigorous I couldn't believe it had come from such a frail, bent form. "And Wheaton? That you?"

"That's us."

The old man's face crushed in on itself as he squinted at Frances. "You been here before, haven'tcha?"

"Once or twice," she said.

He nodded, satisfied. "We appreciate your business." Turning to me, he said, "First time at the Sunset View?"

"Yes."

After we hand-printed our personal information on oversized index cards, he pulled out two keys—real keys, not the credit card–sized swipe kind that most hotels use nowadays—and handed them to us across the Formica countertop. Both keys were attached to old-fashioned hard plastic fobs that featured the motel's name and our room numbers embossed in gold.

"I put you two next to one another," he said. "Rooms seven and eight. They're right in the middle." He pointed a gnarled finger. "Nicest views of the sunset. Course, you missed it tonight."

"Thank you," I said. "If anyone should happen to come looking for us—"

"We don't allow parties here. We run a quiet place."

"No parties," I assured him. "But if anyone should come by and ask if we've checked in here, could you please tell them we haven't."

"You mean lie?"

"It's important," I said.

"I won't lie to the police."

"It wouldn't be the police who come looking for us."

His thick lenses made his watery eyes look especially buggy.

Frances tugged my arm. "No one will come looking for us."

I ignored her. "Is there anywhere to park my car in the back?"

"Don't want anybody to know you're here, do you?" He gave us a long once-over. "You running away from a bad relationship?" he asked me. "You and your mom?"

Frances huffed.

"Something like that," I said. "We'd really appreciate it if you don't tell anyone we're here, but if someone does come by, please let us know right away, okay?"

"You mean like call your room?"

"Yes, would you do that?"

He nodded. "I got a rifle in back. Do I need to bring it out here?"

"No, please. No guns."

He seemed disappointed. "All right. You two in for the night?"

"We're going to go back to Indwell," Frances said. "Percy's waiting for us."

"That's the first place they'll look." I shook my head. "We can't go back yet. Not until we get some answers." I turned to the man. "Yes, we're in for the night."

While Frances made her way to room number eight, I parked the car out of sight and trotted back around the front with my overnight bag in one hand and our sack of rapidly cooling fried chicken in the other.

As I juggled my burdens to fit my key in the door, Frances stepped outside of her room. "Let me take that." She lifted the chicken bag and headed back inside. "We can eat in here if you like."

"I'll be there in a minute," I said.

Room number seven smelled like fabric that had been stored too long in a musty old basement.

Allowing the door to slam shut behind me, I crossed the indoor-outdoor carpeted space and dumped my overnight bag and purse on the first of two double beds. My heavy load landed on the bed's blue-and-gold-flowered spread, shooting a rush of stale air up my nostrils.

When I heard liquid sloshing from inside my purse, I remembered the bottle of anisette I'd been carting around. Wrinkling my nose at the thought of sleeping in that smelly bed tonight, I picked up both my purse and bag and gingerly set them instead on the small table in front of the picture window.

When I shut the drapes, I cringed at yet another blast of 1960s air. I'd have to throw everything into the laundry the minute I got home.

From the lamps on the end tables to the tiles on the bathroom floor, it was clear that nothing at the Sunset View had been updated in recent years. The sink boasted a chained drain plug and separate, twisty handles. The tile around the bathtub was old and cracked, but at least the bathroom was clean. The jalousie window had been cranked open in an effort, I assumed, to freshen up the room a little before our arrival today.

An energetic knock pulled me from my observations. I started toward it realizing when the knock came again, that it was emanating not from the outside door, but from the one that connected my room with Frances's. "Food's getting cold," she shouted from the other side. "You coming over here tonight, or what?"

I drew open my side of the double door to find her standing there, red-faced, hand poised ready to knock again.

"What took you so long?"

"I've been thinking about Dan and Debbie," I said as I followed her in. Number eight was the mirror image of my room. Frances swung her side of the door as wide as she could, adjusting the placement of the small table and two chairs to allow the door's full arc. She and I emptied the bag of food atop the tiny table before sitting down.

"A little cramped, but at least the place is clean." When I fidgeted, the back of my chair bumped up against the inside of the wide-open connecting door. "I'm glad you shut the drapes. I did, too."

"Nobody needs to see inside," she said. "Not even Mr. Nosy Proprietor."

As we began to eat, I continued. "Just because Dan and Debbie have a relationship doesn't mean they're guilty of any crime, but the more I think about it, the more it all fits."

"Sure does," she said as she took a bite of chicken. "This is cold. I knew it would be."

I ignored her complaint. "I think the two of them did it and now they're running scared.

They're getting sloppy, or at least Debbie is. Why else would she risk following Dan tonight? I don't want to wait for the police to complete DNA tests on the syringe caps to say anything."

"That will probably take another week."

"Or longer," I said. "The only reason Bennett and I got our DNA tests done so quickly was because he had the power to get it done fast."

"You mean the money."

"Right. Police departments, especially small ones like Rosette's, have to wait their turn at the testing centers. That could take months."

"In the meantime, I'm still in the hot seat."

"Not if we can push for more evidence," I said. "We know there were no puncture wounds on Gus's body, right?"

"Right," she said.

"Leading us to believe that—if he was murdered—whoever did it used the port on his heparin lock to administer the fatal dose."

"Your friend Joe came up with that idea."

I nodded. "You knew Gus. Would he ever have allowed anyone other than a nurse to inject him with anything?"

"Not a chance," she said. "But they keep saying I could have done it while he was sleeping."

"Sure, if he went back to sleep after you and Percy left and after Kyle took off. But I think it's far more likely that one of the nurses came in, took four vials of insulin from Percy's refrigerator, and injected Gus on the pretense of this being a medical necessity."

"And you believe Debbie is that nurse?"

I sat forward. I'd taken only two bites of chicken and downed a little bit of the cold mashed potatoes, but as my excitement grew, my hunger waned. "She could come and go in Percy's room or Gus's room without anyone giving her a second glance."

"But why?" Frances asked. "What does she stand to gain by killing Gus? She didn't hate him the way most people did. She went overboard being nice to him, in fact."

"Dan was out of town when Gus died, remember?" I said. "What if Dan and Debbie were in on this together and they agreed she would make her move when Dan was away to keep him completely above suspicion? She may have killed Gus so that Dan would inherit his father's estate. Or at least half of it. And I'm sure she expected to share Dan's half."

Frances shook her head. "But Anton told you that the sons don't benefit."

"They didn't know that, though. And remember how both Dan and Harland complained about how much money Indwell cost? Anton suspects that they wanted to staunch the flow of money out of their father's estate. But Gus loved living at Indwell. They knew he wouldn't have agreed to leave."

"So they killed him." She shook her head. "You really think so?"

"What if?" I asked as I put it all into words. "What if Dan schmoozed Debbie into believing that he'd take care of her financially? Or maybe she believed he was in love with her. Maybe he actually is."

Frances frowned. "Women do stupid things for men sometimes, I'll give you that."

"My impression is that Dan didn't seem particularly thrilled by Debbie's attentions today," I said. "And from all reports, he's a player. She must be feeling vulnerable. Santiago raised the alarm, taking their anticipated natural-death scenario and casting a suspicious light on it."

"And now the police think it could be murder."

"Right. She's getting worried Dan has turned his back on her. How better to retaliate than threaten his windfall while also attempting to nullify the murder theory?"

Frances frowned. "Cathy was with Debbie when they found the pamphlet."

"I know," I said. "I've been thinking about that."

"You think Cathy is in on it, too?"

I shook my head. "I don't." I pulled up my phone and began scrolling. "Tooney sent me basic contact information for everyone involved."

"Why did he do that?" she asked.

"Because he's thorough." I found the e-mail

he'd sent me. "Here it is. Would you mind writing this down?"

Frances recorded the phone number on one of our spare napkins as I read aloud. "What is that?"

I turned the napkin to face me and dialed. "Cathy's home phone."

"She was off sick today, remember?"

I'd forgotten. "Thanks." A moment later, when Cathy answered, I injected as much warmth into my tone as I could. "Hi, how are you? This is Grace Wheaton—Frances's and Percy Sliwa's friend?" I said with a lilt. "I hope I'm not bothering you."

In the background I could hear dogs yapping. From the sound of it they were little dogs, and I remembered—dachshunds.

"Grace?" she said with obvious puzzlement.

"Are those your dachshunds in the background?" I asked before she could quiz me on how I'd gotten her phone number. "I love dogs."

I could practically feel her warm up over the phone line. "I have three. They're very energetic." Away from the phone, she shushed them. "Quiet, boys."

Surprisingly they listened to her. One whined, but very softly.

"I'm sorry to interrupt your evening; how are you feeling?" I asked. "I heard you were sick today."

She chuckled. "Don't tell anybody, but it was

more a personal-breather day than anything. Debbie and I were talking about how much has gone on at that place in the past few weeks and she thought we both needed time off."

"I'll bet you do. Speaking of Debbie," I said grateful for the segue, "the reason I'm calling i to ask you about that brochure the two of you found in Gus's room."

"Sure, what about it?"

"I know Indwell wanted you to have a look around, but I forgot to ask you what made you start with Gus's bathroom."

I held tight to the phone.

"I don't know. We just thought that they probably should have cleared that room out first, but they hadn't."

"Oh," I said, disappointed. My shoulders slumped and my sweaty hands relaxed. "So you just happened to breeze through there to check the room's status."

"Debbie was worried that the administration would start forcing *us* to do the cleanup," she said. "She thought it would be a good idea to have a look around to see what we might be facing."

I gripped the phone again. "So this was Debbie's idea."

"Yeah, I told her I'd worry about that when the time came. You know, a cross-the-bridge-when-you-come-to-it sort of thing, but she insisted. Said that the sooner we got in and had a look around the better prepared we'd be for what comes. I guess that's true."

"So Debbie searched through the bathroom cabinets while you looked through Gus's room?" I asked.

"Not exactly. She told me to go through the bathroom cabinets. In fact, now that you mention it, she's the one who insisted that I look under the sink area. I mean, how much could really be in there besides toilet paper? But there it was—that brochure. I found it. But only because Debbie suggested I look there."

"How did Debbie react when you found it?"

"She was excited and happy," Cathy said. "She told me what a great find it was. She kept saying that now Indwell wouldn't be known as a place where patients were murdered. The way she carried on, you'd think she was a part owner of the place."

Frances had been listening in the entire time Cathy and I were talking. I watched as Frances's brows leaped and tightened and leaped again as Cathy described finding the brochure.

"Thanks for clearing that up, Cathy," I said.

"Thanks to you, though, the police are telling us that someone may have planted the brochure there," she said with a sigh. "Nobody can figure out why anyone would do such a thing. It doesn't make sense. Debbie's the only one who keeps insisting that it had to have been there all along. That Gus must have committed suicide."

"I suppose we'll have to let the police sort that out."

"That's what we said."

"How did Debbie take that?" I asked.

Cathy laughed. "She didn't like that one bit. You know how Santiago loves the fact that he was the one who called the police? Well, Debbie really liked being the one to find this clue. If it's not really a clue, then it isn't important anymore. She thought we did a big thing. Turns out it wasn't big at all."

"How do you feel about that?"

"Doesn't bother me." The dogs started yipping in the background again. "I think everything about this situation is weird. But I have to admit that it's kinda exciting, too."

When I hung up, I said, "There it is. Debbie sent Cathy in to find that brochure. She directed her to that bathroom cabinet specifically."

"And the reason Debbie planted it there," Frances said as she reasoned aloud, "was to throw the police off the murder scent."

"And, I suspect, to cause trouble for Dan. She's angry with him. She knows Gus died of insulin poisoning, because she injected him. She also knows that you and I aren't going to stop until we get you cleared of the charge. That means delivering the real guilty party. Debbie's only hope now is to convince the police that Gus injected himself."

"Hmph," Frances said. "I'll bet she would have let me take the fall, too, if it hadn't been for you poking around and asking questions."

I smiled. "Thanks, Frances."

She shot me a glare. "Yeah, but it's only because I pushed you to do it."

Chapter 36

I ZIPPED THROUGH MY CELL PHONE'S directory. "I'm not waiting until tomorrow to tell the Rosette detectives about this," I said as I dialed. "And we're calling Tooney, too."

My call to Madigan at the police station went immediately to voice mail. The same thing happened when I tried Nieman's extension. I left brief but succinct messages for both women.

"What kind of police station doesn't answer its telephones?" Frances asked when my third attempt, to the station's nonemergency number, went unanswered after six rings. I hung up. "Even Rodriguez and Flynn are reachable around the clock."

"True." I dialed Tooney. When he answered, he started to tell me that Anton, Harland, and Joslyn were winding up, but I interrupted him to share our theory.

"I think you nailed this one, Grace," he said. "Again. Where are you right now?"

I told him.

"How about I meet you there? I don't like the idea of you two on your own at a tiny motel that probably considers motion-sensor spotlights the height of security."

"We're in for the night," I said. "But you could take my room and I could bunk with Frances."

She frowned mightily.

"I'll get another room, thanks," he said. "Assuming they have a vacancy."

"I'm betting that they do."

"Great. I'll be there in a little while."

This time when I hung up, exhilaration and exhaustion hit me at once. "We did it," I said. "I know it was Dan and Debbie. I know it."

"And, for the first time, you and I have solved a murder without one of us almost getting killed."

I grinned and stood to begin clearing away our dinner mess. "That makes this win ever so much sweeter."

Frances got to her feet, too, and began crumpling up the paper bags.

I picked up my head. "What was that?"

She stopped what she was doing. "I didn't hear anything."

A second later, the noise came again. Tiny, clicking sounds. I pointed through the open connecting doors. "It's coming from my room."

She blinked, leaning forward, concentrating.

"Maybe I imagined it," I said.

She shook her head. "No, I heard it, too."

I held up a hand when the faint clicking resumed.

"It sounds like someone is trying to get a key in a lock," Frances said.

"*My* lock."

I lunged for the door.

Too late.

Before I could yank my chair out of the way to allow me to swing the connecting door shut, Debbie and Dan raced into my room. Dan carried a gun and pointed it toward the bed. In the two seconds it took for them to comprehend the situation, I banged the chair away and began shoving the door closed.

Still too late.

Dan slapped a purple-gloved hand against the hollow yellow door and elbowed his way into Frances's room.

We shouted for help and turned to run, but Debbie pushed past Dan. She, too, wore gloves. Using both hands, she struck me hard, propelling me sideways and sending my butt skidding along the indoor-outdoor rug.

When Frances screamed, Debbie punched her in the stomach. Frances doubled over, gasping for breath. I scrambled up in time to grab Frances's arm and help her into the chair.

"What is wrong with you?" I shouted at Debbie.

"Keep your voice down," Dan said. Though he trained the gun on me, I couldn't help notice that his hand was shaking.

Debbie waved him back toward the connecting

doors. "Stay out of her reach. I've read up on her; she's a wily one." She crossed to the bed, grabbed one of the pillows, and handed it to Dan. "This will muffle the shot."

He nodded and held the pillow up around the front of the gun's barrel.

Crouching next to Frances, I asked, "Are you okay?"

Wheezing hard, she nodded.

How could they have found us? And, more important, how were we going to get out of this? I ran a hand along Frances's shoulder. "Hang in there," I said.

She sucked in a noisy breath and, gasping, tried to talk. "Spoke too soon, I guess."

I stared up at Debbie's angry face and counted my blessings that she wasn't the one holding the gun. She wouldn't hesitate to pull the trigger. Dan, on the other hand, might. Sweating profusely, the man fidgeted, glancing toward the picture window every couple of seconds as though he had X-ray vision and could see through the heavy drapes.

"You won't get away with anything," I said as I got to my feet. "Your only chance is to run. And you better go now, because help is on the way."

"Yeah, right," Dan said.

"We're not leaving until she writes a suicide note." Debbie pointed at Frances, who still struggled for air. "She has to admit that she killed Gus, and say that the guilt got to be too much to live with, so she killed herself, too."

A surprised laugh bubbled up, despite my terror. "You're crazy," I said. "No one would ever believe that."

"Sure they will," Debbie said. "But even if the police do eventually figure it out, it will take a long time. Enough time to get out of the country with Dan's half of the estate."

"No, it won't." This time my laugh was forced, derisive. "Dan doesn't *get* half the estate. He's only entitled to his share of his father's insurance policy. Gus made Anton his sole beneficiary."

"What?" She spun to face Dan.

I read guilt on his face. He'd already learned the truth.

"Dan didn't mention that tidbit to you, did he?" I asked in a taunting tone. "Didn't you wonder why he was so upset about you planting that assisted-suicide brochure in his father's room?"

"No, that's not right. It can't be." She stamped her foot. "Dan?"

Perspiration dotted Dan's receding hairline. Every time his fingers twitched, I sucked in another breath. We couldn't die here. We'd taken every precaution to keep ourselves safe. Unbidden, my mind swirled with thoughts of Bennett and how hard he'd take the loss. And my roommates— their plans for buying the Granite Building would be quashed. Tooney would be devastated. And maybe even Joe.

I couldn't let Frances get hurt; I couldn't let myself get hurt.

"How did you find us?" I asked. "There's no way you could have followed us here."

Debbie tapped her forehead. "Thanks for the reminder." She glanced around the room. Not finding whatever it was she was looking for, she brushed past Dan, shoulder-checking him as she stormed into my room.

I held my breath. Dan seemed to be holding his. "You can put the gun down," I said. "We're not going anywhere."

"Don't listen to her," Debbie shouted from my room.

A second later she returned, carrying my purse. "What do you have in here?" she asked as she dropped it onto one of Frances's beds. "This thing weighs a ton." She reached in and pulled out the bottle of anisette. Holding it aloft, she shook it so that its contents burbled back and forth. "You two really had a party planned tonight, didn't you? Sorry to spoil your fun."

"Debbie, let's get going," Dan said. "Maybe we should take her advice and get out of here now while we can."

"Don't be stupid," she said as she continued to dig through my belongings. "If Frances doesn't write the suicide note, the police will never stop investigating. If she confesses to the crime, it's solved. Closed. Done. You get your money and the two of us start a new life in a new town."

Dan's expression darkened.

"No one will believe Frances shot herself," I said. "And they certainly won't believe she shot me. Because that's your plan, isn't it? Shoot us both and make it look like a murder-suicide."

"Here it is." Debbie pulled one of Indwell's locator bracelets from my purse. "I had a feeling about you so I dropped it in there yesterday when you were busy showing the police where Percy hid the moonshine." She shoved the bracelet into her jacket pocket. "Amazing little devices, and, if you download the app to your phone, you can trace any of them anywhere. As long as you know the bracelet's individual code." She smiled. "Which, of course, I do."

Dan ran his tongue along his bottom lip. "Go on, Debbie. Give them the morphine. I want to get out of here."

She pointed to a little pad of paper featuring Sunset View's letterhead. "Write what I tell you," she said.

Frances had been able to straighten herself. Her breathing had returned to almost normal. "I will not."

"Oh, yes, you will," Debbie said.

Dan swallowed hard. "What if we don't get the insurance?" he asked. "What if it doesn't go through?"

"We'll figure something else out." She dug through her own purse now. "As long as we're together, right? Ah, here they are." She pulled out two syringes. "Morphine. Easy enough for Frances to have procured from Indwell on her many trips there. Nobody will think twice about the two of you being dead from an overdose. I filled these up specially."

"Nobody will think twice?" I asked. "Are you delusional?"

"All we need is a little time." She wiggled the syringes back and forth. "These will provide that."

Instinctively, I stepped in front of Frances. "And when you dose us—when you pull the cap off of those syringes—will you use your teeth?"

Under any other circumstances, the look on her face would have been comical. "What are you talking about?"

"You pull caps off with your teeth, don't you? Every time you give an injection." Before she could say a word, I turned to Dan. "We put that together today—this afternoon, in fact. You understand what that means, don't you? Debbie left her DNA on those syringe caps—the ones she replaced in Percy's refrigerator—the ones in police custody right now. And her DNA is on the cap Santiago found rolling around on Gus's floor."

Debbie advanced on me. "Doesn't matter.

Nobody's looking for DNA. And once Frances writes her confession, no one will care."

Dan's attention swung between me and Debbie. Every time he moved, his aim shifted, too.

"Except testing is already in progress," I said with far more calm than I was feeling. "You think we kept this to ourselves? We called Frances's attorney immediately. And Rosette's detectives. And our private investigator. They all know everything we do." I purposely left out the part about Tooney being on his way here now. "You're not getting away with it. Not a chance."

Dan looked perplexed. "Her DNA is on those caps?" he asked. Turning to her, he repeated the question, then said, "You're not going to get away with this, are you?"

"They're bluffing," Debbie said.

"No, they're not," Dan said. "And if they arrest you, you'll turn me in. I know you will."

"Dan, baby. Never. They're lying. They're just guessing."

"No, they're not," he said again. And before I could blink, he fired.

The gunshot, though muffled, made me yelp.

Debbie crumpled, grabbing at her abdomen. Crimson blood blossomed and grew beneath her outstretched, grasping fingers. Her mouth made a silent *O* and she stared at Dan, her face a mixture of hatred and disbelief. She fell sideways, her shoulder and head hitting the end of the bed before she toppled, lifeless to the floor.

I made it to her side in seconds, but there was nothing I could do for her.

Dan took a step forward. "She would have turned me in," he said, looking eager for absolution. His lips were the color of dead fish. "I think I'm going to be sick."

Using one hand to cover his mouth, he swayed from side to side.

We had seconds before he'd turn the gun on us.

"I don't have the stomach for this sort of thing, you understand," he said from between his fingers. "I couldn't do it myself. Not to Dad. That's why . . ." Still swaying he blinked, striving to regain control. "I'm sorry. I don't have any choice. You have to understand." Bile must have risen up the back of his throat. He coughed, then choked it back down and turned his head to the side.

I grabbed the bottle of anisette from the bed. Holding it by its neck, I swung the heavy bottle in a wide arc, making contact with Dan's head in a bright, shattering crash. Glass shards exploded over us and licorice-scented alcohol poured down Dan's surprised face.

As the bottle connected, I flashed back to a similar move I'd made a few months back wielding an antique club. That weapon had been much heavier, however, and had packed a much heftier wallop.

Dan staggered sideways but didn't fall as I'd hoped he would. In his shaky hands, the gun wobbled. He fired wildly. Miraculously, he'd maintained his grip on the pillow long enough to muffle the sound. A second later, the beleaguered cushion dropped to the floor.

Before he could get another shot off, I jammed the bottle's jagged edge into his gun arm, using every bit of strength I had. The pain made him gasp, but he still didn't fall. He had too many clothes on for the glass to have enough effect. I thrust the bottle at his face, but he ducked away. When he pulled the gun up again, I knew I was a goner.

Until a second bottle of anisette crashed across the back of his skull.

This time, he fell.

Frances stood behind his bloodied body, holding the neck of the broken bottle like a bat, looking as though she wanted him to get back up so she could smash his head again.

"Thought you needed a little help this time," she said.

"Thank you, Frances." I said. And then I hugged her.

Chapter 37

BECAUSE DEBBIE WAS BEYOND ALL HELP, she was beyond our concern. Dan, on the other hand, began to stir almost immediately. We had mere moments before he'd come to. I grabbed the gun and moved it to the bed, out of his reach.

When I flipped him onto his stomach, he moaned.

Frances delivered a quick kick to the back side of his leg. "Serves you right."

With one knee wedged hard on Dan's back to keep him down, my gaze raced around the room, looking for something to tie him up with.

"The phone," I said, pointing.

Frances lifted the old-fashioned instrument from the nightstand and brought it over. I unhooked the curly cord and used it to tie Dan's hands behind his back.

I unhooked the flat cord from the back of the phone and had Frances detach the other end from the wall jack. Pulling the long gray wire up, I bound Dan's ankles together.

"That should keep him out of trouble," I said. "Now, let's call the police."

. . .

BY THE TIME ROSETTE'S HOMICIDE detectives showed up, a pair of uniformed officers had secured the scene. Frances and I sat on the bed in my room while paramedics tended to Dan's bloody wounds and whiny complaints.

Madigan strode in first, her partner trotting along behind. "What do we have here?" she asked.

The uniformed cops provided a dispassionate account of what they'd found and what steps they'd taken. Madigan and Nieman nodded and jotted notes. After assessing the situation themselves, the two of them came through the connecting doors to talk to us.

"We'll take your statements now," Madigan said. "Separately."

While they interrogated Frances outside, I took up a position in the connecting doorway to watch the goings-on in the other room. Though Dan had regained enough stability to sit up straight, he remained on the floor. The paramedics were having a difficult time bandaging his head and chest as the man rocked side to side, moaning whenever anyone tried to touch him.

"Try to stay quiet, sir," one of the paramedics said. "We need to take you to the hospital."

To my surprise, Dan began to weep. "She talked me into it," he cried. "I didn't want to. I didn't. I swear."

The two uniformed cops were bright enough to

drag Madigan back in to hear what Dan had to say.

"What happened?" she asked.

He touched his forehead, felt the swath of bandages wrapped there, and began sobbing anew. "It's all Debbie's fault. I never wanted to hurt anybody. All I wanted was for my dad to stop wasting all his money."

Crouching next to him, Madigan adopted a more soothing manner than I'd believed her capable of. "It's okay now. Everything will be all right. As long as you tell me what happened. From the beginning."

"It wasn't my fault," he said again. "It was hers."

"I understand completely," Madigan said. "And after a stop at the hospital, we're going to take you back to the station so you can tell us all about it. But first, you have the right to remain silent . . ."

As she recited the rest of the Miranda warning, I blew out a breath of relief. She heard the exhalation, locked eyes with me, and gave a shrug as if to say, "Hey, I was just doing my job."

Sunset View's elderly proprietor poked his nose into the doorway of number eight. "If there was any illegal business going on here, I wasn't aware of it." He blinked big eyes and tried to peer around Madigan to get a better look. "I run a reputable establishment." He craned his neck. "Is that woman dead?"

One of the uniformed cops grabbed the guy's arm. "Sir, I need to ask you to step back," he said as he guided him away.

"This is my hotel," the old man shouted. "I have every right to be here. And those two women were suspicious from the very start."

"Please step back." The cop took him out of my line of sight. "Until we give the all clear I don't want you closer than room number five. Understood?"

He must have complied because I didn't hear another peep.

After Frances and I provided statements, we were told we were free to go. "Thank goodness," I said as we gathered our overnight bags and purses.

"Finally, I say," Frances said.

We'd just stepped out of number seven and were making our way to my car when Tooney pulled in, parking next to the police squad shining its spotlight into number eight's doorway.

"Grace," Tooney said as he raced over to us, "what happened? Are you all right?"

"Don't bother asking about me," Frances said.

Even in the dim light I could tell Tooney's face colored. "I'm sorry, Frances. When I asked, I meant both of you."

"Of course you did." She rolled her eyes. To me, she said, "Let's get out of here. Are you up for driving back to Emberstowne tonight?"

"I am." In truth, I couldn't wait to get back. "But you aren't staying alone tonight. You're coming home with me. Don't even try to argue."

She rolled her eyes for good measure, then jerked a thumb at me. "Can you believe her?" she asked Tooney. Frowning, she faced me again. "Have it your way, Miss Bossypants."

As we made our way to our cars, Tooney nudged me and whispered, "Nicely done."

"CAN YOU BELIEVE IT HAS BEEN ONLY A week since this whole mess got started?" Bennett asked the following morning.

Even though it was Sunday—not a regular workday—he, Frances, and I were gathered in my office, sipping coffee, and waiting for Rodriguez and Flynn to make an appearance. Tooney had gotten in touch with them both last night, but apparently Rodriguez had insisted on coming in today to get the full story in person.

"Only a week?" Frances asked. She clucked her disapproval. "It feels like a lifetime. When I think of how close I came to being incarcerated . . ." She affected a shudder.

"I spoke with Lily Holland early this morning," Bennett said. "She assured me that she's following up to make certain that this matter is expunged from your record and your reputation remains clear, Frances." He leaned forward, returning his coffee cup to its saucer, then addressed me. "Gracie, my girl, you were in the thick of things again. Despite our best efforts, we can't seem to keep you out of trouble."

"It isn't just me involved in these situations," I said. "You're still recovering from being shot. This time, they were after Frances. I was an afterthought."

"But you're the common denominator," Frances said. "Ever since you came here, life has gotten dangerous for us all."

"What are we to do with you, Gracie?" Bennett asked.

I was spared answering when a voice hollered from the other room. "Where are our ace detectives?" Rodriguez called.

I got to my feet as he strode through the door between our offices.

Flynn followed behind, scowling. "When are you two going to learn to leave police business to the police?" he asked.

When a third party came through the door, I knew my face gave away my surprise. "Good morning," he said.

"Joe? What are you doing here?" Back to using his cane, Joe Bradley followed Flynn. He wore an eager expression, as though he wanted to cross the room far faster than he was able.

"Detective Rodriguez invited me along. I hope you don't mind."

"Sure, because it's never a party at Marshfield until the coroner shows up," Flynn said.

Joe's brows jumped and Rodriguez slid Flynn a baleful glare. "Good thing you're not on the welcoming committee, amigo." He turned to me and winked. "I think my partner hasn't had his morning coffee yet."

"It's on its way," I said. "In the meantime, have a seat. And tell us everything you know."

As we settled ourselves, coffee and pastries arrived. Flynn was the first to help himself. "You guys always do set out a nice spread," he said.

Even though that was probably the friendliest thing the young cop had ever said to us, Frances harrumphed. "Don't get used to it."

Once the servers left, Rodriguez cleared his throat. "We had a nice conversation with the Rosette cops last night, and they were kind enough to provide an update this morning," he said. "As you know, Dan has been charged with murder. What's frightening is how easily he could have gotten away with it."

"Gotten away with killing Gus, maybe," I said. "His ultimate goal was to gain control of his father's money. That was never going to happen. Too bad Gus never shared the provisions of his will with his sons. He might still be alive today."

"Very true," Rodriguez said.

"That nurse Debbie was a real pro," Flynn said. "The Rosette cops are looking into her background. There are a couple of unexplained deaths at elder-care homes she may have had a hand in when she worked at those facilities."

"How did she get the job at Indwell if she's been under suspicion in the past?" Bennett asked.

Flynn shook his head. "She was never tied to any of these deaths. Not officially. It's only now, after the incident at Indwell, that the Rosette police are having those other places take a closer look at Debbie's involvement."

"It may turn out that she's innocent, but Flynn and I suspect she was one of those angel of mercy types. Dan claims that Debbie assured him this would work because she'd done it before."

"Angel of mercy?" Flynn snorted. "More like vulture of mercy."

"Once the two of you"—Rodriguez pointed to me and Frances in turn—"came up with the brilliant idea of testing the syringe caps for DNA, Debbie was never getting off scot-free. She just didn't know it yet."

"Thanks to Joe and his observation about the heparin lock, we knew to focus on the nursing staff," I said. He nodded acknowledgment. "That helped immensely."

"And seeing them together at the restaurant," Frances said. "Well, I didn't see them personally. But when Grace hustled me out of there, I knew something was up."

"The thing is," Rodriguez said, "they could have gotten away with murder if it hadn't been for that other nurse sounding the alarm. That was the one variable Dan and Debbie hadn't counted on."

"Why did she leave one syringe cap?" I asked. "She had to know it was there."

"According to Dan, she didn't realize it was missing until she put the empties back in Percy's room. She intended to go back for it after Gus was declared dead and taken away. She intended to replace Percy's empties at a later date as well. She never expected anyone to notice the irregularities so quickly."

"Yeah, if it weren't for Santiago, Gus's death may not have raised an eyebrow," Flynn said. "It's a good thing he caused the ruckus, otherwise those two murderers would've skated."

"What are you saying? We should be grateful to Santiago for getting the police to arrest me?" Frances puffed herself up. "I'd like to hear you say that if you were in my shoes."

"No one is happy that you had to go through all that," Rodriguez said soothingly. "But because of your involvement—and Grace's—justice prevailed. You should be very proud of how you handled yourself throughout this ordeal. If it weren't for you, this crime may have never been detected, let alone solved."

"*Hmph,*" she said, but I could tell she was pleased.

Chapter 38

EAGER TO RESUME THE LESSON BENNETT had initiated more than a week ago, I met him in his study, as agreed, immediately after work Friday afternoon. "I'm finally caught up with everything I ignored last week," I said. "And I can't help thinking about what you were going to show me before Frances's phone call threw our lives into a tizzy."

Bennett glanced at his watch. "It's after five o'clock on a weekend night," he said. "Shouldn't you be out on a hot date instead of spending time with your old uncle this evening?"

I laid a hand on his arm as we made our way to the second-level dead-end corridor that had perplexed me last time we were there. "My evening is completely free, and I'm absolutely delighted to be spending it with you."

He patted my hand. "I worry about you, Gracie. I worry you spend too much time here and not enough time enjoying life."

"If we could manage a few months without a murder investigation, that would help," I said. "But . . ."

He turned to me.

"If you must know," I said with a grin, "I do have plans tomorrow night. With a young man."

"A date?" He arched one white brow. "Anyone I know?"

"An honest-to-goodness date. The first one in a long time. And yes, you've met him."

Bennett made a small noise that I took as approval. "I hope you and Dr. Bradley have a wonderful time."

I stopped to face him. "How did you know?"

Bennett tucked my hand deeper into the crook of his arm and resumed walking. "I can tell by the way he looks at you."

"Really?" I found myself warmed by the thought.

Bennett smiled down at me. "Really."

When we got to the fawn-colored corridor with the skinny window far to my left and the wide one to my right, I ran my hand across the long, curved wall between them, shaking my head.

"I can't figure it out," I said. "You've hinted that there's a secret space around here, but I can't imagine how that can be, not with a two-story library just on the other side."

"You worked so hard to help Frances," Bennett said with an indulgent smile, "it isn't fair to make you work to uncover any more. I give."

Amused, I watched as he pivoted and made his way to the oak stairway leading up to the next level. Placing his left hand atop the acorn-shaped finial that topped the staircase's handrail, he smiled. "Observe," he said.

Using both hands now, he twisted the acorn counterclockwise.

There came a soft *click,* followed by a gentle rumbling that sounded a lot like wood moving smoothly along a ball-bearing base. As though someone nearby was opening a heavy pocket door.

Bennett pointed behind me. "Take a look."

I turned.

The fawn-colored wall was opening, moving from my right to my left. There wasn't a secret door or a hidden panel that popped open; the entire curved wall was sliding sideways. I felt my eyes widen and my mouth fall open as the area beyond the moving façade was revealed.

"What is this?" I asked.

Bennett remained silent as I stepped closer to examine the unusual space. The wall had disappeared—exactly the way a pocket door might, except on a much larger scale—allowing us access to a narrow ribbon of walkway that followed the same curvature of the missing wall and the second floor of the library behind it. A skinny stairway led up to my left.

I pointed. "May I?"

"I'd be disappointed if you didn't."

I crept slowly up the stairs. There were about a dozen. "Stone," I remarked as Bennett followed. "These have been here for a long time."

"They're part of the original plans," he said.

At the top of the steps, a narrow doorway. "No lock?" I asked.

"Anyone who's gotten this far deserves to be here," he said with a smile.

I opened the door, crossed the threshold, and drew in a gasp of delight.

That we were above the library wasn't a surprise. That there was this space, this glorious, sun-filled, *second* library—one that offered a 360-degree view of Marshfield Manor property—was.

"Breathtaking," I said as I took a tentative step toward the nearest bookcase. "The library ceiling is directly below us. Is it safe to walk?"

"Perfectly safe," he said. "Marshfields have traversed this floor many times over the decades."

"But the mural on the ceiling below," I said. "Won't a lot of foot traffic disturb the plaster behind it? Won't it crack?"

"I don't anticipate a great deal of foot traffic up here, do you?"

I laughed. "Good point."

Unfurnished, the oval room was wide open and bare, except for the books. They occupied every shelf of the waist-high bookcases that lined the room's perimeter.

"This is amazing," I said as I reached for the nearest volume. Less than two seconds later, my mouth dropped open for the second time that day. "Audubon's *Birds of America*?"

Bennett nodded.

I scanned the shelves again. "These books," I said, finding it difficult to form words. "These are all first editions?"

"Mostly," he said. "I keep a few sentimental favorites up here, too. Some of those aren't quite so valuable."

"But," I said, "but you have hundreds of first editions downstairs. All over the mansion."

He seemed amused by my flustered response. "But these are the ones I treasure most. I knew this space existed, but it had gone largely unused for decades. Back in the early 1990s, I brought in experts on book preservation to advise me on temperature, humidity, and other important considerations for preserving paper. With their help, I had it converted to what you see now. I call it the Library Annex. Or Annex, for short."

"This is beyond belief."

"I take it you approve?"

I carefully placed the Audubon book back where I'd found it. "How could I not?"

Bennett allowed me to explore the Annex for the next hour or so. Finally, I admitted that it was too much to take in at once and we headed back down to his study.

"When can we visit the Annex again?" I asked.

Bennett shook his head. "Gracie, when will you learn? This home is yours now. Every inch of it. Come and go as you please."

"You are too generous," I said.

He reached an arm around my shoulders and hugged me tight. "No, I'm family."

AFTER DINNER, BENNETT AND I RETURNED to his study to chat.

"You heard that Frances has decided to bring Percy to Emberstowne to live?" Bennett asked.

"She told me," I said. "I quote: 'Well, since everybody in town now knows what went on at Indwell, there's no point in hiding him anymore.' She's hoping to hire a part-time caregiver next week."

Bennett sat back. "I knew she wanted him out of Indwell as soon as possible. I didn't realize she was moving that quickly."

"There's still a question of where he'll live. That's up in the air. She thinks it's improper for him to move in with her if they're not married."

"Plus, her house is not wheelchair-accessible."

"Exactly," I said. "And then there's Kyle."

Bennett raised his eyebrows. "How does he figure into this?"

"Apparently, this incident at Indwell gave Kyle the leverage he needed to convince his parents that he ought to be allowed to live on his own. With a caregiver, of course. He and Percy get along well enough. They want to try rooming together out here."

"I give them credit," he said.

"As do I."

"Speaking of roommates, I know that you're moving forward on the purchase of the Granite Building. Any news in that arena?"

I nodded. "Barring any surprise from the building inspectors, we should be able to close on the property within thirty days."

"Bruce and Scott must be so relieved."

"And excited. I am, too. This is a whole new adventure for all of us," I said. "And Gus's friend Anton has agreed to work with us when we're ready to expand."

"That's wonderful news."

I inhaled deeply, then exhaled. "Life is good right now," I said. "Let's hope things stay quiet for a little while."

"For a long while."

Bennett had barely gotten the sentiment out when my cell phone rang.

"It's Bruce," I said, then answered. "We were just talking about you."

"I hate to bother you while you're busy with Bennett," he said haltingly, "but this involves him, too."

"What happened?" I asked.

Bennett sat forward and I instinctively tightened my grip on the phone.

"Nothing yet," Bruce said, "But . . ."

He let the thought trail off for too long.

"What is it, Bruce? What's going on?"

413

"The phone rang here at home," he said. "It was your aunt Belinda so we didn't answer. But she left a message."

I sucked in a breath as my heart rate ratcheted into high gear. "What is it?" I asked. "What did she say?"

"It's about your sister," he said. "Liza's being released."

Center Point Large Print
600 Brooks Road / PO Box 1
Thorndike, ME 04986-0001 USA

(207) 568-3717

US & Canada:
1 800 929-9108
www.centerpointlargeprint.com